DEMON DANCE

Book 3 of the Vampire Gene

Also by Sam Stone

In the Vampire Gene Series
Book 1 - KILLING KISS
Book 2 - FUTILE FLAME

A Vampire Gene novel
HATEFUL HEART

DEMON DANCE

Book 3 of the Vampire Gene

SAM STONE

Dedication

For David and Linzi.
For listening to my story ideas and letting me talk myself into further development! Thank you as always for your love and support.
Also for Frazer: thanks for making me laugh and keeping me grounded.

Special thanks to:

My Editor Terry Martin and his lovely wife Liz: who have believed in The Vampire Gene and taken this whirlwind journey all the way with me. Phew we've finally done it! Sally-Anne and Jane: the administrators to Rhuddlan Castle for allowing me access and being so friendly and helpful. Rhuddlan Castle herself for being such a welcoming and beautiful old lady who I found truly inspiring. Simon Clark, Raven Dane and Geoff Nelder: for amazing and encouraging pre-publication reviews and comments. My siblings, who have been nagging me constantly for Demon Dance almost as soon as they finished reading the Futile Flame. And finally to Judy Broadbent for her never-ending enthusiasm.

Remember?

I'm Gabriele Caccini, a four-hundred-year-old vampire. I started this story with a search for my perfect mate. I found Lilly while stalking a victim at Manchester University and we began our lives together. But I became concerned when I learned that Lilly was a direct descendant of my own daughter, Marguerite. Even though I always wondered why Lilly was the only woman to survive my bite and to be reborn as a vampire, I was determined to be happy and we set out to travel the world together.

All seemed idyllic until a strange entity appeared in our lives. This unusual creature was capable of sapping our vampiric energy and I was afraid for my newborn lover. That's why, for Lilly's sake, I was forced to seek out my maker in my quest for answers.

I already knew I was a descendant of the infamous Borgia family of Rome because my vampire 'mother' was Lucrezia Borgia – herself turned by her brother, Caesare, after an incestuous relationship, but I didn't understand the implications of our entwined ancestry. Although I had been estranged from Lucrezia since my turning, I began to secretly meet her. I needed to understand her life, and learned of her seduction by her brother and her terrifying escape after he made her into an undead creature.

Later, Lucrezia was aided by a gypsy traveller named Miranda who taught her a form of magic using herbs that enabled her to hide from her obsessive sibling. But Caesare eventually tracked her down, stealing her away to the fantastical underground world of the Allucians; a petite and magical race whose children were being born with golden and watchful eyes.

Lucrezia managed to escape from their world, but was haunted by the memory of an infinite corridor of doors, each one representing a different time and place.

By this time, for better or worse, I had told Lilly the truth of our shared heritage, and met with her and Lucrezia as my maker's intriguing story unfolded, in the hope that this would tell us something about the entity that was hunting us. This powerful force turned out to be Caesare! Since leaving the Allucian city through one of the mysterious doors, Caesare had become an insane and corrupt shade, switching the focus of his obsession and spending his time presenting 'trophy' killings to Lilly and I in some crazed attempt for appeasement.

As Lucrezia finished her tale to us, the impossible happened and a twisted and monstrous Caesare appeared in central Manchester and wreaked havoc before our eyes.

There was a battle and Lucrezia was able to defeat him using the magicical knowledge she'd acquired from Miranda.

Dazed and shocked, we returned to our cooling coffee only to find the world around us changing. Lilly, Lucrezia and I found ourselves transported back to the corridor of doors.

Lilly became entranced by a particular portal. Helplessly drawn, she stepped through and the door slammed shut behind her, separating me from the only woman I've ever truly loved.

Seconds later, Lucrezia and I were back in the café in Manchester. I was distraught, not knowing quite what had happened or what I should do. Then, my mobile rang. It was Lilly! She was in Stockholm, and this isn't my story anymore … it's Lilly's …

Prologue

Loss

Gabriele stared at his phone as Lilly hung up. He was confused, scared. In the four hundred years of his life he'd never felt this vulnerable.

'What's going on?' he asked Lucrezia.

'I don't know. I've never known anything happen like this before.'

She fidgeted in her seat. Around them the café at Harvey Nicholls was buzzing with the usual trade. No one had noticed the strange threesome vanish, nor that only two of them had returned.

'This is crazy,' Gabi said. 'She says she's in Stockholm. How did she end up there?'

Lucrezia shook her head, avoiding Gabi's searching gaze.

'You know something,' he insisted. 'Look at me!'

When she did, her eyes confirmed this was the Lucrezia of old.

'She's alive. What else matters? And she's safe isn't she?'

It was all wrong though; people and vampires didn't just appear and disappear like that. He'd lived in this world long enough to know that it wasn't possible.

'Whatever's happened,' Lucrezia continued, 'it's all right now.'

Gabi looked around the café once more. He wasn't so sure. This place felt wrong, Lucrezia felt wrong. Yet moments before the anomaly everything had been so good. Right then he didn't trust his own world or reality, and he didn't trust her either.

'I shouldn't have brought you into our lives.'

3

'That's right blame me. Everything's about me and biting you. You wouldn't be here if I hadn't, and you wouldn't have met Lilly.' Lucrezia stood, her anger flaring.

'Where are you going?' he demanded.

'You're such a whiner, Gabriele. I can't stand listening to you anymore.'

Lucrezia turned on her heels and Gabi was alone again, just as he'd been before he found Lilly. Nausea pulled at his insides. He couldn't shake the nagging thought that his world would never be the same again.

He was drawn back to his phone, still gripped firmly in his right hand; his only link with Lilly. He hesitated, then redialled the number she had called from.

'The number you have dialled is not available ... The number you have dialled is not avail-'

Gabi hung up. He would just have to wait, but patience had never been his strong point.

The King's Castle

Harry sits down beside me as I work on my journal. He's irritable tonight. Long flowing hair falls over his face as he gazes over my shoulder. He's tall. He was once a Viking – not that it would have made any difference to his height. It does however, have much to do with the powerful muscles in his arms and shoulders, naturally built up from the days when he wielded a hefty broadsword. He's anything but fragile and, with his centuries-old vampire blood, so strong and powerful he could destroy the world – if he chose. But Harry's days of war and pillage are over. Now he is nothing. Not even a king any more, just a blood-sucking fiend. Like me.

We live in a castle in Sweden. It has been converted with all the conveniences that anyone could wish for, yet outside it appears to be something out of *Chitty Chitty Bang Bang*. The exterior is now painted an eggshell blue. It's a bit twee and fairytale for me, I prefer my home in North Wales, but Harry likes it here. He feels safe on his home territory, in one of his old fortresses. Once made from huge imposing stone, it was redesigned in the nineteenth century to appear like some fairytale castle. Throughout the years I've been unable to persuade him to leave Sweden for any length of time.

The sitting room is spacious, with reproduction furniture. I don't like the old stuff. Everything has to be as modern as possible, though I compromised a little because the castle wouldn't seem right with the minimalist style I prefer. Harry feels happier when he is surrounded by things that remind him of the past. He has his paintings, and they are his little pieces of history.

They line the walls, reminding him of his warrior days. Renaissance art, created centuries after his birth, but depicting battles and raids. He still glories in his battle prowess. Some of the pictures even feature images of me as I had posed for his artists more years ago than I care to remember.

Harry stands up and fusses around me like a child waiting to ask a parent a crucial question that they know the grown-up won't like. I put my laptop aside. He feels my gaze and looks up. His eyes are an intense green, just like mine. In fact people could be forgiven for mistaking us for brother and sister. All of the carriers of the vampire gene are genetically similar and that is because we all descend from the same source ...

Guilt ripples through my stomach. The hairs on the back of my neck prickle and I feel a momentary nausea. I quell the panic that threatens to consume me and instead turn my attention back to Harry's fears.

'What's wrong?'

'You're going to contact him now,' Harry states, collapsing onto the sofa beside me.

After centuries spent in my company, albeit intermittently, he knows me so well.

'Yes. You've always known I would. It's time.'

I glance at my laptop. For some time now I have been recalling the past, writing a journal to help me make sense of all that's happened.

Harry rocks forward. His agitation and fear warp the air around us as he paces the tapestry rug before the huge open fireplace. I say nothing. I've long since learnt it is better to let him find his own articulation, rather than to pre-empt him. In the old days I had a penchant for interrupting him as he spoke. It caused arguments that I soon wished to avoid. I didn't want us to part on bad terms.

'What of me?' he asks finally. 'What of us?'

'We are a family,' I answer simply. 'Nothing can change that. I'll always be there for you if you need me.'

'I had hoped, had desired ...' he trails off.

Harry holds his hands out before him, they quiver. I turn away. I can't bear to see him like this. I have destroyed him, as I have so many others throughout the centuries. He was once a king and he should be always regal and strong, not this weak and pathetic creature in love with a woman he can never have.

'Lilly.' His eyes are haunted; they plead for something I can't give.

'Let's hunt,' I say.

A pale green light ignites in his eyes like an emerald beacon. He loves to kill, has never mastered the art of a 'small feed'. Out of all of them, Harry is my most brutal child. His biggest kick is fucking as he feeds. The victim can be willing or not. It doesn't matter to him. For that too I have my guilt-cross to bear because for all the threats and reprimands I make, he is still a loose cannon. And I know soon I won't be around to stop him doing precisely what he shouldn't.

It's raining and the night air feels like liquid blackness on my limbs as we fly high above the city. Stockholm is an exciting hunting ground. Like any city it is full of evil and there are many who deserve to die. But Harry isn't particular. He'll take young or old irrespective of their nature. As we swoop towards the city skyline, I know it won't be long before he homes in on some poor innocent.

'There!'

I feel his excitement as he closes in on a young man of about seventeen.

'Wait,' I call.

I give an initial scan of his victim's blood. We have to be extra careful in this city; there are so many strains of Harry's bloodline living unwittingly among the masses. None of them know that they are descended from a philandering king. The boy is blond, nothing strange in that, but if there is one trace of the gene in him, he'll turn.

I cloak myself in invisibility and move closer. Harry's potential meal shivers as I slip around him; sniff him, a gentle taste of the dried perspiration on his throat. His hand flies to his neck. He's scared and stands rooted to the spot in the dark street. He can sense me, but not see me. Harry moves forward, I bare my fangs and he backs off. He knows better than to interfere with my checks. The boy's sweat is on my tongue, I savour and swallow. I see his gene pool swim out like lines of light from his aura. It stretches for miles in directions that I recognise. I see faces I've seen a hundred times in these lines and it leads forwards and backwards, into the past and into the future. The gene codes are coloured variants that represent the families and they are visible to me now. I follow the lines, analyse them, right down to the longest, oldest face.

Then I see it, faint, but undeniable.

I turn and fly away, grabbing Harry and pulling him roughly with me.

'Lilly!' he grunts.

'Not suitable,' I tell him when we're miles up in the air.

I look down at the pin-point boy scurrying away as if he knows that his life has almost been stolen. And it has. He will never know how his ancestry saved his life this night, but in some small recess in the back of his mind, he may wonder if there really are monsters hiding in the dark.

I gaze out at the myriad of lights glowing from the expanse of the city. From above it is like a collection of small, bright, islands broken up by the dark paths of water running between each part.

I pull on Harry's hand and we fly outward towards the Baltic Sea, above the belching chimneys of the oil refinery at Nynäshamn and out over the coast.

'Come, Harry,' I say, as we land silently on an oil ring just offshore. 'When all else fails we may take a little here from the foreigners.'

I scan and find the least likely link. Our feet barely register on the metal stairwells as we climb down into the heart of the rig.

Harry follows me eagerly as I track the aura of a man working below. We weave in and around the maze-like corridors until we find the tantalising source that has pulled us through the dark structure.

'I don't like the smell,' Harry complains as we round the final corner. 'It makes the blood taste like oil.'

'No it doesn't,' I laugh. 'You're such a baby.'

In the gloom, the man seems dark in colouring, perhaps of Asian origin, or perhaps he's merely covered in grime. He's an engineer. We watch as he takes readings from a panel of clock-shaped gauges. He's a short man in his early fifties. His fingers are stained and filthy from long-term contact with oil and grease, emphasising the rough cracks in his dry skin. His hands are those of a worker. I pity him as he writes on a clipboard and then hangs it up on a hook by the panel, not because of his choice of job, but because this is the day he will die. He turns to face us and Harry has him by the throat before I have a chance to check his gene code.

Fangs flash luminous; the man shudders and groans as Harry feasts. He slumps in Harry's arms, and eventually slips free and collapses on the oily floor, dead and drained of blood.

'That was very careless,' I say, pursing my lips. 'What if he comes back?'

'Haven't you ever had unprotected sex?' Harry says. He thinks it's funny to disobey me, but I'm definitely not laughing.

'Well, you may have just made a baby, that's for sure.' I bend down and lick the cooling throat of the engineer. I swallow. His gene code is rapidly dying.

'Well?' Harry asks.

'Never. Fucking. Do that. Again!'

I stand, brushing my hands down my long woollen jumper and black leggings. I feel tainted. I hate checking the newly dead, but I resist the urge to spit on the deck as we emerge with the body onto the rig's deck.

'Your kill. You fucking get rid of it,' I say.

I'm furious. I make Harry carry the corpse and he jumps over the side of the rig, flying out to sea to dispose of the evidence while I wait on the top, watching his form diminish as he gets farther away. Maybe this one will swim back to the rig and take out all of his friends before he understands he can control it. But then, maybe not. I think he was safe, though the link dies almost as rapidly as the body does and so it is hard to tell for sure.

Harry disappears and I turn away. I push aside my fury. It is pointless anyway. Controlling him is impossible, but at times I could fucking kill him.

A young man scurries furtively along the deck with something hidden in a roll of newspaper. He's a black American in his late thirties and even in the chill of night he's wearing jeans that fall off his backside, the crotch is halfway to his knees, and an off-white sleeveless t-shirt. His hair is covered by a baseball cap worn with the peak in reverse.

For his lack of fashion sense alone he deserves to die.

He gasps as I allow him to see me and he almost drops his prize. The newspaper slips away revealing the contents. It's a bottle of rum. Naughty. I believe that alcohol is banned on oil rigs. But then maybe I'm wrong …

'How'd you get here?' he asks. 'Who brought you aboard?'

'Fancy sharing some of that?' I say, smiling.

It takes him a moment to comprehend what he is seeing. I am all white fangs and blazing green eyes. Corny I know, but I just love the drama sometimes. His eyes widen and his mouth flaps as he attempts to yell; fear paralyses his throat but his mind screams in recognition. A psychic flash of a child listening to the tales of an old West Indian Grandmother. *Granny was right! A Sucoyan! They exist to rip the souls from men.* I nod as I acknowledge his cultural name for my kind. Drool slips down his chin, his chest heaves. And then, some primitive instinct for survival kicks in. He runs.

I shake my head: maybe his Grandmother should have

explained the first rule about running from a predator – the hunt only excites them.

I follow him eagerly as the chase takes us back below deck. His breath is ragged as he clatters and stumbles down the metal stairs, heading for the mess area. Below I can hear the revelry of the men as they play cards. There is the faint, echoey sound of voices coming from a television set. In the kitchen there is the sound of dishes being stacked into a dishwasher. Farther below, I can hear the tapping of fingers on a computer keyboard as someone writes an email, creates a spreadsheet or merely completes the rig log.

The man stumbles. He's trying to call for help but is unable to draw a sound through his frayed breath. He casts a backward glance but can no longer see me. His beating heart leaps in relief as he begins to hope I was a hallucination. The taste of false security vibrating through his aura is almost as delicious as his fear. I lick my lips and wait outside the mess room for him to arrive.

He almost collides with me as he runs down the final flight of stairs. The rum bottle finally drops from his fingers and I catch it before it hits the deck. Then I look directly at him.

His eyes meet mine. His breathing evens out, serenity replaces the fear on his face as the tension leaves his brow and his cheeks slacken. I walk past him, stop a few feet away and curl my finger. He follows.

'Pull your jeans up,' I order and he does as he's told; like a good victim.

In his cabin I check my food as he squirms with excitement in my grasp. Unlike Harry I don't have unprotected mealtimes and I don't fuck my food, but I still feel the buzz of exhilaration in the pit of my stomach as I smell the hot, warm fluid beneath his skin. I lick his throat, while forcing my will into his mind. He is pliant. Willing. Anticipation builds in his blood. As I pull him against me I feel him harden through his baggy jeans. But his sexual lust will go unfulfilled, unlike my blood lust. My teeth tease the vein in his neck, waiting for that moment when his sexual energy pumps the blood faster and stronger as though offering itself as a sacrifice to his new goddess.

I hold off, teasing myself until I almost collapse with thirst. The smell of his warm skin is like a drug with its combination of oil, blood, sweat and pheromones. He falls weak in my arms, but I clasp him easily despite his muscular build. My mouth clamps on the vein and I suckle it in an intense love bite until my fangs take on a life of their own and plunge into the skin, finding the blood source immediately. I drown in his life.

For a moment I am completely consumed with the intensity of blood lust. My head swoons. A rush of invulnerability sweeps my limbs.

I pull back. Staggering, I drop my victim, wiping my lips with a shaking hand. I feel like a reformed alcoholic who has bitten into a brandy liqueur. I force the lust back down inside me – for now it must remain unquenched. This boy is not really deserving of death, even though he has no taste in clothing, but there will be others who are.

A few minutes later I'm licking my lips and fangs clean and my victim is sleeping off what will feel like the biggest hangover he's ever had. I wonder how he will explain the hickey to his friends and I stifle the laughter that threatens to burst from my lips. I am high and wired.

Harry enters silently and glances down at the sleeping man; a cynical smile curls his lips.

'You're still playing with your food, I see.'

Taking his hand I smile up at him. Harry's mood has lifted, as I knew it would once he fed. Hunting is the only connection he has to his previous life and world. At least when he hunts he feels in control. Once more he is the predator and king.

Hand in hand we take flight and head back inland. There is more food to hunt this night, and I am eager to begin.

Behind The Door

Beyond the first door the environment had a surreal element, as if the leaves and plants, dew and flowers, were all brand new. It was as though the world was turning for the very first time, the very first day. Its design, a pattern or blueprint felt like an experiment. Definitely cleaner than the world I knew; a far better place than the dark, old, gothic city of Manchester.

The air sang with elation. Daisies grew alongside tropical plants, like no landscape I had ever seen. Perfection was the only word that could describe it. All the plants and trees, foliage and bushes you can imagine grew in this one place. I felt the closest to nature that I had ever been and though I turned and glanced back at the doorway, seconds before it closed, I felt no urge to run back to the corridor of doors.

I saw Gabi clawing at the wind that pushed him back; his nails raking the air as though he were fighting for his very life. Lucrezia had said, 'The door you need will call you.' And it had. This door, with its marble renaissance frame *had* called to me. I'd heard the music beyond and I'd been pulled like a Pied Piper's rat right through the door to my fate.

'Lilly!' Gabi screamed.

I turned my head in time to see him thrown back from the doorway by the invisible force.

The door slammed shut and promptly disappeared. I felt a brief moment of angst and then the singing world sucked me in. I was propelled farther away from the doorway into the perfect-length grass. A row of lilies in full and ideal bloom stared open-mouthed like singing children in a church choir as I passed. I was mesmerized and completely unafraid.

The music was so perfect that it brought tears to my eyes but I couldn't place the instrument that played. It was as though the plants and trees were a choral arrangement and every bend and twist made in the gentle breeze created a new and immaculate sound. It had a strange effect on me; I skipped through the forest and gardens without a care in the world and passed by a lake and a river, all within minutes. It was as though the world I'd left didn't matter anymore.

'I must have fallen down a rabbit hole,' I giggled. 'Alice must have felt just as strange.'

This world was everything. Possibly the Allucians had rebuilt their garden, or maybe I had arrived at the time it was first built. If so, then finding the corridor to return wouldn't be that difficult. One thing was for sure, I felt no threat. In fact, I felt completely and utterly alone, as if I was the only person alive on earth: a thought that should have terrified me, but it didn't. Looking back, I understand that my senses were being deliberately numbed, but I didn't realise that at first.

I came to a halt at a river and watched the steady flow as it stretched on farther than the eye could see. The liquid was clear and pure. I bent down and ran my finger tip into the water. It felt like velvet washing over my hand. In the middle I saw a fish jump as it swam against the current. Then another. Then several fish leapt in and out of the water as though they were putting on a display just for me. I sat back on the cushioned grass bank, cross legged and watched. The fish never tired, they merely dwindled until they had all swam away.

The night drew in, and still I sat by the river, my head resting on my hands. I felt intensely calm to the point of sedation. It was very strange. Not like me at all.

Night fell tentatively; afraid of the unknown. When fully dark it was blacker and more complete than I had ever seen. Then the moon appeared like an actor who had missed his cue. It beamed down on the lake, and the light stretched gradually outwards like a dimmer switch slowly being turned up. The clear water no longer appeared to be black ink, but rather the scene of a romantic setting.

'Bravo!' I said, clapping my hands.

Nature hushed. Full dark froze. The moon blinked. I lapsed into semi-consciousness and waited. I think it was then that he noticed my presence.

Daylight sprang into action in a burst of brightness and I came out of my trance, wondering if I had fallen asleep and the morning had merely woken me. I blinked, my eyes adjusting to the sun again. I glanced up into the immaculate sky and noted that the moon had completely disappeared. The river was still flowing serenely but the fish were hiding or maybe they hadn't started their tussle with the current yet. There was a stillness and silence that hadn't been there when I arrived.

'Please sing again,' I whispered lying back on the bank with my arms under my head.

The nature-song began slowly, cautiously, and then resumed with eagerness as though the world had found a voice once more. Around me the breeze picked a playful fight with a rose bush of the purest red. I was hypnotised by this world; calm beyond anything I'd ever felt before. Even the blood lust was still and the fear of starvation never entered my mind.

What are you?

The wind whispered around my ears, the sun scanned and caressed my skin as a splatter of rain cooled and soothed in its wake.

'I'm Lilly ...'

Lill ... ay ... The wind picked up my name and hurried it through the trees and it warped and changed with nature's Chinese whispers.

Lil ... ee ...

15

Lil … leeth … Lillith!

'No, it's … never mind.'

I never thought it strange that the plants were talking to me. It was as though this was how the world was meant to be. But somehow we had lost the art of communication. Or maybe the plants had stopped talking. Either way, it didn't really concern me. I was in a lovely dream and I never wanted to wake from it. It felt like heaven.

An interesting word.

'What is?'

Heaven!

I opened my eyes. A brilliant white shape floated before me. At first I was unsure what to make of the light, for light is what formed the creature. Light, beauty, love. There was no sense of anything evil and since my rebirth I had always sensed evil in man. I sat up. The shape backed away. Of course he would know I was evil. I don't know what possessed me to think 'he' but it just felt right. So, from then on he had a gender.

What are you?

'I'm a …' I wasn't sure what to say. How could I tell *him* I was everything against creation? 'I'm a woman.'

But then what did it matter? This was only a dream after all.

I felt eyes scanning me as he moved closer. Could this creature of light tell I was much more than a woman? Did he know that I was a fiend and something to be feared? He danced about me, a rapid whoosh of light and air that spun around my body so fast that it sucked the oxygen from my lungs. I felt dizzy, confused, weak. It was as though every part of me was being examined by an invisible force.

'Please!' I gasped.

The next thing I remember, I was laying flat on the grass. The light blurred above me and I peered through the slits of my eyes at the shape. He was made up of a million fireflies. His form was indistinct. He warped in and out of different shapes. One moment I saw the shape of a lion, a bear, a carp, a beetle. Constantly changing as though he couldn't decide which form suited him best. Then he became more ape-like until finally he settled in the form of a man.

'Ah. That's better. You were making me dizzy with all those changes.'

Features formed in the face, as though being moulded out of clay, the light thickened and became more solid. A perfect, slightly cynical mouth, curved up, opened and closed as though testing to see if it worked. My eyes took in the solidifying shape of an Adonis body.

'Well, hell! Why not make it as immaculate as possible?' I laughed.

The scene, this dream, was as bizarre as any I had ever had. I was determined to remember it. Even the absolute beauty of the man that grew before my eyes into the most astounding and absolute specimen I had ever seen.

I applauded again.

'Amazing! You should have your own magic act!'

He mimicked me, clapping his hands together in a joyous and excited way. I laughed and his mouth jerked up, opened and a strange snigger burst forth, unforced, but not natural.

'You'll need to practice that. Don't worry, laughter just happens at the right moment. But you have to feel it. Right here,' I told him indicating my stomach.

His hand went to his own stomach and then I realised he was completely naked and totally unaware. He was, indeed, a very fine specimen.

'Oh well, it's only a dream anyway.'

Where did 'you-come-from?' he asked.

His voice was slightly hoarse, as though he were a coma victim waking after years of sleep. His vocal cords were unsure what to do. And so, his speech was disjointed; half spoken through the wind, half from his larynx. I watched him swallow, moistening his throat, and open his mouth to try again.

It seemed to be a tremendous effort, as though he had to

concentrate all his strength and energy into making the sound from his throat.

'You must be an Allucian,' I concluded. 'Lucrezia said that your people spoke with telepathy.'

I ran through my memory of the conversation, just a few hours ago now, but it felt like an age. Lucrezia, Gabriele and I were in Harvey Nicholls café, in Manchester, and she had told us her story. She had explained how she had been captured by the Allucians and was being kept as a plaything for her obsessive brother Caesare. And then, Caesare had appeared. There had been a battle and Lucrezia had destroyed him. It was all coming back, but it was so distant and unreal. Somehow I'd ended up in the corridor of doors that Lucrezia described.

Yet, unless I had slipped into an alternate time or universe when I stepped through the door, I knew that this world was, or had to be, illusory. According to Lucrezia's story, that was altogether possible.

That left me with the dilemma of where I was, of course, and who this man or creature was. But I soon decided he wasn't an Allucian. He was too tall. Lucrezia had described them as a tiny race of people, pigmy in size. Their colouring was far different too. Black, shiny hair and intense brown eyes as I recalled, with olive skin. This man was pale, almost stark white, as though the sun had never touched his flesh. He had a sandy, golden-blond, mass of long hair and stood over six feet tall with blue or green eyes. I wasn't quite sure because like his form earlier, the eyes kept changing, as though they hadn't quite made up their mind what colour they wanted to be.

'You're like an angel ...'

My heart leapt as the implication of my words sucked deeper into my brain, holding fast like a rock in dried tar.

In The Beginning

What I was imagining was completely impossible. There were no such things as angels, but then, I'd once thought vampires didn't exist either and here I was, living and breathing and eating people to survive. So, I reasoned that if there were demons like Gabriele and I, then surely there had to be something that balanced that out. So angels were infinitely probable, and that opened the world up to a whole lot of other possibilities too.

Everywhere I went, he followed. He was as curious about me as I was about him. I didn't find his interest intimidating or worrying but rather natural under the circumstances.

'*Are* you an ... angel then?'

'If you want me to be.'

He smiled and then peered into my eyes so intently I felt that my very thoughts were being ripped from my mind.

'Pack it in!' I said. 'That's like rape you know.'

He was a little confused as though the words I spoke meant nothing, yet he'd spoken to me in my own language. Surely he understood me?

'I don't recognise some of your words,' he answered with a voice like pure honey, smooth and beautiful, incredibly sexy. 'I don't think they have any meaning.'

'Well, of course they do! It's part of my speech.'

'Where did you come from?' he asked.

'The corridor. The doors.'

He shook his head. He didn't understand at all. This was an

innocent time, a beginning world; so new and clean and polished. Even so, he must have come from somewhere. He spoke my language after all.

'I'm translating ...' he said.

'Translating?'

'Yes, everything you say. I have a different language to you. But some of your words don't fit.'

It all felt so surreal. My life was like one long passageway of changes and insecurity. Just one year ago I was a normal student attending Manchester University and then after a night of great sex, with a really gorgeous guy, I was a vampire. I'd been with Gabriele ever since. Just as suddenly, here I was in the middle of some freaky bloody garden talking to someone that could be, well, God.

'What is this place?' I asked.

He stared at me in surprise. Then glanced around. 'I don't know.'

It was as if we had both been displaced in time to this huge garden.

'So, you don't know where you are either?' I asked.

'Oh yes. Of course I do.'

'But you just said ...'

'I know where I am, I just haven't named it yet,' he answered, and a strange pricking echoed in the back of my skull.

I felt dizzy, confused. Suddenly this world seemed less benign. It occurred to me that my emotions or feelings were being controlled, that so far the feeling of security and safety was coming from some other source than me. The garden *did* have some kind of calming effect and I'd responded to it as soon as I'd entered.

'What are you?' I asked.

He examined me with big eyes, one blue, one green and I knew the answer already and couldn't say. This place felt like the beginning of time, because maybe it *was*.

Panic set in.

'I need to leave now. I need the doors. Can you show me the doors?'

He shook his head. The word confused him because it described a thing that didn't exist in his world.

'You are a Lillith,' he stated. 'The trees told me.'

'No ... I'm ... I'm a woman. Well no actually. I'm more than that. Lilly is my name.'

'Your name is Lillith then.'

I couldn't be bothered correcting him again. It didn't matter anyway. What did matter was finding the doors, or waking up, if this was a dream. I felt an urgent need to leave, yet I realised very quickly that leaving might not be that easy. I shook myself mentally. What was wrong with me? Why had I been so docile? It was as though the atmosphere was soaked in valium and I had taken too much.

'I must go,' he said.

'Where?'

He was silent for a while, gazing up at the sky thoughtfully. I waited. Something about him made me feel like I must be patient and so I turned away and pretended to examine a rose bush.

'I have more to do,' he said simply. 'This is only the first part. I have to duplicate it all over the planet.'

'This is *Earth*, isn't it?' I asked turning, only to discover he was gone.

I was talking to myself; even the plants didn't respond.

Left to my own devices once more I began to explore again. This time I tried to retrace my steps to the point of entry. If I had entered through a door, then it must be there somewhere in order for me to exit.

Lillith, the wind whispered, and I glanced around.

'It is hardly fair that you have a name for me and I have none for you.' I was too afraid to use the name I had in my mind.

'It is hard to translate, and you would not understand it if I used my own words.' He stood in the clearing exactly where the door had been as though he was waiting for me to find him.

'Still it would be nice to call you something.' I thought back to my Sunday-school days. The many names of the almighty had once been drummed into my young brain and they rolled through my head recited parrot fashion with the same emphasise as the times tables.

'Adonai,' he murmured ripping it from my mind as it floated to the surface of my memory. 'Names are important.'

I folded my arms around myself. 'Why?'

Nothing exists until it is named, the wind answered.

And so he was named and therefore he existed. There was no denying that.

'The door has gone,' I pointed out. 'I'm not sure how I can get back.'

Adonai looked around him at the space he had just vacated. He raised a hand sweeping it over the air as though he could feel the door lurking behind an invisible screen. He frowned. His fingers glowed in the sunlight with the residue of power left from the door.

'Strange. There is no creation that fits this ... and yet it existed.'

'Exists. It does exist! What does it feel ...?'

His hand went out as though he needed complete silence to concentrate. My arms fell to my sides and I stood, feeling awkward, as his hands caressed the air.

'Time,' he murmured finally. 'I can see ...' The air shuddered around him. He staggered back. 'No!'

His eyes fell on me. They were cold blue. The air rippled where the door had been and I realised his probing had brought forward something of the door again. Quickly I ran towards it realising that this may be my only chance to return, but Adonai caught my arm before I reached the spot. I tugged and pulled towards the doorway, but he was incredibly strong and no matter how hard I pulled, his hand remained vice-like around the top of my arm. Seconds later the air stabilised and the shimmer disappeared leaving nothing but space and oxygen in its wake. Adonai released my arm.

'Why did you stop me? I need to go home!'

'There's only one way for you to travel through time now, Lillith. This thing you call "the doors", this can only be crossed one way.'

His body began to glow and once again became fractured light. He grew so bright that my eyes could barely focus on him because the light was just too painful. Then his form blinked once, twice, before he completely vanished.

'How then? How can I return?'

There was a decided absence in the space he'd occupied. The air was hollow. I walked around it. Prodded it. The air dimpled under my fingers. I pressed my hand forward, felt resistance. It was as though the air around his exit point was surrounded by a film or bubble. I pressed harder to see if the film would break or give. It shuddered and pushed back, as though an invisible hand were squeezing my fingers.

'Strange.'

The film was cloying and cold. My skin felt like it had been dipped in treacle; the more I pulled back the more the invisible tar sucked at my flesh. I tugged back my hand. Then sat down on the warm grass and stared at the space until the moon pushed the sun away.

Adonai came and went as the days wore on, and night and day passed by fluently; the rehearsal was over. This was the real thing. The world was born. But despite my questions and pleading, he refused to explain his ambiguous comment and the mystery to my future remained ever present, a puzzle I had to unravel alone.

At least there were consolations.

I felt no hunger in the garden and after the intensity of my blood-cravings to not feel anything was a strange sensation. It was as though all of my physical needs were met all the time. In many ways this was precisely as Lucrezia described the Allucian world to be; perfect. Although I knew that I was not underground, deep inside the thick rock of a mountain. This was something else entirely. It was possible that the Allucians had visited this place through their corridor of doors and brought back the knowledge that helped them to create their world initially. If they had, then surely there was a way to return. The implication that I was stuck here forever, as Adonai had said, was not acceptable.

'I'll find a solution,' I told the wind. 'I've always been good at problem solving. I'm female after all and we are the stronger sex.'

The wind huffed against the trees in silent laughter.

Chapter 4 - Present

The Trinity Klub

The club is bulging. I push my way through the bodies, brushing against auras. The proximity of so many humans almost makes my stomach retch. I hate crowds. I am by nature a loner these days. And the gyrating sexual energy that flows through the crowd repulses me. The consolation prize is the blood. It floods the air along with the hot scent of perspiration.

I took only a little blood from my last victim and so I'm still hungry. As I look around the club I don't see anything I fancy eating. Harry has found a pale, slender redhead. She looks like Nicola Roberts from the pop group Girls Aloud, complete with plaster of Paris make-up. She's wearing hot pants and a cropped top that barely covers her tiny breasts. I use the blanket of the crowd on the dance floor as an excuse to brush the damp bare flesh on her waist with my hand. I lift my fingers to my lips and taste her sweet perspiration. Colours burst into the air before my vampiric gaze, lines of heritage. The lines stretch up and out and stop several feet above her head. I've seen this before. She is a long way from her home and there is no nearby connection to her lineage. It is good news for Harry because there is no trace of our bloodline in her gene code. I meet Harry's eyes and nod. He moves in rapidly meeting her eyes. Within minutes he's pulled the girl close and their hips bump together as they dance. Before long he leads her away from the crowd. Unconcerned I watch them leave, assured she is safe for any kind of fun he wishes to have with her.

Across the room a group of boys part to reveal a gorgeous blond Adonis. He reminds me of the love I lost. Even from this distance I can see the green twinkle of his eyes, see the seductive dimples in his cheeks and chin. I turn away rapidly. Everywhere I go in Stockholm there are constant reminders of my one-time lover. How can I still hold a torch for him, after all this time?

'Hey beautiful.'

I turn and glance at the swarthy man who just breathed in my ear. He's in his late thirties. Cute. Dark hair and nothing like Gabriele or any other male from my gene pool. But none of that makes a difference; what does is the fact that he has his hand on my waist and he's stroking me. He's skilled. His fingers weave hypnotic patterns over my skin. I am frozen to the spot.

That's his first mistake. I don't like to be touched.

'Want to get some air?' he asks.

I let him take my hand and lead me outside onto the balcony. It's a cold night and we are alone except for a tall, stocky, bouncer taking a cigarette break. We look out over the city. Multicoloured lights litter the streets. I am mesmerised by the beauty of the cold air, of my breath huffing out like steam. It is one of those silly delights that my vampiric sense really enjoys.

'I'm Stephan,' he tells me as he places a joint in his mouth and flicks his lighter expertly.

He takes a long pull into his lungs and then offers it to me.

'I don't smoke,' I answer but I don't bother giving him the lecture that smoking will kill him eventually. He'll be dead long before then anyway.

'I watched you inside the club. Your boyfriend went off with a redhead.'

'He's not my boyfriend.'

'Ah. Good. Because I think you are the most beautiful woman I have ever seen.'

I raise a cynical brow. The fluency of his words tells me how often Stephan has used them. I sniff the air around him as he inhales the weed again. He smells of sex. Cigarettes. Weed. And something else. Cocaine. Then I see the particles of white powder, briefly reflected in the moonlight, around his nostrils. I turn to walk away. He's too boring to bother with.

'I want you,' he says catching my arm.

I glance down at his hand. 'Let go.'

'I always have what I want.'

'You're not my type. Sorry.'

Stephan tightens his grip and chuckles. It is a dark sound and it implies hidden knowledge. I turn just in time to see the bouncer heading my way.

'You've got to be kidding me ...'

The bouncer grabs my arms and they pull me towards another door at the other end of the balcony. I don't resist, even though I could shake them off easily if I wanted to. But there are too many people around and I'm curious to see how far this will go. I let them pull me into the other room. The glass door is closed behind us and I find myself in a small office which contains a desk and a futon covered in luxurious cushions in various shades of red silk. I look around. Other than the balcony, two doors lead off from the room. One, I suspect leads back into the club; the other is probably a bathroom.

'Leave us,' Stephan says and the bouncer departs.

'Is this how you get all your dates?' I laugh. 'You could just try wining and dining a girl; it might well have saved your life.'

He chuckles. 'Saved my life? Young lady I don't think you realise who you are dealing with. I own this club.'

I run my finger along his desk as I recall the rumours I'd heard about the Trinity Klub and the mafia who owned it. Stephan's name and face float behind my eyes as I recall a scandal in the newspaper recently. The report flashes before my eyes. The curse of a photographic memory.

Young woman throws herself from club owner's balcony ... Investigation inconclusive.

'Mmmm. Yes. I do. But do you know who you are dealing with?' I meet his eyes.

He steps back when he sees the venom in my expression. He

blinks. Swallows. Then smiles. *Never smile at a crocodile...* I smile back.

'Come here,' he orders.

'What if I scream?'

'This room is sound-proofed,' his smile widens.

'Your biggest mistake of course was touching me,' I say stepping towards him. 'I really don't like to be touched. Especially when I haven't given my permission.'

'You better get used to it bitch. I'm going to touch all I want in the next few hours.' He reaches for me and I let him grab me; his fingers bite into my arms. 'You're going to do everything I ask.'

I laugh in his face. Then flick my tongue out over his cheek, testing him. His heritage lines stretch out, far away from Stockholm and no hint of my DNA. Very, very safe. It seems Stephan is of Russian decent. He pulls me close. He's taken my tasting as a sign that I like him after all. Foolish mortal.

My fangs burst free of my gums as I rear and strike in one fluid movement. I bury my teeth in his face and rip back, taking a strip of his cheek with me. There is a sickening tear as his face shreds. Stephan screams. His hand flies to his face and he stares in shock at the blood covering his fingers. As he tries to push the flapping skin back in place. If he survives our encounter his looks will be ruined. But he won't need to worry about that.

'What the fuck ...?' He staggers towards his desk, shocked and dazed.

I see the alarm button just in time. I grab him, snatching his hand away from the desk and crush his fingers in mine. I squeeze. Bones cracked in my grasp. He screams again. I sigh. It's getting boring again.

'Where you going honey? I thought you wanted to fuck? Oops. My bad. You wanted to rape, didn't you? Is that how you get it up, Stephan? You have to have the rough and tumble first?' I throw him back on the futon and reach for the zipper on his trousers. 'Well let's see what you have in there then. I'm feeling hungry.'

Stephan screams like a girl. His hands beat at me, but his blows have no more strength than that of an insect. I laugh when he pulls back his uninjured arm, fist clenched. His blow lands on my cheek. The fingers in his hand snap like twigs and his knuckles crumble. Both of his hands are now destroyed and with it the fight goes out of him. I bet this is the first time he has ever been bested by anyone, never mind a female. I slash away his pale cream trousers; his blood has ruined them anyway. Stephan cries and sobs as I expose his stomach.

'Please ... Mercy.'

'Did you have mercy for that poor little girl you raped and threw from the balcony Stephan?'

I smile, all fangs and Stephan recoils, 'Wha ... t are ... you?'

'I could come out with "I'm your worst nightmare" or some clichéd crap like that. But I reckon that would be lost on an arsehole like you. So I'll tell you this, that blood-sucking monster you had childhood nightmares about exists. It's real. I'm the bogeyman. I'm going to eat you, because you've been a bad, bad man.'

His cries become incoherent as I get to work on him. I bite, scratch and tear until his guts are smeared all over the futon. The red silk cushions darken and change colour to a deep, black purple. Blood falls onto the cream carpet in an interesting splatter pattern.

'Your biggest mistake was touching me,' I say again as I lick at an open wound finally drinking my fill. 'I really don't like to be groped. Maybe in death you will learn some manners.'

His eyes bleed tears as his mouth leaks gory saliva. He's dying; it will be slow and agonising. And as much as I'd like to, I can't afford the luxury of leaving here unless I finish him. I reach down. Taking his mangled face between my hands I twist his head sharply, snapping his neck. But I'm aware of the valuable lesson he has just learned about life and death. Power is a tenuous possession. You are only strong if there are others weaker than you. I'm Lilly. I'm *Lillith*. I'm the

Adam

I missed Gabi. It was like an agonising ache in my heart. I worried constantly about how he must be feeling and what he might be doing to try and pull me back into my own world. Once the original apathy had worn off all I could think about was returning home. It didn't matter that Adonai tried so hard to distract me. I walked through the garden in a panicked daze, constantly searching for that elusive exit.

'I think you may like this Lillith,' Adonai said as I found him waiting for me by the pool.

'What is it?'

'I made something,' he smiled proudly.

'You what?'

'There!'

I turned to see where he pointed and noticed a weeping willow, drooping into the water. The branches were like flowing hair and I admired its beauty.

'Very nice. But it's a tree: you've made trees before.'

'Not that,' answered Adonai.

I stared again, carefully scrutinising the tree and branches. Then I saw the clay figure staring blankly back at us. The brown of its husk almost matched the bark of the tree. It was an accidental camouflage.

I laughed. 'Oh my!' *A man! But only a clay one. That would have been creepy – if he had created the real thing …*

'Look closely.'

The figure was a beautiful and perfect mimicry of the human form. Its face was happy, and the lips curved up in a natural

31

smile, leaving indents and laughter lines in the cheeks and around the eyes. I moved closer.

'He's beautiful!' I gasped. 'Shame he's not real.'

'I haven't quite finished yet,' Adonai sighed. 'It was much more difficult than the other pieces I've created. But you can see what I'm trying to do can't you?'

Adonai pointed out all of the figure's details proudly.

I stared around at the garden, at the river, the grass, the fish, the insects. The answer to one puzzle presented itself at last to my sluggish brain.

'This is your art.'

Adonai stared at me for a long time before turning and looking around at all he had created. 'Yes ... In a way it is. And now you are here and I have someone to share it with.'

A dark horror shivered up my spine.

'But I have to leave, return to my own time.'

Adonai shrugged, 'You must know that is impossible. I have so much more to show you.'

But I didn't want to know anymore. Didn't need to know. Was afraid to know. What Adonai revealed would blow a huge hole in the history of the world. Or would it? Maybe Adonai was God after all ... even though he saw himself as an artist and not a divinity. But I was still too curious to know just what he was. Was he alien? Or was this just some alternate reality I had stepped into? All I wanted to do was demand to know where he came from, but I was too nervous to ask.

To distract my thoughts I stroked the lines on the clay man's face. My hands ran over his arms, every muscle and curve had been defined in the clay. He was, in fact, perfect in every sense. My fingers brushed his hand and the thumb twitched. I jumped back.

'He moved!'

'Of course he did. But he isn't quite ready yet. For that I need your help. He won't work until he has a name.'

'A name?'

'Yes. I told you. Names are very important. They make us who we are, Lillith. And you are very good at helping me with that ...'

Adam.

Oh no. Oh my God, no!

I couldn't name him that. But the thought had popped into my head and immediately Adonai blinked.

'I knew you would find it. "Adam" it is then.'

'No,' I shook my head. 'Not that. This is too surreal. I think I must be losing my mind. Or dreaming.'

I couldn't really be in the Garden of Eden and this man of clay couldn't be Adam because if it was, then Adonai was *really* God.

The clay began to change colour. It lost its dark, red hue and melted into an olive brown. Adam's hair darkened and the clay strands separated in the breeze. His head became a mass of flowing, long hair that grew around his shoulders. I stared down at his shifting limbs. The arms and legs twitched and flexed as though he woke from a deep sleep and was stretching his muscles. He was naked, and very well made. I stared back into his face, a slight flush colouring my cheeks. Adam's eyes blinked to reveal they were a rich dark brown, yet vacant, confused, dazed as they struggled to comprehend all that he saw just like a newborn baby.

Adonai stretched out his hand and placed it on Adam's head. His fingers glowed for a few moments and I watched in fascination as Adam's vision cleared and his eyes focused steadily on me.

'I have given him some innate knowledge,' he explained. 'Now he can function as the other animals do.'

'But he isn't an animal. He's a man. He should have the choice to live as he wishes.'

'And you think he does not have free will? But of course he does. Just like the animals do.'

'Free will? The animals have free will? They can think for themselves?'

'Of course. They couldn't possibly work unless they had a choice on how they wanted to live.'

Adam reached out a hand and his fingers brushed my face, 'Beautiful.'

I stepped back out of reach, revulsion shuddered up my spine. 'How would you know? I'm the only woman you've ever seen.'

I turned to Adonai and found he had gone. So that was it. He had his own agenda. Adonai had made me a mate. Oh dear, he really didn't understand anything about women.

I turned back to Adam. 'What on earth am I going to do with you?'

'Lillith ...' he said.

'Come on, you might as well explore your new home. But I wish Adonai had made you some clothes. At least then it wouldn't be so obvious that you like me ...'

Adam followed me around and I felt obliged to show him the acres of land that consisted of the garden. I avoided the fruit trees; I wasn't going to be blamed for that one! He smiled indulgently as I pointed out the river and the leaping fish. It was as though he already understood everything.

The animals came out from the trees to greet Adam. Most of them had hidden from me all this time. I saw two of everything. The garden was the original Noah's Ark. There were rabbits hopping side by side with loping wolves. A chattering monkey played with a lazy python in a tree. An antelope and a leopard gleefully chased around an expanse of open land like children playing 'Tag'. A lioness came out of the trees and walked towards us. She rolled over on the grass before our feet and allowed us to pet her. Her mate, a proud and perfect lion with a beautiful long mane, stood back and watched.

I pushed aside the thought that Adonai now had male and female humans as well. Except, I'm not human, and I sure couldn't make babies with Adam.

I was amazed and thrilled by the animals. Until then I had barely caught a glimpse of any of them. Although I had been aware that recently the night had become peppered with sounds, such as an owl screeching, the discordant howl of a wolf, or crickets chirruping, mixed with the occasional elephant call.

'So, that's your world. Now I have to get back to mine,' I told him and tried to walk away.

'This is your world now, Lillith. There is nowhere else for you to go. Why do you resist it?'

I turned and stared at Adam in surprise. How much knowledge had Adonai given him?

'You don't understand. This is *not* my world. I have to get back to Gabi!'

Adam shrugged. He had the future all mapped out, but he sounded like Adonai and the more I thought about it the more I suspected that Adonai knew exactly how I could return, but he really didn't want to help me.

Adam stroked my arm and I shuddered, jumping away as though I had frost-bite.

'Don't ...' I warned. 'You may be the only man alive, but that's no excuse to think you have the right to touch me.'

The faint smile fell from Adam's face. Fortunately he knew nothing of violence, his whole demeanour was innocent and he didn't pursue me further, merely sat, naked, under a tree. Then quietly he picked a daisy from the ground and scrutinised it.

'Beautiful ...' he said, holding the flower up to the light.

I shook my head. Adam found the flower every bit as fascinating to touch and admire as he did me, but the flower didn't object to being admired. It was hard to dislike him though; he had the simplicity of a child and his innocence was quite endearing.

I left Adam and walked back to the clearing where the door had once been. How was I ever going to find my way home?

The only way back is to go forward, Adonai had said and his words rang in my head until my heart throbbed with anxiety. I fell asleep on the doorway, hoping that if I stayed there then a new opportunity would present itself and a new door would open.

'Paradox,' said a voice, and I opened my eyes to see a beautiful dark haired woman sitting opposite me before an open fire.

She was wearing multi-coloured clothing. A wide skirt of bright pink, a pale blue top that tumbled off one shoulder and a dark purple sash around her waist. The sash had tiny bells sewn along the edges and it matched the swatch of cloth that was tied around her hair, half headband, half scarf.

I sat up, looked around, and watched her carefully as she swirled a ladle in a large pot above the fire.

'Paradox is my biggest dilemma ...' she continued.

'What a strange word,' another voice said, and I turned to see a blonde gypsy leaving a barrel-shaped caravan. The second woman walked towards the fire, swaying her hips; the coin covered belt around her waist jingling. I must be dreaming. I rubbed my eyes, but felt completely awake. I knew who I was staring at but couldn't quite believe that this was Lucrezia. And across from me had to be Miranda! Lucrezia had told Gabriele and I of how the gypsy, Miranda, saved her from her brother Caesare. Miranda then taught Lucrezia her witchcraft in order to stay hidden, which she managed to do for almost two hundred years.

Somehow I was in their reality. A few hundred years before my own time! I must have crossed another door.

Lucrezia danced around the fire. The tinkle of the coins was her music. She banged wildly on a small handmade tambourine that consisted of a shallow wooden drum and some pierced coins. It was roughly covered with stained calf-skin. Miranda watched her for a moment. Lucrezia swirled and leapt, her bright red skirt whipped around her legs, flashing her white calves. Around her ankles she wore ribbons with tiny bells sewn on, which added to the music of the dance.

'You're improving,' she said. 'But you still dance like a demon.'

'I am a demon,' Lucrezia laughed, her movements gradually slowing to a halt.

Miranda laughed. 'That you are ...'

'What's a paradox?' Lucrezia asked as she sat down by the fire and slowly began to untie the bells from her ankles.

Miranda stared into the orange flames and didn't answer for a moment. I tried to talk, but no sound came out and so I stretched out my hand to Lucrezia to get her attention, but it was as though I wasn't there because she showed no sign of having seen me at all.

Miranda glanced up suddenly, staring through the flames in my direction.

'I'm you,' she whispered. 'And you're me. Or there will be a paradox ... Do you understand, Lilly?'

'Lillith.'

I woke slowly. The vision faded from my mind but I was reluctant to let it go. It was the closest I'd been to my world in weeks. I could not understand why I had been driven so hard to enter the doorway in the first place. It was as though I had no choice; that a contradiction in time would occur if I resisted. The dream suggested it, but then maybe that was just my subconscious. And I believed that dreams didn't mean anything anyway.

'Lillith!'

My eyes fluttered open and I stared into Adonai's multi-coloured gaze. His hair was lighter today, his eyes greener.

'Stop it!'

'I don't understand,' he replied.

'Don't use his image. Don't you dare try to look like him ...'

Adonai's hair darkened, his eyes changed back to one blue, one green. 'I did not wish to offend you. I thought this was a form you liked.'

'It is! But not ... I need the real thing, not a doppelganger. No one could be Gabriele, but Gabriele. Do you understand?'

Adonai blinked and shook his head, 'What a strange being you are. There is all this ...' He indicated his skull briefly. '... confusion!'

'I shouldn't be here, Adonai! I told you!'

'But you could be happy here. Tell me what you need; I can make it for you.'

'I need to go home. I need Gabi. Can't you do that for me?'

Adonai shook his head once more. I wasn't sure if this meant he couldn't help me or that he didn't want to.

'You should be satisfied,' he said.

The Phone Call

I find Harry waiting for me in the hallway as I come out of the bathroom wrapped in my robe. Hair washed, nails scrubbed, there is no evidence of the murder I committed the night before. I meet his eyes but he drops his gaze immediately. He will do everything he can to try and help me feel less guilty for what he believes will be 'me losing it' because I always refuse to kill. But the pride I see briefly in his expression is enough to make me toss my head back and tell him the truth.

'I didn't lose it. I killed in cold blood, okay? The fucker groped me, and you know how I hate that!'

Harry's deep, rich, laughter, echoes through the castle. 'You need to come with a public health warning! "Mauling this blonde will seriously damage your health!"'

I laugh until my sides ache. Harry's sense of humour has always entertained me.

'Well, that and I could see he was a murdering, rapist-bastard son-of-a-bitch who was a danger to women,'

'You've been watching too many vigilante movies.'

I smile. 'Nah. I just have no respect for life.'

I walk into my room and pull the towel from around my head letting my long damp hair cascade over my shoulders and back. Harry follows and watches as I sit down before my dressing mirror and begin combing my hair. He perches on the edge of my bed.

'So, how was the redhead?' I ask over the whir of the dryer. 'Was it her real hair colour?'

Harry meets my gaze sheepishly in the mirror, and nods.

'No more details than that?' I laugh.

'I don't kiss and tell!'

'Okay. I respect that in a man. I guess ... But you used to *brag* about your conquests.'

'Yeah. I know. But I'm trying to change.'

'Did she live the night? At least tell me that?'

'Yes. And she'll have trouble walking for a few days ... but that will be a very good memory.'

I laugh. 'Saucy boy.'

Harry glances around the room, his eyes falling casually on the packed cases by the door. For a moment his face becomes more serious.

'You know, you could come to Wales with me ...' I say into the mirror.

He shakes his head but his face is thoughtful. 'You know I'm happiest here. But even so, this is a meeting you have to have alone.'

I stare into the mirror, watching the door close. My eyes fall on the phone. Then flick towards the clock. A few hours to go. I had waited long enough, after all, to ring Gabi. But there was no point in calling yet. *Right now he doesn't even know I'm missing.*

In an hour, by London time, Lilly, Lucrezia and Gabi will all be sitting in the café at Harvey Nichols in Manchester. Lucrezia will tell them the rest of her story and then Caesare will appear and cause mayhem. Lucrezia will kill him. Lilly, Gabi and Lucrezia will calmly return to their cooling coffee and then ... it happens.

I have gone through this in my head so many times, exploring how crucial my timing must be; how the phone-call mustn't be a minute too soon, but should be as soon as Lilly disappears. And yes, oddly, I have to refer to myself as a whole other person because in the world, since her birth, I've felt this strange tremor, and I believe it is because there should never be more than one of you living in the same time and place. But it was unavoidable.

Soon the world will become right again; at least my world will. I hope.

I glance at the clock once more. I've waited an eternity, yet these hours creep by slower than the years ever did. I can't wait. But I have to. Preventing paradox has been the bane of my life.

I switch the hairdryer on and run it over my hair. Gabi will see many differences. My hair is so much longer than the Lilly he knows. She has a bob, mine flows long and wavy, down to my waist. They say the eyes are the mirrors to the soul; I wonder what Gabi will see when he looks into mine. It won't be his love reflecting back. It can't be, after all that has happened.

I sigh.

My heart hurts. Anxiety. Fear. Every emotion you could possibly imagine ... except love for him, because I don't think I can feel that anymore. The distance between us has been exaggerated by hundreds of years in my time. But still, my feelings are irrelevant. I don't want him to be distressed ... Gabi waited so long for love, had it so briefly, that it still feels unfair that I was ripped from him. Or at least will be ... soon. There's nothing that can be done to stop it, otherwise I'd be a paradox myself.

I dress with careful simplicity. As with all things, one had to be prepared for every eventuality. So, I slip on a fitted black designer t-shirt and some tight black jeans. Over which I pull on a pair of black knee length boots. Finally I put on my jacket, a black leather bomber, with soft cream faux fur around the neck.

Picking up my cases and handbag, I check my pockets for my tickets and passport. For once, I'm travelling traditionally with a direct flight booked to Manchester. From there a hire car waits. I will drive to my castle in North Wales, a mere hour and a half away. This is the place I have chosen to meet Gabi once more. It is a world that over the centuries has become close to my heart and the castle at Rhuddlan has often been my home, even though externally it appears to be a tourist ruin.

Harry is nowhere to be found when I leave my room. Clearly he doesn't wish to say goodbye and I feel a moment of angst at his stubborn and often childish behaviour. Sometimes I believe that my child had not evolved beyond the years of his change, and in many ways that is true. Harry was born in a time when women were servants to men and in a world of violence and greed. Now he has the world at his finger tips and still he struggles to change and grow.

I get into the waiting limousine outside and my driver stows my bags in the trunk while I retrieve my mobile phone from my purse. I glance at my watch. Two minutes. My heart is in my mouth. Nausea pulls at my insides. I feel like a teenager about to ask her first crush for a date, afraid of rejection. And yet, for Gabi the moment of my departure has only just occurred. I flip open my phone and dial his number. Even after all this time I haven't forgotten it.

I press *call.* The phone rings. And rings. It seems an age as I wait for him to pick up. Fear clutches my heart. I swallow as the sickness grows more intense. Any moment I will vomit over the immaculate interior of this car. Panic sets in. Unreasonable angst twists my mind and heart in knots. *My timing must be wrong. Maybe I have remembered the dates incorrectly. Yes – I'm a year late! I must be. Too late!*

My fingers are numb as they hover over the cancel button.

At last Gabi answers. I don't give him time to speak, I'm too afraid that I won't be able to tell him I'm there.

'Gabi! It's Lilly. I know this is really strange after so long, but I need you. I'm in Stockholm.'

I am gabbling. A gibbering wreck I wait for him to answer. Wait for acknowledgement even though I know the gulf between us is now too wide to surmount. My brain is mush, so much so that I barely take in his reply.

'How can that be? You've only just vanished?'

'What?'

'Just ten minutes ago … Darling, I'm so relieved to hear your voice.'

'Ah, I have so much to tell you.' My voice seems fake to my ears.

I feel dazed. My call was made right on time but now the moment is here I am afraid of the future. Perhaps I should have just left him alone.

Chapter 7 - Lilly's Journal
Leaving The Garden

Eve was beautiful, with long dark flowing hair and a physique to match that of Adam. Although I didn't make much effort to really get to know if this equality stretched to mental capacity also. She was a little sycophantic for my tastes. Always following him around and if not Adam, then it was me she hung around.

'So now you've created woman ...' I sigh as Adonai proudly shows me his beautiful, naked creation.

'Yes Lillith. Do you think she is an effective woman? Perhaps you could help her development ...'

'I know where this is going. And I'm not prepared to be the snake.' I told him walking away.

Adonai watched me leave; I could almost feel his confused expression burning into my back. He didn't understand my lack of enthusiasm for his world. The 'paradise' thing wore thin after a few days. The truth was, there was only so much nature and beauty a person could take. There just wasn't anything to do. There was no need to attempt to survive. I felt no hunger, or cold and my body only craved sleep when my obsession drove me to mental exhaustion.

There was no stimulus in the garden, nothing to motivate any of us. Yet Eve and Adam were content to waste away their time lying around languidly. Or they would merely walk in and out of the waterfall as though it were the most exciting experience of their lives. They were simple, and yet they knew as much about me as Adonai did. Often I came upon them sitting by the river watching the fish leap, or petting the horses of which, by then, there was a full herd. Always Adonai was near.

One morning as I sought out Adonai, I came across the three of them by the river. Adonai was pointing to a space on the other side of the water, where a giraffe family wandered, chewing occasionally on the leaves of a tall tree. As I approached I heard them talking and it was a language the like of which I had never heard. It was as though their words were music. It sounded like bells and chimes in a variety of tones and pitches. And it hurt!

I fell to the ground clutching my ears as blood oozed from them. The sound of their alien speech and laughter was like sharp knives being plunged into my ears. I screamed. Adonai stopped talking and turned to me. For a moment Adonai, Adam and Eve all seemed to be wearing the same dark, blank and cold expression and then their faces changed. Adonai rushed forward and kneeled beside my prone form on the cushioned grass.

'Forgive me,' he said. 'I never meant to harm you.'

'It was the music,' I cried. My ears hurt so much I could barely hear his reply, it was only by watching his lips move that I could make out what he said.

'My language is old and you were not made to hear it.'

'It was beautiful ...' I protested. 'So why ...?'

'Why did it hurt?'

Eve helped me sit upright as I nodded. The pain was receding from my head and the blood had stopped flowing down the sides of my face.

'Old magic.'

'I don't understand ...' I said.

'You will, in time. You have much to experience first.'

My ears healed as he spoke. At least that was one supernatural element I had retained. As soon as I was better Adonai left the garden for the day. I watched him disappear, back near my original entrance point. This was his favourite exit point.

I began to suspect that I was an experiment, a lab rat, and that the three of them were merely scientists observing my reactions and learning all they could. There was no obvious reason for this paranoia other than the fact that Adonai clearly had a method to leave and wouldn't share it with me. Also, he would often skulk away out of earshot with Eve and Adam and they would talk for hours in their music-speech. As time went by the snatches of speech I heard stopped hurting my ears but remained no less alien in their sound and I never learned to understand it. I felt as though I was constantly excluded from this private club of theirs. So as the weeks wore on I became more determined to leave and find my way home.

Every day I returned to the exit point of the door and stared at the air shimmering around it. It was still there. I just knew it. But what if I tried to leave the way I had come?

Once I turned around to find Adonai watching me, his expression blank.

'What will happen if I try to cross the door ...?'

'It would be dangerous.'

I shook my head. 'I don't believe you, Adonai. What is this place, really? It feels like a recreation just for me. As though this place is a holding cell, and I'm a prisoner.'

'You can't go, Lillith,' Adonai said.

'I can. And I will. Even if I walk the entire length and breadth of the Earth to find another doorway.'

The air shivered and the ground at my feet shuddered. My arms flew out to steady myself. It felt like the world's first earthquake.

'Why would you invent that?' I asked Adonai. 'So many people will die because of earthquakes.'

'I didn't. The planet has a will of its own now.'

'You can't stop it?'

'Why would I want to?'

'I thought you wanted perfection?'

Adonai shook his head in that fatherly way he had adopted when speaking to me, 'Lillith, nature is perfect. It has its own purpose. I wouldn't change it, even if I could.'

As always these conversations ended with my frustration. My mind was on its own wild tangent. Probably from lack of any external stimulation, and for a twenty-first century girl, that was hard to take. Imagine being without your mobile? Your laptop? Cars? TV? All of the things that I was used to, had grown up with. It was no wonder I obsessed so much about who Adonai really was. I went from believing he was God to convincing myself he was the devil and I was trapped in some form of hell. For this place was hell to me, not paradise, not beauty but confinement and it kept me apart from all I had known and loved.

'Come away from the gateway,' Adonai pleaded.

I didn't answer.

'You can't go back to your time Lillith – don't you see that?'

'You constantly speak in riddles. Why won't you help me instead?' I asked.

'He's trying to protect you ...' Eve said.

I ignored her. I was sick of her following me around, mimicking my gestures, imitating my smile, copying my walk. I sat down on the grass looking intently at the rippling and shifting space before me. The air shook again. I sat forward.

It's unstable. At any time it may reappear and I'll step back through to find Gabi and Lucrezia waiting for me, I thought.

'Lillith,' Adam called. 'Come and see the animals with us.'

As if on cue the lioness appeared and rolled down on the grass beside me. I ran my hands over her back and stomach as she squirmed and played like a kitten.

Eve, Adam and Adonai drifted away leaving me once more to my thoughts, but the lioness kept me company for the rest of the day, occasionally licking my face with her rough tongue.

The days passed into weeks, the weeks into months and then the months into years. I spent my days and nights by the door. It was a reflective time. As always Adonai came and went through an exit point near the doorway I had entered. This taught me that there was a way to leave. But caution held me back from following him. After all, I didn't know where he was from or where he went to. Even so, I watched carefully and after a time he began to ignore my presence. I rarely responded when he spoke to me anyway. He couldn't understand me, or my motive for wanting to leave his perfect world. Maybe I had been an experiment but I merely became a disappointment because I refused to interact with his other toys.

The animals began to procreate more and more, and often the lioness and her cubs played around my feet.

'You're the only company I need,' I told her as she purred under my touch.

The lioness visited me regularly up to her old age and she died one day by my side as her great-grand-cubs frolicked in the field nearby. She had an affinity with me and I often wondered if the animals had also been snatched from another time. Forced to be benign, these lovely and powerful predators, had families, aged and died, but had little other motivation for living. The lioness was a huntress just like me, and in the garden we were both neutered. I'd even tried to force my fangs forward and found they wouldn't come.

Unlike the animals, Eve and Adam did not reproduce, nor did they age. This sinister realisation made me wonder just what they really were. Or why they were here. But it was a problem that remained unsolved. I withdrew further into myself after the lioness died. Rarely speaking, refusing to be touched. Isolation can paralyse the most loving heart. Loneliness became unimportant, and the obsession with my life 'before' the garden became a vague memory.

That is why Adonai stopped watching me completely. He felt I had given up. That was the day I saw the barriers between the worlds Adonai inhabited. And when I realised he no longer worried about me that was also the day I chose to leave.

He arrived unannounced as always and the edge of the garden was shimmering with the resonance of his recent emergence. He ignored me when he arrived. I wasn't part of his bigger plan – it was his two human-like creatures that interested him, even though I had inadvertently named them. I believed without doubt that the garden was indeed an unknown world, but probably had nothing to do with the biblical legend. My presence there had merely shaped it to look like the Garden of Eden I heard of so often in Sunday school as a child.

As Adonai left the clearing, I glanced up at his entrance point. There before me, briefly, was a reflective image. It was as though a large mirror had materialised in the space. I saw myself for the first time in years; ragged, my hair was Rapunzelian. My clothing was worn and aged, little more than rags. But my face, though pale and drawn was as perfect as the day that Gabriele transformed me into his vampire mate.

I stood up. My lengthy lethargy should have made my limbs waste away, but my muscles were solid and defined as they had always been. Because I couldn't die, I was immortal, no matter what situation I found myself in. I walked to the mirror; my image shivered on the surface while behind me the perfect world stayed still. I didn't belong here, I'd said it all along, and this reflective image showed that my form was out-of-step with the world around me. I reached out placing the palms of my hands against the surface. It felt like the skin of a pond; behind it the world bulged. I pulled my hands away, walked round it only to find that at the back it was the same.

Excitement gathered in my chest. This was indeed a portal of some kind. It was clearly and significantly different from the door by which I had entered, but was by no means any different in some respects. At the front again I pressed my hands deeper into the shiny, glutinous surface and my fingers pushed through. I felt a tar-like tug and so I held my breath and stepped forward.

I can at least peek inside.

My face met resistance and I had to close my eyes against the pressure. But once the surface skin of the portal was broken I opened my eyes.

Beyond the portal was a myriad of doors, all like reflective glass. I moved closer, allowing the suction to pull me through. And I left the garden forever, without even saying goodbye. But as I stepped into Adonai's illusive world, I looked back and saw him staring through the portal. I turned to face him, but he said nothing. His face was solemn. He didn't follow me as I had suspected he would.

Had I finally gone forward in my attempt to go back?

The Corridors Of Reflection

The corridor of reflections showed me centuries, past, present and future but all of the ones from my time were barred to me. In this at least, Adonai, had been right. I couldn't re-enter my time, but I could move away from this primitive world and live in the real world a little closer to my centuries.

The corridor was infinite. No matter how far I travelled there were more routes to explore, although I learnt this all by sheer error.

The moment I crossed the portal was a defining time. As I looked back at Adonai in the garden the portal closed. I knew this because the reflection thickened and froze. The image became an ice carving. The fluidity solidified and I knew I could never again go back through that route.

'You must have known,' I said to Adonai's frozen, captured image. 'You said all along that the only way back was to move forward. And yet, you seem to have the freedom to go anywhere you please. Okay. So if I've used this door I can't use it again. That's fine. I need to get back to my century anyway. I was sick of your bloody garden.'

The portals were like two-way mirrors, I could see the worlds beyond them. That at least would help me find the closest one to home. The first one I studied showed me a town in Europe in the 1950s. Beyond the portal was a street filled with old cars that reminded me of Laurel and Hardy movies I'd seen, although it could have been anywhere in Europe or America judging by the occupants that walked unwittingly by. It was as good an entry point as any. I pressed my hand against the mirror, felt briefly the buoyancy of the portal and then it froze me out.

'So, not that way then ...' I sighed, moving onto the next mirror.

This one showed a Roman city. As soon as I touched it the scene froze. Another reflection revealed nineteenth century London. I watched in awe as the city moved. Yes. That was Waterloo Bridge. A gold carriage drove past with a procession following close by. The Coronation of Queen Victoria. *Close enough!* I threw myself forward. The image froze, hurling me backwards into the corridor.

'Shit! Fuck!'

I'll be stuck here forever, I thought several portal rejections later. *Maybe there is a knack to it. Perhaps I need to enter the other side ...*

Traversing the reflections only revealed new destinations and every one I touched froze. I sat down on the floor. The corridor was tiled in a multitude of materials: earth; marble; sod; brick; wood. It was a manifestation of every kind of material that was developed throughout the centuries. There was even some form of metal that I had never seen before. I didn't ponder too much on this at the time because my head hurt when I tried to analyse the corridor. It wasn't meant to be understood.

I tried a few more portals. This time not stopping to look and choose a specific time or place, because maybe I didn't have any choice. But each time I tried I was barred. After a few hours, I became more and more annoyed, and typically threw a tantrum because I couldn't get my own way. I picked up a pebble from a beach-like section of the floor and hurled it with all my might at the nearest mirror. I wanted to smash and destroy every single portal. But as I turned away there was a distinct lack of breaking glass. I looked back at the mirror and saw a dimple in the surface where the pebble had travelled right through. The surface rippled with the aftershock.

Jumping to my feet I ran to the doorway and gazed beyond

into the world. For a moment my confused mind couldn't make sense of the chaos I was seeing. It looked like a battle was taking place and it was in a landscape that was oddly familiar. I watched some kind of warrior running riot with a huge sword. He was chasing an old peasant. There was definitely something wrong with the power balance of the battle. This wasn't soldier against soldier – even I knew that with what little history I'd studied at high school.

It was a Viking raid. I could tell by the helmets and the dirty sheepskin clothing. The villagers were losing, despite a few valiant efforts with pitchforks and axes.

'Vikings? Let me see … if I can remember my history that is nine hundreds? Tenth Century then!' I muttered to the portal. 'Seems a familiar time. But then if you let me through I won't fucking care where I end up.' I stepped forward. 'Although you'll probably freeze around me …But anywhere would be better than being stuck in here any longer.'

I jumped …

… right into the raid.

The sound of screaming hit me as I landed smack in the middle of a haystack just outside a barn. I fell forward with the force of entry and did a near perfect roll, jumping immediately to my feet. Battle-noise roared around me, with the clang of broadswords and the snarl of men as they savagely hacked each other to pieces. It was painful to my ears. I hadn't heard this much noise in years.

I smelt blood. It was the most glorious thing I'd smelt since I found myself in the garden. My vampiric hunger surged up in response. Back in this world, my reflexes returned to normal, my fangs burst forth. I had almost forgotten that I was, in fact, a murdering fiend in my own right. Being amongst such brutality, therefore, shouldn't have been such a shock. But it was. I felt confused and disorientated, and stumbled backwards into the open doorway of the barn.

I'd left a world of almost absolute quiet and was plunged into this insane situation. The screaming of women and young girls echoed through my brain, making my heart pound in anguish. It was horrible. The noise hurt my eardrums almost as much as Adonai's ancient language had. My vampiric instincts of self-preservation kicked in.

I scanned the barn, realised I was alone. Outside I heard the pound of rapidly approaching feet. Above me was a second tier in the structure. I leapt up just as a burning torch hurtled inside, catching the dry straw alight immediately. The ground burst into flames below my feet. I looked down, then around, remembering Lucrezia telling us that she had been burnt at the stake and then miraculously healed, but I wasn't prepared to learn how painful that really was, or even if I too could survive such destruction of my body. I felt an unreasonable sense of panic.

I think I had become institutionalised. In the garden the fight had been taken from me but at that moment all those desires came back in a consuming rush. I was starving: all the years of not feeding were pressing down on me. I looked frantically at the flames rapidly climbing up the wooden walls, fuelled by the straw. It was terrifying and exhilarating. The structure of the building was swiftly becoming undermined. I was trapped.

And then I saw a faint light from the fires outside, gleaming in through a hatch above me. Climbing a small stack of straw bales I reached the window and pushed it open.

A battle was in full force in the field below: I stared down at screaming and running peasants. Utter chaos reigned. A Viking grabbed a young girl by her hair and yanked her back, dragging her shrieking and crying along the ground. A male peasant with a pitchfork ran to her aid and was skewered on the broadsword of another Viking before he even raised his arm above his waist. A small boy was decapitated as he stood in the bedlam tearfully calling for his *madre*.

An old woman lost her arm as she raised it to fend off the blow of a Viking. The sword cleft her face and head in two like a ripe melon being split by a carving knife. Her blood splattered in every direction as the Viking yanked his sword back but it became wedged briefly in her neck. The body lifted as he tugged and as he leaned over her it looked like they were joined in a macabre dance. Then he pressed his foot down into the centre of her chest. The sword slid free and the Viking kicked the corpse away and laughed as he turned to rejoin the fight.

I slid down the twenty or so feet of roof and landed sure-footedly in the middle of the brawl. The first Viking, who was wearing tan coloured buckskins and a sheepskin vest, tied with a brown leather make-shift belt, was in the middle of raping the young girl. Her cries of pain as he rutted with her made me feel a vigilante urge to rip out his heart. But soon her tears began to annoy him and he slit her throat, climaxing second after her life's blood seeped away into the already blood-stained soil.

I was behind him as he stood and I back-handed him, sending him sprawling, neck-broken across the carnage that he and his marauding buddies had left behind.

The noise around me retreated as I picked up the broadsword the dead Viking had dropped. I turned to face the astonished faces of the other Vikings who had seen me, a petite and ragged woman, kill their friend.

'Come on! You murdering bastards,' I yelled. 'I'll kill you all!'

The full force of blood-lust was on me. It pounded in my head, aching and throbbing like the onset of a crippling migraine. It made me insane with rage. My fangs were out in full view, my sword raised. One of them was foolish enough to run forward. I swung the sword with perfect reflexes and his head rolled at the feet of the others.

'Haxa!'

The name they called me, I later learned, was their name for witch. But these cries were no less than I would have expected in this bizarre and dangerous era. I stalked towards the men.

They stood their ground for a fraction of a second longer and then, with a cry of 'Demon!', howled in fear and rage, the group turned and ran.

'Clearly not the *berserker* warriors that history painted you to be,' I jeered after them. 'Viking honour means nothing in the face of a demon then? Arseholes!'

I gave chase as they ran through the village. I was enjoying their fear; it fed my fury as much as their blood would feed my veins. I was so hungry. I howled like a banshee and the stench of urine assaulted my nose as one of the Vikings pissed his pants at the sound of my feral cry. They scattered and ran in different directions and I gave chase to a small band of them as they fled through the village screaming in abject terror.

I heard whimpering inside one of the buildings and instead of enraging me it halted my fury. I stopped in the village square, turning around slowly, scanning every corner. Around me the myriad of noises was a total distraction after the absolute silence I'd had grown used to. Sensory overload was enough to drive me out of my mind. I could hear the crackling of several bonfires, the slight groan of buildings as they slowly disintegrated in the flames. The laboured breathing of the dying merged with the frantic crying of horses pushed too hard. It was difficult to distinguish some of the sounds as they blurred into one. I took a deep breath, pushing back the noises into categories I could recognise. Then I listened.

A faint sound. A quiet, murmur of fear, the smell of rape. My eyes fell on the one untouched building in the village as a cry echoed through the smoke-filled air. There was at least one alive to save. Although I didn't understand why I even wanted to interfere, but the urge was so immensely strong that I found myself running towards the building full pelt.

I kicked down the door and found a whimpering woman lying on the floor. Her skirts were flung up, and I could see and smell damp semen on her thighs. The Viking responsible was fastening his breeches. He reached for his sword as I burst in but I had him by the throat before his fingers could gain a good purchase on the ornate hilt of his weapon.

The hunger was ripping up my insides, my body was beginning to cannibalise itself and the physical exertion of the fight had expended more energy than I'd realised. The smell of blood had made me crazy. I had to eat. I pulled him to me, plunged my fangs straight into his throat and gulped and chewed as he flailed against me. His struggles were pointless of course. He had no chance. His thrashing arms gradually lost their strength and once he was drained I threw his body away as though it were an empty milk carton.

I felt better. Calmer. The blood lust had been appeased, at least for that moment. I flexed my limbs as the strength pumped back into them and the momentary wooziness I'd experienced from the lack of blood quickly diminished. My pounding headache cleared and the battle noise no longer hurt my ears as much.

I looked over at the body of the Viking, noticing how he still gripped his sword. It had a beautiful and ornately designed handle and scabbard. I threw aside the one I'd been carrying and I picked up the dead Viking's hand. I snapped his fingers and took the sword, examining it carefully. Then I reached down and unfastened the Viking's belt, taking it and the scabbard.

As I fastened it around my waist I turned to the woman, who was cowering up against the wall. She was silent but afraid. I gasped. As I met her gaze it was like looking into the eyes of my mother. She was the very image of her. She stared back, terrified as my fangs slipped back into my gums. But she didn't scream. I wiped the blood from my mouth with the back of one hand as I held out the other to her.

'Come with me, I won't hurt you.'

And she believed me. She stood, straightened her clothes and we left the hut standing as the rest of the village burned. The Viking raiders were nowhere to be seen, had run away for the time being, but I was aware of them at the edge of the village, perhaps thirty or forty waited there as I led the woman away in the opposite direction; deep into the Italian landscape and away from the corpses of the villagers.

'What's your name?' I asked as we weaved through the neighbouring woods.

'Maria Serafina.' Her voice was steady. 'You saved me!'

'Not soon enough,' I sighed.

'I was no virgin, but a widow. I am grateful to be alive; he would have killed me. God sent you to save me.'

'Of course he didn't!' I said shaking my head, but then my mind flashed to all the barred doors. Perhaps something or someone had meant for me to be here at this time and to behave as I had in response to the brutalities of the Vikings. 'Come,' I said again. 'Let's get you away from here. I promise I won't hurt you.'

'You are an avenging angel,' Maria said.

I shook my head in denial, but maybe I was to her. This was a superstitious world and I would rather have her think I was an angel than a demon. That would make life far less complicated if I had to remain here for any length of time.

We found a clearing a little more than a mile away. Maria collapsed down on the grass, all of her remaining strength evaporating once we were clear of the village.

I gazed down at her unconscious frame. I was afraid for her though I didn't understand why I even cared. There was a nagging feeling in the back of my mind. Something about her survival was important. We were still too close and so, shrugging, I picked her up and ran on, covering the miles in a short space of time.

Before dawn, and after resting awhile myself, I picked up the Viking sword and left Maria huddled up against a tree. I ran back to the village, combing the area for any further survivors, or indeed any more Vikings to eat, but they had taken their dead and the village was in ashes. I stood where the barn had been, looking for the tell-tale shimmer of the doorway back to the corridor of reflections. But it was nowhere to be seen and I wondered if the flames could have closed the portal, or whether it was true that I could only enter one way. This did leave me with a dilemma for the immediate future but it was pointless worrying too much about it. I was here, in whatever time it turned out to be and at least I had escaped the stasis of the garden. Anything would be preferable to that.

I searched the remains, picking up provisions and clothing that I thought we might need. On a washing line hung a thick woollen cloak. I took it and pulled it around me, aware that my clothing, even though they were little more than rags, might seem strange to the people in this time.

As the sun rose, a small whimpering sound reverberated around the remains of the village. Immediately I became alert again. I raised the broadsword. The cries were strangely echoed, but muted as though the person was afraid to be found, but was in so much pain or discomfort they could not help making this slight sound. I walked through the burnt, muddy street and realised the sound was coming from a well in the middle of the square. Hurrying forward I looked down into the scared, glowing eyes of a five year old girl. She had been thrown down the well to drown but had somehow managed to wrap herself around the bucket that hung by a tenuous thread.

'Stay still,' I called.

I sheathed the sword and reached for the rope seconds before it snapped. For a moment I didn't have the grip I needed to pull the girl up. The rope burnt my fingers, slipping and ripping through the skin until I tightened my clasp. As the bucket fell down lower to the water, the child yelped but didn't scream. Once my hold was secure I pulled again, slowly and more in control this time.

'Don't be afraid,' I said again.

Although she didn't understand my modern day Italian completely, she realised that I was trying to help and she held on, looking up eagerly into my eyes.

Pulling her completely out of the well, I lifted her trembling body into my arms wrapping the cloak around her. Then, as dawn broke, I ran with supernatural speed out and away from the village.

When I returned Maria Serafina had built a fire and was huddled close to it. She took the little girl from me and sat her down next to the fire. They shivered, but not from the cold. I understood the chill that took them. It was shock mostly, and the cold was seeping out from their souls after the horror of the night they had survived. It would, I imagined, live with them for all of their lives. I gave Maria the supplies I'd found and both of them nibbled on some scorched bread and chewed on a hunk of cheese.

'You helped me. I can help you,' Maria said some time later.

I looked at her, vaguely amused but my cynical smile disappeared when I met her gaze.

'I knew you would come. I'm a herbwife. I dreamed of you.'

I tried not to laugh, for if she had been blessed with the gift of prophecy she surely could have warned her village of the marauders.

'How can you help me?' I asked politely instead.

'The villagers didn't believe me. There have never been raids this far inland before. But I saw it all.'

'Why didn't you leave before it happened?'

'I couldn't leave my village. They needed me. Besides, I had to wait. My dreams told me you would save me. And now I am with child from the Viking. That is my destiny.'

I didn't argue, but I knew it was too soon for her to know if she was pregnant.

'I need to help you now. You need to learn the ways of the herbwife and protect my heirs until the right time.'

'Look, you've been through a lot. You aren't making much sense,' I said. 'Maybe you should rest.'

She blinked, and then nodded. Before long she settled down with the little girl, whom she called Angelina, huddled against her. I watched the flames, occasionally adding more fuel to keep them both warm as they fell into a deep sleep. Later I slipped away and back to the village to scavenge more things; cooking pots and any food I could find for them. A few blankets and a sheepskin robe had survived the fire, I bundled these up, along with a calfskin water carrier, which I filled from the well.

Once I knew they could survive unaided, I intended to leave and try to find another route back to the twenty-first-century and to Gabriele. But little did I know that my destiny for the next seven years would be with Maria Serafina and the child she gave birth to.

Rhuddlan Castle

The landscape welcomes me back as I drive my hired car through the grim outskirts of Manchester, down the M56 and into the beautiful Welsh scenery. I see the red dragon, emblazoned on a road bridge as I cross the border from England into Wales and take a deep breath. Relief. Strange, considering all that I have seen in the world; it feels like coming home.

I turn off the A55 at the Prestatyn and Caerwys exit and drive through small villages, passing the familiar signs for Trelawnyd, Gwynaesgor and Dyserth and carry straight on the main road towards Rhuddlan. Driving home I can barely wait to see the fortress. Anticipation wipes away all of the anxiety I've been feeling on the journey from Stockholm to England. The beauty of the landscape helps me centre my emotions as I near my destination.

The castle now stands in ruins. Or at least on the surface it appears to be so. It, like me, has survived for centuries but still remains strong. The castle, now a tourist attraction, hides a secret beneath its foundations. Here lies my lair. Carved out for me over a hundred years ago, it has since been improved with all the modern conveniences I love. Furthermore, the Celtic foundations hold a power that has shielded me whenever I wished to hide.

I turn my car into Castle Street and drive up towards the castle car park. It is 5.30pm on Halloween. What an ironic time to return to the stronghold of my most powerful lair. There are cars parked everywhere, up and down and on both sides of the already narrow street.

'Ah. I should have realised!'

The castle is hosting a Halloween party and hundreds of people will be admitted to the grounds. I'm lucky to find a spot and quickly park my inconspicuous Polo, leaving my luggage inside the trunk. I cloak myself in invisibility and walk into the grounds, planning to retrieve the bags later. First I need access to my home.

The car park is full with the usual attractions. It has four port-a-loos in place, next to a stall that is being set up for refreshments. Beside this is a burger and hotdog stall. I can smell the burnt-fat odour of cooking meat as the helpers stack food onto the hot barbeque at the back. I wrinkle my nose in distaste but my mouth waters. It has been a long time since I ate anything so normal and basic, and I'd always loved hotdogs, but these days my diet is strictly liquid ...

I browse the stall positioned just outside the main shop. They are selling glowsticks and tickets for a 'spooky walk'. I grimace.

I walk on towards the bridge. Two more stalls before I reach it, but I'm not sure what they are selling. One looks like a game of some sort, but without seeing anyone playing I'm not sure what it is about. The other, I realise, is housing a fortune teller; an elderly woman in an ill-fitting wig, gaudy clothing and stick-on talon nails. A send-up gypsy, but I stay clear just in case.

I reach the bridge just as the sound of a crowd begins to crescendo behind me and I glance around to find a procession of people, dressed in varying Halloween costumes: witches, ghosts, ghouls, and ironically, many vampires. They are carrying glowsticks and torches and the whole parade descends on *my* castle in a mad flurry. A little girl runs ahead of the crowd. She's dressed as a witch with a black and silver boob tube and a black net skirt, under which she is wearing black and silver striped tights. I step back as she barely misses running headlong into me and her glow stick whips the air inches from my face.

My fangs are out in anger within seconds. I'm not averse to biting the innocent. More and more children carelessly run forward following in her footsteps until I'm knee deep in them. I back up to the edge of the moat and drop down from the bridge without making a sound as the people rush across above my head and into the ruins. Their excited chatter is almost painful to my ears as I hear bits of their conversations. I don't care for crowds … I don't care for humans generally.

'Does my make-up glow yet? Is it dark enough …?

'Let's play a joke on …'

'I want a hot dog, Mummy …'

'Can I have a glow-stick …?'

'Do you think the "Spooky Walk" will be as good as last year …?'

On and on, their thoughts, their words, tumble over me, until I feel smothered by the throng, suffocated by their fevered party madness, drowning in their deluded excitement.

I squeeze myself against the moat wall, placing my hands flat against the cool stones, and experience the Celtic power in the ruins. The castle's aura vibrates with recognition and I am welcomed home. My fangs retract. A sense of calm rolls over my body and the noise of the swarm zones out. Everything around me grows quiet. My fingers probe the wall and promptly find and open the only fake brick there. Behind is an electronic keypad and I press the numbers of my security code. The tunnel door grinds subtly open beneath the bridge and I slip inside as the noise and frenzy above begins to escalate and a loud PA system blares out music.

I rest against the wall inside as the tunnel door closes. The brick comforts me, pushing away the last sounds of the outside lunacy. I stroke the walls; feel the greeting as my fingers rustle with white power, sparks crackling from their tips in the dark. The first stage is traversed and I know that my entrance was unobserved by human eyes. Time to move on.

There is a myriad of tunnels beneath the castle. They are buried so deeply that the humans have never known they were there. No matter how intelligent their x-ray equipment becomes it is unlikely they will discover my hidden world. That is because the castle itself holds a spiritual power that can't be measured by technology. It sits on a spiral of interlinked ley lines.

My eyes adjust to the gloom, but seconds after the door closes the lights switch on and the staircase becomes illuminated. I begin my descent; round and round – over a thousand steps down into the bowels of the earth. I hurry down, eager to be in my lair and truly away from the hubbub above. Even though I can no longer hear the crowd, the castle foundations quietly register their presence like a security camera system monitoring visitors in a top secret facility. There is a low hum in the air. The castle wants no invasion into its inner sanctum, any more than I want people to find my lair. So my secret is safely tucked within her womb.

As I reach the bottom of the stairs the lights above switch off and the corridor before me brightens. There are no magical torches lighting by themselves here, as Lucrezia had described in her tale of the Allucian city, this is modern technology. I have it regularly maintained. Although the engineers who created and built the system will never remember the existence of what could possibly be their greatest achievement.

I find one such technician servicing the heating system as I open the doorway to my home. He is young, around mid-thirties, and he's wearing an overall with the words 'British Gas' emblazoned on his top pocket. His hair is almost black and I can't make out what colour his eyes are because he is working with them half closed. He is sleep-walking. He, like a computer, was programmed some years before to respond to my distantly sent command. I telephoned him as I reached the arrivals lounge at Manchester and spoke the words that activated my hypnotic power over him.

Job done, the man begins to pack away his tools. As he fills his bag his demeanour doesn't change. He turns to leave without acknowledging my presence.

Once he's gone I close the door and listen to his slow, steady ascent back up the stairs. He will wake as he leaves the grounds and will believe that he was called out to make an emergency gas repair somewhere. Actually he had checked and serviced my heating system. Not that the cold really bothers me but I do like a comfortable room temperature and the furnishing in the stronghold would become damp and spoilt if the place were left unheated all the time.

Being beneath so much earth also meant that an air-conditioning unit had to be installed. It would be unlikely that I would suffocate, and for years I had nothing of this nature down here, but air from the world above is pumped in and circulated nonetheless, keeping the environment below comfortable and fresh.

I twist around and gaze into my hallway. It is large and sprawling with a high ceiling, and leads to a huge staircase. My lair is a modern-mansion below sea-level and sits in the middle of the ley lines. It is this magnetic power and energy that feeds the power circuits. With the right knowledge, self-sufficiency is achievable.

'Let there be light,' I say, and the lights switch on in the hallway. Art deco candelabras also flicker into life on the landing and I take the stairs two or more steps at a time. I half run, half walk along the top balcony to my room, eager to be with the possessions I've accumulated over the years.

In my bedroom I am surrounded by original art-deco furniture; a dressing table of shiny black wood inlaid with a curved gold pattern around the drawer handles; a matching chest of drawers, stretching almost the entire length of one wall is complimented by two bedside cabinets on either side of a huge four-poster bed draped with red velvet fabric. Rich, cherry velvet drapes hang from the walls in two points, giving the impression of windows. I lie down in the centre of the bed, arms outstretched, and absorb the dizzying power of the ruins and the ley lines, feeling the renewing influence pour into my limbs.

I am relaxed and at home for the first time in a year. The castle has become the focal point of my power source and these regular top-ups energize and regenerate me, making the years of waiting so much more bearable.

'Music,' I say, and the room fills with Vivaldi.

I sleep for a while, drifting into memories of how this all began, where the knowledge of the universe's power came from, and how I, the youngest vampire, became the oldest.

Maria Serafina's Knowledge

I threw the broadsword down as we began to pack up our camp. We had decided to move on, find somewhere safe to stay further inland. But as I dropped the sword, Maria Serafina gently took my arm.

'You need to keep this Lilly. It has some significance for you.' She bent down, pointing at the handle, and there for the first time, I saw the triskele.

'I don't understand,' I said examining the rough carving. 'It's just some Viking sign, crudely cut into the metal.'

'Yes. But it has meaning ...' explained Maria, her finger tracing the three curves. 'These represent the past, the present and the future. And that is exactly what you hold in your hands, Lilly. After all, you came from the future didn't you?'

I stared at Maria. 'How do you know?'

'Your aura,' she answered, shrugging as though it were the most obvious thing in the world. 'It shimmers. It is part here, and part not. You are still in your own time, but so are you in all times.'

I shook my head. 'That's not possible. Yes. I am out of my own time. I admit that, even though I don't understand how *you* know that. But right now I'm here and I'd like nothing more than to return home as soon as I can.'

Maria patted my arm sympathetically. 'You will go home, when the time is right. But your destiny is to stay here for now. I have much to teach you.'

'Well, whatever happens we need to get you and Angelina to a safe place. Then we'll see.'

It was then Maria told me about the village nearby; it was a *Castrum* which meant we would have to sign up to the charter and agree to the laws of living within a fortified village. If we did this they would welcome us. It seemed they had recently lost their herbwife and so Maria Serafina's skills would be much needed.

'I heal the sick, help mothers give birth to their babies,' she told me. 'They believe these skills to be magic, but merely it comes from knowledge passed through my ancestors. Magic is a different skill altogether ...'

'Where is this village?' I asked.

'It is not far,' she said. 'Angelina is drained and still in shock. The sooner we get there the better I can treat her.'

We arrived in the village at dawn. It was built within a fortress and Maria explained that it was ruled by a Lord who had sworn to protect the people from the invaders. The Viking had not been the first to invade their lands. The Saracens were there first and so there were many fortified villages like these, scattered along the outskirts of the mainland.

The stronghold was built around a church and a small castle where the Lord resided.

'I'm not sure,' I said because the church worried me.

Maria looked at me and followed my gaze to the wood and stone building with the huge crucifix built into the wall above the doorway.

'It's just a church,' she shrugged. 'You can go there; you are no soulless demon.'

'How do you know?' I asked, my eyes scrutinising her impenetrable expression. 'And how does a village like this really feel about a herbwife? *You* could be in danger here. Christians have a history of fearing magic.'

'The priests have very little say over the traditions of the past. Why would you think me in danger from them? My kind is respected by Lords and peasants alike. If the sick need a cure, you wouldn't go to a church to find it, you'd visit a herbwife.'

Her words did little to reassure me but they did begin to give me an insight to the beliefs of the people of this time.

Angelina slept most of the way in my arms, and I wrapped the robe around us both. The robe hid both my strange clothing and the broadsword, which remained fixed around my waist at all times during the journey.

'Before we go in,' Maria said, 'I need to change your appearance.'

'The cloak hides my clothing ...'

'No ... your hair.'

'My hair?'

'You look like a daughter of the Vikings with your golden locks. And your height will emphasise that.'

For the first time I realised how much taller than Maria I was. In my own time, five foot six or seven was tall but not extraordinary. The people in this time seemed far more petite. Maria herself was barely five feet tall. I would appear like a warrior, especially with the sword, and the villagers would be immediately suspicious of me.

'But how can I disguise my height? My hair, I could dirty it I suppose ...'

'Look,' Maria said gesturing towards the stream that ran through the woods.

I placed the sleeping Angelina gently down on a soft grassy patch beneath a large oak and followed Maria to the stream's edge.

She pointed at my reflection in the water. My fiery green eyes and fair hair were a giveaway. But as I watched the image changed, my eyes darkened, my hair became a rich chestnut brown and the pale whiteness of my skin turned into a deep olive.

'The height will matter less now. It will be good for the villagers to have a warrior anyway. You will be far more accepted in this guise ...'

'Oh my God,' I whispered. 'I *am* Miranda.'

Maria had unwittingly used her magic to give me the aspect of the gypsy Miranda, who saved Lucrezia from Caesare and taught her the magic she needed to hide from him. The dream I'd had came flooding back.

Paradox. I'm you and you are me ...

Miranda had said that there would be a paradox if I didn't meet up with Lucrezia.

You must go forward in order to go back! The wind whispered and I turned around expecting to see Adonai. But all I found was Maria Serafina staring at me curiously.

'How long will this last?' I asked.

'For as long as it is needed ...'

She reached for my hand and drew the triskele in my palm tapping it three times with her middle and her forefinger.

'It is the intent behind the change which will make it happen.'

'What do you mean?'

'I've given you the power. Focus your mind on your face and the triskele image.'

I stared into the water and slowly saw the image of Miranda fade.

'Excellent!' Maria gasped. 'I did not expect you to learn so quickly. Now, bring the disguise back, change yourself.'

Changing to Miranda was much more difficult than I had thought it would be. It required more focus and a memory of her face pressed firmly in my mind.

'Try again,' Maria encouraged when the image slipped away from me and my features reappeared.

This time I closed my eyes, thought of my dream, remembered Miranda's expressions. The slight curve of her eyes, the sharpness of her nose, the flashing white teeth.

'Yes ...' Maria breathed.

I opened my eyes and Miranda's image was truly there. I felt my face, explored the cheekbones that were higher than before, touched the lips that held a sensual semi-arrogant curl. I was Miranda.

'I never knew … All this time! It *was* me.' My mind tumbled with apprehension. Anxiety burned in my throat and chest. This couldn't be possible, could it? If I really was Miranda, then there was not going to be any quick solution to going home. I had a destiny to fulfil.

Behind us Angelina moaned in her sleep. I turned.

'What about Angelina?'

'She won't remember your previous form,' Maria said. 'When she opens her eyes she will see you as she thinks you have always appeared.'

I lifted the child up once more and we turned and headed towards the village.

At the gates we were halted by a sentry.

'I'm Maria Serafina – herbwife from the village by the sea …' she told the guard, pointing back in the direction from which we had come. 'We were attacked by a Viking raid. We are the only survivors. We ask sanctuary from your Lord.'

The sentry bowed to Maria. 'Of course … You are welcome here.'

The sentry barked an order to a nearby male peasant who came scurrying forward.

'Take them to the *Castrum* and have them presented to the Lord. They must be treated with respect …'

'We have much need for your kind, lady,' Vicente Agostini, the Lord, said bowing his head towards Maria. 'And who is this with you?'

Vicente's dark brown eyes watched me under black brows and a mop of curly long hair; curiosity brightened his pupils. And a familiar smile curved his lips. He found me attractive.

'My niece. She is a warrior; trained in the mountains. And the child is Angelina, now orphaned. But I am willing to raise her as my own.'

Vicente nodded, his eyes skittered away from me quickly as

Maria mentioned the mountains. 'Good. We have recently lost our herbwife. You would honour us if you took on her role here. And the warrior would be welcome as your niece of course.'

'My wish is always to serve ...' Maria said. 'And Lilly will be of great use to you if we are attacked. She saved our lives.'

Easy. Too easy. But I, cynical as always, had my doubts.

Accepted into the community of the *Castrum*, we had to make our mark on the charter which meant that we must live by Vicente's rules. Maria scribbled a symbol on the page that represented her and Angelina drew a rough circle on the charter and then they turned and looked at me. The scribe passed a fine feather quill to me and I stared down at the paper, with its variety of names and marks and quickly I scribbled my name as Lilly Caccini. In some strange way, calling myself by Gabriele's surname made me feel closer to him. Even though I was in the world seven or eight centuries before his time.

The scribe glanced at the parchment and blinked. He hadn't expected me to be able to read, let alone write. He looked at me curiously but I just shrugged and turned back to Maria and Angelina instantly forgetting his interest.

I wonder if this charter survives the centuries? I thought.

Immediately after signing we were taken to the house of the late herbwife, which was a hut made of wood and mud, with a straw roof.

Inside the hut was a huge fireplace, which was the centre of what seemed to be a living and eating space. There was a large roughly carved kitchen table and chairs, and a crude bench, scattered with straw filled cushions. The walls were covered in shelves stacked with pots full of herbs and oils; these it seemed were the tools of the herbwife. There were two more rooms off from the main room, which were small bedrooms. Each contained a straw pallet and blankets. Having slept purely on grass for the last year or so in the garden, the idea of any kind of bed seemed like a luxury. And so I was pleased when Maria gave me the smallest bedroom and put Angelina on a pallet before the fireplace in the main room.

The villagers came to the door bringing gifts as soon as we arrived. Hot broth, bread, packets of flour, milk, butter, fruit and all manner of plants. Some brought blankets and clothing. Maria thanked them all graciously, accepting everything that they brought.

'It's an honour they are doing us,' she explained. 'By bringing us gifts, no matter how meagre, they show their appreciation of our presence here. And they earn themselves a blessing from the herbwife.'

'What's in the mountains? Vicente seemed a little nervous once you mentioned I was "trained" there.' I asked as the door closed on the last of the peasants.

Maria placed a bowl of broth down on the table before Angelina and turned to me. She nodded towards the door of one of the bedrooms. I followed her inside.

'In the mountains it is said that there is a monastery where females are trained to be warriors. Strong, brutal and magical. The warriors have pure intentions and for this reason are all virgins. By implying you are one of them I have made you beyond reproach. And the local men will not try to become familiar with you. Also, if you do display any of your superior strength it will not be analysed too deeply. There are a lot of superstitions about the mountain warriors, but behind it all is always the greater good. The warriors are deemed holy.'

'Thank you,' I said. 'That is a perfect alibi.'

'One other thing,' Maria said. 'Feed outside of the village. I understand that you have needs that must be met, but they may well raise some suspicions.'

'I will.'

And as if my hunger had been waiting for her words, the first cramps began. I left the cottage cloaked in invisibility and casually walked past the sentry and out into the woods.

Samhain

I wake. I am aware of the blood pumping above me to the beat of the music. The castle walls are vibrating subtly with the auras of the visitors. The ley lines are feeding on their energy. I'm hungry, but calm. Time to go for a walk among the mortals.

I open my wardrobe and pull out a long black crushed velvet dress. I strip, shower and quickly slide the dress over my naked body. Then I reach in and find a cloak – I must merge with the revellers.

Walking among them, refreshed by the ley lines, I'm no longer anxious. The crowd parts for me as I cross the bridge and enter the main fortress walls. I am visible but invisible as I am one among many in this throng. I am the thing they pretend to be, but tonight I go unnoticed. I stroke the walls and the power caresses me back, with a languid flick. The castle too is enjoying the energy generated by my return and for a time loneliness is assuaged by the people once more crammed inside her walls.

'My beauty,' I whisper and she throbs in response.

It is a powerful night and the moon is full. The organisers couldn't have staged that if they had tried. The moon is adding to the glow created by the artificial lights around the castle walls and inside her turrets. Samhain: the end of summer and the night when the dead and the living can co-exist side by side. Or so it is believed.

A male voice echoes through the night over the PA system, telling the visitors the timetable of events. I tilt my head and look at the sky – fireworks are due to go off at 9.30pm. One hour from now.

Inside the walls is a roped off arena where a medieval reconstruction fight scene is taking place. Two men battle with broadswords for the amusement of the crowd. They are dressed in armour but have no trouble lifting the light-weight fake weapons. *If only they had fought with the real thing. They'd find them so much heavier.*

I walk on.

'... and don't forget to take a stroll down our spooky walk.'

Hunger.

I move through the castle, tag onto the trail of the next group going on 'the walk'. I merge with the night as the tour begins.

'The castle is haunted,' the tour guide says. 'A beautiful young woman is said to have died within its walls ...'

Many beautiful women have died here, and many men. I smile. Rhuddlan is over seven centuries old; she has seen many births and deaths within her grounds.

'Her husband was jealous ... strangled her in a fit of rage ... and now she haunts the woods ...'

I suppress a giggle. There is no such story; the castle would not have allowed it. She is an exacting mistress when it comes to death. Natural causes. Or punishment for the murderer. I'd seen that punishment first hand ...

We are led across a back bridge into a small stretch of woods. It's dark, and blood begins to pump erratically through the crowd as their adrenaline levels increase. A woman dressed as a witch recites a poem with a hidden warning as they pass into the woods. There is a body hanging from a tree, a patch of land has been turned into a graveyard and a tall girl flits around the trees in luminous white, her face painted with glow-in-the-dark make-up. Among the gravestones lurks a man dressed like a zombie straight out of a Michael Jackson video and he reaches out to the screaming people as they pass by. They are thrilled and scared but overall the crowd feels safe. On their return path a body drops down from a tree and swings before them on a hangman's rope.

Then I see him. He's not part of the tour, he's skulking farther back and there is something shiny in his hand.

The tour guides hurry the group along and out of the woods, but I fall back among the props. I stand by the hanged-man's tree and watch the out-of-place man. He's tall and excessively thin and he's wearing the mask of an old man. His clothing is tattered, ripped jeans and worn shirt, covered by a dirty sheet that's meant to be a cape. Although it is dark I can see everything clearly. I want to see what he will do. He watches as the props are put back into their original places and the actors group together to converse before the next tour arrives.

'Did you see that woman's face when the corpse dropped,' the tall female ghost laughs.

'Yeah – hilarious,' a grim reaper chuckles.

'When's Gareth back? I need a loo break …' says the zombie.

'I think he's here now,' points the ghost and a new zombie, also in a tattered red jacket, appears.

'Great – need to dash.' The first zombie scurries away and out across a field in the direction of the castle, but not back through the official walkway.

The man in the old man's mask begins to follow him. He's carrying a switchblade and it flicks open. I see the sharp silver edge gleaming in the moonlight as he swings his arm, walking, for the entire world, as if he were out having a stroll.

'Positions everyone; here's the next group.'

The actors fall back into their roles and begin scaring the new arrivals. I follow the man in the mask as he skirts across the grass back towards the castle.

It isn't long before the zombie begins to cast glances behind him as though aware he's being followed. Some humans do have a sixth-sense about these things and he has two of us on his tail. Besides, the masked man isn't being very quiet; he constantly flicks the knife switch to retract and to open and the clicking noise echoes over the empty field in time with the loud music.

As the zombie turns again the masked man drops down into the long grass unseen. I'm invisible, so neither of the men can see me.

At the top of the hill people are beginning to congregate in preparation for the fireworks display which has been prepared over the other side of the River Clwyd. The zombie reaches the bottom of the hill. Finding himself near some bushes, he casts a final look around and unzips his trousers. As he relieves himself the masked man decides to make his move.

I am on him, silent as the evening's breeze, before the switchblade flicks open for the final time. He barely struggles as I pull him down and rip off his mask. Beneath it I find a skeletal face, starved and tormented. His eyes are wild. He's an addict in the throes of a severe trip; blood too tainted to be drinkable, but that doesn't mean I'll let him kill an innocent on the castle grounds – even if that innocent does pee on the grass! A murder here would taint the ley lines.

The man's feral eyes bulge from his scarecrow face as he sees my elongated fangs. His body jerks and spasms beneath me. White foam bursts from his lips. I turn him on his side into the recovery position. Maybe the trip is a particularly bad one, but seeing a real live vampire won't help his grasp on reality.

I force my mind into his, calming the hallucinations, levelling his sanity, imposing a suggestion. *Leave. Go to the hospital for help. You don't want to take drugs anymore.*

I wait, holding the man still while the zombie zips up his pants and climbs up the hill, skirting around a group of children playing 'limbo' with a long glow-stick. He doesn't realise that he has just escaped death for real. Then I release the addict. He stands, staggers a little, and then begins to climb the hill carefully. I watch as he sits by the side of the castle, taking space between a cuddling couple, and a sulking boy from one of the families out for the evening. The couple glance at him nervously. He is obviously out of place. I turn my attention from him as he gets up and makes his way through the crowd and out of the grounds.

I'm sure of the persuasion I exerted, it has never failed me this close to such a powerful source of magic.

The mob is thickening. The limboing children are making a nuisance of themselves by blocking the walkway and the parents aren't paying any attention to them. Typical.

I look once more at the sky. It's almost time for the display. Glancing across the river I see the swirl of torches and the movement of two men preparing to light the fireworks. I fall back, huddling under the second bridge as the first ones are lit. I listen to the thrilled cries of the children and adults as the sky lights up. The brick beneath my back feels warm and I experience the grateful beat of the castle's power as she acknowledges my reluctance to spill blood on her grounds.

'Us girls have to stick together,' I whisper.

Leaving the crowd before the display ends, I fly to Rhyl. I'm hungry and have to feed – tonight though I feel no urge to kill.

Landing on the promenade I wander along the sea front. It's littered with chip-shop paper, empty cans and the occasional broken bottle, yet there's a bin every fifty yards. Humans amaze me. They never fail to self-destruct and they're intent on taking the planet with them.

The tide is in. Out to sea I observe the distant lights of an oil rig and farther along the rotating blades of the wind farm. I turn away, walking past the cheesy amusement arcades and wander up through the centre, looking for a likely snack.

A young couple are kissing in a car parked on double yellow lines. There's another car farther down with hazard lights on. An AA van drives up and the driver of the car, a woman in her forties, jumps out to greet him. She looks relieved.

A man staggers down the street, muttering to himself.

'Damn bitch ... whore! Gone left me for that knob ...'

He's drunk. I smile, reach into his mind and find the image of his lost love. My hair shrinks back into my scalp, turns a sickeningly vile shade of shocking pink. And the jade green of my eyes turns to grey. I make myself visible.

'Sandra ... is that you?'

'Yeah. Come 'ere an' give us a kiss love ...' I say.

He kisses me; there is no trace of my gene code in his blood. He's safe. I lead him back towards the promenade and down onto the darkened pathway that runs the length of the beach. His blood is full of cheap whisky, it gives me a minor buzz and then my system clears the intoxicant away and I am left with the taste of misery in my mouth. His liver is halfway to shutting down completely, if he carries on drinking like this he will be dead within the year. No matter. People die. Yet the sour sadness remains in my gut. Loneliness is the worst human emotion to swallow.

I feel a momentary distaste as I consume the last mouthful of blood. I push the drunk away wiping my lips with the back of my hand and leave him slumped against the rail. He'll live tonight, but what happens to him beyond that is not my problem.

Entering my lair just before dawn my mobile phone rings in my pocket.

'Lilly!'

'Gabi ...' His voice is everything that I remember it to be.

'You said you had things to tell me ...'

'Yes.'

I have put the meeting off. Gabriele thinks I am still in Stockholm. He has missed me in his life for only a night, but he has been absent from my life for hundreds of years.

'When can we meet?'

'Soon.'

'I don't understand. What's happened Lilly? Are you alright? How did you end up in Sweden?'

Questions. And all the answers are desperate to be spoken but not yet.

'It's not time.' *I'm not ready.* 'I'm writing a journal for you. So that you'll understand what happened.'

Why after all these years, all this waiting, why am I suddenly so unsure?

'Give me a date, a time. Or I'm flying to Stockholm tonight.'

'I'm not in Sweden now.'

He falls quiet. The silence screams along with my heart. I need to get this over with.

'Okay. In a week.'

'Where?'

'I'll text you an address closer to the time.'

I hang up, turn off my phone and lie down once more on my bed. This time sleep is not an easy companion. Gabi's voice still echoes in my head and the memory I have of him remains like the perfect and evil dance of a demon. He's untainted. My fear of meeting him again is irrational, but somehow I almost feel that I am protecting him from me.

I remember how I felt when I first saw him. How that same emotion was intact on the last day. That's the thing with us immortals; our memory is infinite and a curse. If only it was that easy to forget...

Chapter 12 - Lilly's Journal

Ancestry

As Maria predicted, she was pregnant. As the months in the *Castrum* passed it became more and more evident.

No one there questioned her, but occasionally I caught one of the villagers staring with curiosity at her swelling stomach as she tended the sick, helped women birth their children or mixed some potion to cure a rash.

As for me, there was loneliness and isolation. I hunted less and less, taking only a little blood and never killing those stray humans I found wandering the woods outside the *Castrum*. I was always afraid that suspicion would come my way. In the first few months I spent more time watching for a sign of a shimmer in the fabric of this world, always hoping for that doorway home, or at least back into the corridor of reflections. There once more I believed I could move through the portals into a new era closer to my real time.

Sometimes I thought I saw the air shiver in some obscure part of the village. Once, by the well, I was sure I saw a door and ran towards the spot. I walked in a circle around the suspect area, examining the rippling centre only to discover that yes, there was something there. A kind of hollowness beckoned, but when I reached out the void collapsed in on itself leaving me standing with my hand massaging nothing but air. It took a few moments for me to realise I was being watched, but the villagers were tolerant of my odd episodes.

'She's from the mountains ...' I heard an old woman whisper to a frightened child as I rushed by. 'She sees things in the world we could only imagine.'

'Why?' asked the child, a little boy of six or seven.

'She's holy,' the old woman answered, and I tried to pretend I had not heard their whispered discussion from across the *Castrum* square as I stared for more than an hour at the still and unmoving place near the well.

I waited until all eyes tired of watching me and turned away before fading into the background. After that, I moved amongst the villagers more discretely. Perhaps these were missed opportunities, or maybe they were never there and only figments of my imagination. Or, on that particular day, there had been a door – but not for me. So, I searched all day, most days, though never found an exit portal.

Maria was understanding and sympathetic, always waiting patiently for my return to the hut. Every evening after supper, as Angelina slept in her make-shift bed by the kitchen hearth, Maria would sit down with me and begin her tuition.

'Lilly, you have much to learn,' she told me. 'Tell me the names of these herbs and oils and explain their uses.'

I studied with Maria willingly. It filled the long and lonely evenings and somehow I knew that the things she taught me would one day become important to the future. I picked up the first jar. It was unlabelled, so I opened the lid and smelt the contents, then lifted out one of the pale green leaves of the herb inside and studied it for a moment before saying what I thought it was.

'Boswellia – treats joint aches and pains. It's also known as Frankincense.'

The next jar contained a flat, fan-like leaf.

'Ginkgo – it can help a number of ailments. Though mostly used for mental infirmity, it's sometimes used to help improve the fertility of a couple, especially when the man can't quite …'

'Yes. Yes!' laughed Maria. 'Excellent. And now the others.'

I went through twenty jars of oils and herbs carefully

identifying their contents, proving to Maria that I had retained all the things she'd taught me over the last few months.

'Good,' Maria said when I placed the lid back onto the final jar. 'Now for something which can only be given from one herbwife to another.'

Maria placed her hands in mine. Her palms were so hot I almost felt my skin blistering. 'Stay still, close your eyes. Do you remember the day we arrived in the *Castrum*?'

I nodded, 'Yes of course.'

'I gave you something then, the power to change your image.'

I nodded again.

'I always promised to explain how I did this and it is now time. Lilly below this hut is a power source. This is a *lei riveste*. This means it is your power, Lilly.

The power was female. It was obvious that lei meant 'she', but the whole phrase translated into English meant that 'this applies to you'. Therefore it applied to all herbwives. At least that's how I understood it. It also meant that men were not suitable subjects to learn this purely feminine power.

'A ley line?' I asked. Of course I'd heard of them. They were said to be all over the world and were supposedly a source of magical power, but I hadn't really thought about them before.

'The *lei riveste* is there for the herbwife to use. We can see them, like a faint but preternatural river under the surface of the earth. They are what we and the whole of our universe are made of. They are the veins of the planet. They pump life through the world.'

'And we are all made of this energy? This power?'

'Yes. And a few people have the knowledge to tap into it and use it.'

'Use it? How?' I asked.

'I have to give you the sight,' Maria answered. 'It's a ceremony and is much more complicated than the mere illusion power I gave you before. It will take a whole day and then you will have to practice using the ley power thereafter until it becomes second nature to you.'

'Right.'

'I can only give this to someone who truly opens up and accepts the sight.'

'I'm willing, but what do I gain by this?'

Maria smiled. 'A worthy question, Lilly. You gain everything. Even the power to find your way home when the time is right.'

'Then obviously I accept.'

The thought of going home brought an ache into my chest. I knew that out there, in the future, Gabriele would be born, would one day meet Lucrezia Borgia and be turned into a vampire. This would give him four hundred years alone, always searching for the one woman who would survive his deadly bite. And that someone was me.

'But know this. The journey to the "sight" is not an easy one. You may not like what you find when you get there.'

'That sounds ominous. Can you enlighten me a little more than that?' I smiled.

Maria shook her head. 'The experience is different for everyone.'

'Okay. I have nothing to lose. Let's do it.'

Maria set up her tools. She mixed oils and herbs from jars she had never shown me.

'We begin at dawn,' she told me. 'Now sleep, for tomorrow will be a gruelling day for you.'

'And what about you?' I asked glancing at her stomach. 'Are you up to this?'

'It is you who will take a journey. I will merely be your guide.'

I went to the small room I called home and listened to the quiet preparations Maria made as she placed the herbs and oils into a mortar and began grinding them with the pestle. I drifted off to sleep as rain patted onto the roof.

The next morning, Maria woke me early and I wondered if she

had even slept as she was still wearing the dress from the day before. I came into the main room to find Angelina's pallet empty.

'She's gone to a neighbour today. There must be no interruptions.'

'But, Maria,' I said, 'peasants call here every day. There's bound to be some interruption.'

'Not this day,' she said. 'Today is Samhain. The villagers will not leave their houses unless necessary. It is the day the dead can commune with the living. And they are always afraid.'

'Oh that's just nonsense,' I laughed but Maria's face became serious.

'No, Lilly. You will see. Today is a very important day.'

I put myself completely in her hands. Maria made me strip and wash by the fire and then lie down on Angelina's pallet while she anointed my skin with the concoction she'd made the night before. It had a clean smell which cleared my head, like eucalyptus and a scent I didn't recognise. Outside was deadly quiet. It was as though the herb-hut was in a cocoon, I couldn't even hear the rain on the roof and yet when I glanced towards the shutters I could see the gentle slither of water dripping down between the gaps.

Maria placed several crystals around my head, as well as one over my heart, throat and abdomen. Then finally she placed one on my forehead.

'The third eye,' she told me.

Something about the ceremony was familiar. It was as if I had experienced this before. Maria had said that my aura was constantly shifting, that I was in all times as well as in this one. Perhaps this event had happened in a past time already, even though for me the moment was now. Whatever it was it didn't matter, but I did experience an overwhelming feeling of *déjà vu*.

The chanting was like a song I'd heard before. Maria sang words that I didn't know, but were vaguely familiar. My body began to vibrate. At first it felt like the sensation of lying on a boat, the gentle sway and movement of a river but then my limbs began to throb. The air sang with an intense thrum, a high-pitched sound that perhaps only a dog would hear under normal circumstances. Maria continued to sing and her voice merged with the sound, seemed to create it and the vibrations racked my body in a sensuous ripple.

I floated up. I had been too young to fly, Gabriele had always flown with me, and so I was apprehensive as I rose up towards the ceiling. I turned and saw Maria still sitting in her chair, heard the singing and there, lying on the pallet, was me. Afraid, I tried to cry out, but my astral body could make no sound in the real world. I fought to go back down to re-enter my body believing something was wrong, but before I could figure out a way to move by my own volition I was rushing upwards, out through the roof of the hut, and there was nothing I could do to stop it.

I could no longer see myself or Maria. Even so, I could still hear her song as I rocketed up into the air. Outside rain poured down on the village. I couldn't feel it. I tried to see my hands, arms, legs but there was nothing there. Yet, I had an awareness of my body. I had a feeling of being there, just the same as when I took on my invisible form except, I couldn't feel anything. My usual vanished state still had solidity, but this was ghost-like, ethereal.

I wondered if this was the 'journey' Maria had mentioned. Astral projection. That was it. I'd read about it somewhere and Gabi had told me that on occasion he could do this. This meant that my body was still with Maria but my spirit had left, but where was I going?

As if in response to the question my cosmic form began to move. Higher and higher I climbed above the world, drifting up into the clouds unchecked, up and out into the waiting darkness of the galaxy. Panic began to set in. Maybe I had separated too far from my body and would find it impossible to rejoin? The drifting was endless and I had no control of it. Or did I?

'Stop!' I thought.

I jolted to a halt above the Earth and stared down on the

familiar globe. I'd seen this picture a thousand times or more, could identify areas of land, sea and mountain peaks. This was Earth. I was above it and I could see something else. It was like veins criss-crossing all over the planet. Lines of molten energy flowing through the land, rippling under the sea, and crawling through and around mountains. The ley lines were everywhere and I could see them as clearly as I could see everything else.

There was a change in Maria's song. I could hear it, even here. Sweet and pure I felt tears start in my eyes at the beauty of the song. I realised it was the song of the Earth, and the herbwife always heard it. It reminded me of the garden. The first sound of the world sparking to life as the trees whispered, the flowers bloomed. And Adonai. It was all interlinked somehow.

'Down!' I commanded.

I floated down gently. There was no plummet or sickening rush, merely a light rocking sensation, like being in a hammock. I entered the Earth's atmosphere and then I could feel the breeze, taste the clean rain as I drifted down.

Something else caught my attention as I drew nearer to the village. It was the beat and flow of the river that sustained me. Blood. Rippling and rushing through the veins of the village occupants. For the first time I really *saw* it. The blood held links to their heritage, and those contacts stretched out wide over the village and fed into several different sources. Although in this small world there were many bloodlines interweaved within families.

I peered into the house of an old couple. They sat at the hearth, a child crawling at their feet and the bloodlines flowed into the child around the couple and into a woman who swept the hut floor with a broom. All family. All the same heritage. I drew back from the hut, scrutinised the village and followed bloodlines as they wove all over from hut to hut, even within the *Castrum* stronghold. The Lord was connected to several families. I knew then that bastard offspring from his ancestors had married into the villagers. A few small babies were even connected directly to him. A perk of his position no doubt.

Eventually I drifted back to the herb-hut. Maria's song still rang in my head and I looked down at her as I sifted through the cracks in the roof. Maria was in a trance-like state. She hummed and sang, her body still in the chair beside my inert frame. Maria's bloodlines pounded painfully in my head. I saw her ancestry stretch out beyond the village and back the way we had come from her original home, but it was the beat within her that was the most intriguing. I could see that the unborn child was a boy. His lines stretched out in all directions but the strongest link was to the silent body, lying on the pallet before the fire. Me. The baby was linked somehow to me. And I didn't know why.

I plummeted back into my body with a sudden jolt.

'Oh my God!' I gasped sitting upright.

Maria didn't stir but continued her chanting. I realised that by focusing hard I could still see the bloodlines flowing out from her body. The most intense of which was one line that came directly from her stomach into mine like a bright umbilical cord of pure red light.

Chapter 13 - Lilly's Journal

Bloodlines

I woke as though from a dream to find Maria pouring broth into two bowls and placing them on the table with a hunk of bread and some fresh butter. I found a coarse blanket wrapped around my naked body. I stirred slowly, my limbs still feeling the paralysis of long sleep.

'Lilly ...' Maria said. 'You must eat and regain your strength.'

'I ... had ... the most peculiar dream.'

Maria smiled.

'Come, let me help you dress.'

She dressed me as my limbs slowly regained their vigour. I felt drugged, limp, wrung out.

'What happened?' I asked, stumbling down into the chair at the table.

'You've been on a very long journey.'

I tried to think but couldn't piece together all that had happened. 'I can't remember ...'

'You will soon. Don't worry. You've been through a very difficult experience.'

'I saw the lines ...'

'Yes,' Maria nodded.

'And something else ...'

She stroked my head and handed me a spoon. The broth was warm but not too hot and as I sipped it a surge of hunger swept my body until I picked up the bowl and guzzled it down. I reached for the bread and butter as the warmth of the soup spread through my stomach. I ate greedily, wiping the bowl with the bread to ensure I didn't miss a drop of the delicious food.

'I'm so hungry,' I said glancing apologetically at Maria as she ate her soup daintily.

My eyes fell on her stomach. I stopped chewing as the memory poured back. I squinted at her, trying to see the baby's bloodlines once more. But nothing happened.

'What is it?' Maria asked.

I shook my head. 'Nothing ... it's just. I dreamed something strange.'

'Whatever you saw, it wasn't a dream. It was real.'

'Oh.'

Maria stood and took my bowl over to the fire and the remaining pan of broth. She refilled the bowl and placed it before me.

'I'm always amazed that food sustains you,' she said softly. 'And yet there's still that need for blood.'

'Yes. Gabi and I discussed it many times. I think I could live without food though, but not the blood. Food helps the hunger, but doesn't ease it enough.'

Maria nodded, 'Yes, I've noticed when you've hunted you don't eat for several days afterwards.'

It was strange being scrutinised by those wise eyes. I knew the question was coming, but waited to be asked rather than volunteer the information. Maria filled my bowl several times and watched me eat until all the broth was gone. The she settled down in her chair by the fire and indicated I should sit in the other beside her but I stood before the fire instead. I watched her stomach rise and fall with her steady breath as she gazed into the flames. The heat made her cheeks pinker than usual, but she was relaxed and calm.

'You've looked at my stomach over twenty times in the last few minutes,' she observed.

I became very still. Then moved slowly to the chair beside her and sat down. She was quiet. The only sound I could hear was the soft whistle of her breath and the occasional crackle of the log burning in the fire. I relaxed back into the chair my mind trying to shape all that I had seen into the appropriate words.

'Maria ...'

She waited patiently as I halted.

'I saw the ley lines ...'

'Yes ...'

'They were like veins. It was as you'd said. The blood of the Earth. The vitality. It's energy. And it's everywhere, all over the planet. It was incredible.'

I fell silent and Maria waited, knowing there was more but I couldn't shape the words, couldn't tell her that I'd seen inside her belly. It was difficult to reveal that I knew she was having a boy and that somehow, that child would go on to be part of my own bloodline. It seemed impossible.

Maria smoothed a hand over her stomach as we sat in silence, and I knew the child was kicking inside her as though impatient to be born. She deserved an explanation, but I wasn't sure that this information was relevant to her or the future. It was merely coincidental. After all if I hadn't been there the Viking would still have raped and impregnated her. Then I remembered his raised sword. He hadn't planned to leave her alive. I had saved her and the child. *Paradox.* The word floated to the surface of my brain once more as I remembered my dream of Miranda.

Everything was relevant, who was I trying to kid?

'I saw some other lines ...' I said finally. 'bloodlines. Lines that showed me the ancestry of all the villages and the ancestry of your son.'

Maria's hand froze over her belly.

'I saw inside you,' I continued. 'Saw the baby. Saw how he will grow and be interwoven with my own ancestry. My own *future* ancestors. Yet, you aren't the source of the connection. It was ...'

'The Viking!'

'Yes.'

Maria stood, and paced the room before the fire, her thoughts spilling out over her face, went from confusion to concern in the blink of an eye.

'It isn't important though is it?' I asked.

'Everything matters, Lilly. Every deed we do affects the future. You saved my life and ensured that your own bloodline was started.'

I was surprised that she understood the implications so well.

'Yes. And I killed the Viking. So what impact does that have? Maybe one negates the other?'

Maria sat again, but her hands clasped each other. 'I see now how dangerous it is for you to be here.'

'Do you?'

'What would happen, for example, if you killed my child by accident?'

I didn't know what to say. Fear welled in my heart as I explored the possibilities. 'Or what if … I'm not around to save his life, like I did yours?'

We talked into the night until we exhausted ourselves with worry as well as the day's exertions. Finally, in the small hours we both fell into bed, and slept like the dead.

Blessed

The very next day Maria's waters broke and the baby was born. We had no more time to think or worry about the paradoxical nature of my presence at his birth. I just had to roll up my sleeves and deliver him while Maria, wracked with pain, yelled out orders to me and directed me how to help her. For a twenty-first century girl who's never stepped foot in a hospital, has no siblings and has always been grossed out by the thought of pregnancy and labour, this was obviously a tall order. It was my first and only delivery and it was as horrible as could be imagined. It was like a blood bath. I was constantly aware of my lack of skill and knowledge. Everything was down to me and it could all go dangerously wrong. Without a doctor or a medical facility to fall back on Maria could die. Of course Maria was naturally strong and robust, as much a woman of her time as I was of mine. None of my fears ever occurred to her.

Despite all the blood at no time did the hunger raise its ugly head. I was too engrossed in the process of keeping them both as safe as possible and so after hours of labour the baby boy came yelling into the world. I pulled him from Maria as she directed me, then passed him to her to cut and tie the cord. When this was done Maria held the baby up to me and I took him carefully, afraid he would break. Swaddling him in a soft blanket that Maria had prepared in advance, I placed him gently back into his mother's arms.

'What will you call him?' I asked, as she instinctively pressed him to her breast.

'I always assumed I was barren,' she told me. 'My husband

94

blamed me constantly for our lack of offspring. When he died, there was no man in the village willing to take me as a wife. I was a good herbwife but a failure as a woman.'

Maria looked amazingly calm and fresh considering all the pain that had so recently wracked her small body.

'That's horrible,' I answered. 'Men are such pigs sometimes ...'

'They never blame themselves. It is always the wife at fault.'

I nodded in response, lost for words. I watched her struggle with the baby, trying to make him latch onto her breast, but he turned his head away and cried.

'I feel blessed,' Maria said. 'And so, I shall call him Benedict.'

And as though he understood, Benedict latched onto Maria's breast and began to suckle ensuring that his life would continue and that his limbs would grow strong and healthy with his mother's milk. I thought again of Adonai's words. *Nothing exists until it is named ...*

Later, as Maria slept, I wrapped Benedict up once more and held him carefully. I scrutinised his fair skin and fine, downy blond hair. He had blue eyes, but I'd heard that all babies' eyes were blue when newborn and so I didn't worry too much about it. He opened his mouth and yawned, gave a little sneeze and drifted off to sleep in my arms.

I was terrified that I might inadvertently hurt him but didn't know what to do with his small body, or where to put him.

The door of the hut opened. Angelina walked inside.

'Can I come home?' she asked.

'Yes, of course. Maria had the baby, look.' I felt a little guilty that I had forgotten to fetch her with all that had happened. Angelina had been at the farmer's house for two days by then.

'He's so tiny!' She kneeled down beside the chair and peered down at Benedict sleeping soundly in my arms.

Angelina stroked his small fingers in wonder, then stood up and ran to the door again.

'Where are you going now?' I called.

'To tell Elspeth, the farmer's wife, about the baby.'

A few minutes later, the farmer and his son arrived with a large cradle. I directed them in, gesturing for quiet as they placed it by the fire. Maria was soundly asleep in her room and I didn't want them to wake her. Inside the cradle was a fresh straw mattress. I placed Benedict into the cradle and watched him.

'Blessing ...' I murmured in English and the farmer stared at me surprised.

'You speak odd words ...'

'Benedict,' I answered. 'That's his name.'

The farmer left, bowing as though he were at the cradle of the Christ child. I met the eyes of the son, he was a boy of nineteen and his eyes were filled with lust. It was then I realised I was only wearing my nightshift. His eyes followed the curve of my breasts and trailed down my body. I stood by the fire. The shift was practically see-through in this light. I moved away from the fire standing instead behind the cradle.

'Get out!' I snapped.

The boy blinked, surprised at my recognition of his desire.

'Your eyes defile me. Get out before I tear them from your head.'

The boy scurried away, terrified. I closed the door behind him, slamming home the deadbolt that Maria rarely used. Resting my back against the door, I sighed. I believed my time here was coming to an end. I had to leave Maria, Angelina and Benedict before my presence jeopardised their existence in the *Castrum*.

Benedict moaned a little in his sleep, and I stood over him, terrified that he may stop breathing. Already I loved the little boy as if he was my own. He was the closest I would ever get to having children. Not that it had ever bothered me before when I had Gabi and we'd been so happy. Children had never been part of that world and I knew that. Something about being with Benedict gave me a different kind of happiness.

I gazed around the hut. It was makeshift and dirty. Little better than a hovel, but there was always food on the table and the people of this time knew nothing else. It was home to me. Maria and Angelina had become family over the last few months. The urge to return to my time had lessened and a kind of acceptance of this era had set in.

'You'll learn patience,' Maria had said and she was right.

I had learned to wait. The moment would arrive, the door would open again; it had to. I was here for a reason and all I had to do was wait. Fate would show me what I had to do. But I wasn't some simple peasant. I feared mistakes, understood implications, worried about that word, that terrifying word; paradox.

Benedict was a blessing. I could see that immediately; not just for Maria but for me. He made me realise that there was nothing I could do that wasn't already in the plan.

A harsh wind blew against the front door, rattling against the bolt.

'Adonai ...' I whispered almost expecting a response, then wondered why on earth I had thought of him at that moment.

I sat down in the chair beside the cradle and the fire, warming myself as I listened to Benedict sleep. Gazing into the flames I imagined the garden, thought about Eve and Adam and especially Adonai, whose presence and motives I still didn't understand. Maybe I'd had my first lesson in patience there. How long had it really been? Ten years? Or one hundred? I didn't know for sure.

I leaned back in the chair and drifted into sleep listening to the rise and fall of Benedict's chest. In the other room Maria slept the exhausted sleep of the new mother and outside the rain fell on the thatched roof in rhythm with the breathing of its occupants. My heart rate slowed to match the rhythm of the occupants as my eyes closed and I began to drift into a steady, calm sleep.

I felt strangely at peace.

Doors

Seven years passed from the day I arrived in the middle of the Viking raid. Seven years of study and direction from Maria until she believed I was ready. I knew all that she knew about magic, except for one final thing; how to find the corridor of reflections.

'All witches study for seven years,' Maria said, adopting my word for what she was, though only in a joking manner.

'Yes. I see that now. There is much to learn, skills to hone.'

Benedict was outside playing with the neighbours' children. He was a beautiful child with fair hair and green eyes. Eyes that were shockingly like mine when undisguised. The love I felt for him was completely uncompromising and we were inseparable. The small boy went everywhere with me, except when I hunted in the night while he slept.

I wore Miranda's face with the ease of an old coat, never letting her aspect drop even for a second lest I forget to replace it. Constantly living this lie had become my reality. When I saw my reflection in the river, or some incidental shiny surface, I had grown to accept it as this mysterious gypsy beauty. I forgot my own face and grew to like the slight cat-like curve of my hazel eyes, admired the constant shine of the rich dark hair that was as familiar to me then as my own blonde curls had been. Benedict, however, brought back the memory of my old self. As each year drew to a close he began to look more and more like Gabriele, and the love I'd felt for Gabi was replaced by the motherly emotions I had for

Benedict. It was almost as though I never expected to go back to my old life.

I felt completely at home in the *Castrum*. The people accepted my strangeness and I was never bothered by the men of the village. They even stopped looking at me with barely disguised curiosity or lust. Of course, I dressed like a man most of the time; male breeches, a sack shirt and an old and worn sheepskin jerkin over the top. On the coldest days I wore my cloak and, always tied to my waist from morning till night, was the Viking broadsword. I think the heavy clothing, which disguised my curves, went a long way to making me appear less female. Despite all this, my hair had grown long and I wore it in a plait down my back.

'Lilly!' Benedict yelled rushing into the hut. 'Come and see the boat I made, it floats on the river.'

I ran outside with him, playing at the riverside as though I were the child. Benedict had that effect on me. He made me feel that life was pure and simple and nothing bad would ever happen again. His boat did indeed float. He had artistically scraped out and hollowed a fire log, adding a mast in the centre on which he had tied a piece of scrap fabric from one of his old sack shirts.

'See,' he laughed, his bright green eyes shining in the brilliant sunshine.

'It's amazing! You are such a clever, talented boy, Benedict.'

I lifted him up with ease as he threw his arms around my neck. He was tall for six, but light as a feather to me. He had inherited his fair colouring from his Viking father as well as his height, but his quick mind and creativity were definitely from Maria.

The boat sailed away down the river, the current rapidly taking it away and beyond the village. I ran for a while with the child in my arms, up to the edge of the village, where I stopped and Benedict and I watched it float away beyond his human vision but not beyond mine.

I kissed his head. A small bead of his perspiration pressed into my lips and I licked them instinctively. Dizziness and nausea wracked my body and I staggered against the sentry gate, almost dropping the boy to the floor. The sentry rushed forward to help me, holding my arm. I placed Benedict down carefully, resting my head against the wall until the nausea passed. I glanced up; Benedict's bloodlines erupted from him as he stood gazing at me with curiosity. My stomach lurched and I bent double as though I was going to vomit.

'Lilly? What's wrong?' he asked, with such distress in his voice that I forced a lie from my lips.

'Nothing. I'm fine ...' But the lines were infinite and my eyes traced them, seeing the faces, some familiar, some not, all leading onto one source. Me. It was a perfect circle. The bloodlines showed Benedict's heritage and it came from me and arrived at me. Impossible!

I straightened up. 'Let's go back.'

The sentry scrutinised me with worried eyes. He'd touched me when I felt faint. This could mean his death if I made an issue of it.

'Thank you for your help,' I told him, my eyes soft and reassuring.

I took Benedict's hand and we walked back to the hut.

'Lilly nearly fainted,' he said as soon as we entered and Maria looked at me with concern. 'She looked like she was going to be sick, too.'

'Are you ... hungry?' she asked.

I shook my head.

'She looked at me like I had grown a great snake through the top of my head,' Benedict continued.

I glanced at him surprised. But then ... why not? Why shouldn't he have inherited some of his mother's power?

Maria looked from one to the other of us before her eyes rested uncertainly on her son.

'Benedict, go and find Angelina. Tell her we need some water from the well,' Maria said.

'You're just trying to make me go away so you can talk,' Benedict answered.

'Yes,' Maria nodded. 'But also I am concerned that she may be alone again with the farmer's youngest boy, Alberto.'

Benedict nodded, 'I'll get her.'

He ran away quickly in the direction of the farm. Angelina was thirteen and at a dangerous age for a girl in the village. Soon Maria would have to speak to the farmer about a marriage. She had tried to avoid it, wanted Angelina to be older before she became too involved or interested in boys.

'So,' Maria said, turning to me, 'what happened?'

'Maria, you remember when you gave me the ley line sight, and I told you I saw bloodlines, the heritage of Benedict? I've never seen it since, even though I've tried on many occasions. I began to believe that I did imagine it.'

'I understand. But I told you that what you saw was real.'

'I know. And I always believed you, but sometimes doubted myself. I saw them again. Today. I kissed Benedict, and his sweat went into my mouth. I tasted him and then I could see the bloodlines clearer than ever.'

'Here. Taste me. See if it happens again.'

Maria held out her arm and I pressed my tongue lightly against her skin, quickly whipping it back into my mouth to swallow the slight salty moisture extracted from her flesh. Maria's bloodlines burst forth spanning backwards and forwards and this time I saw her descendents interweaved with mine. Her son, Benedict, was a direct descendant of my mother and there was a branch that led away into a different direction. Another family link – an extremely powerful family in Rome.

'Oh no!' I said. 'That's how this all happens.'

'What is it? What did you see?' asked Maria as she drew me into her arms.

'The future. I saw the future. Gabi and Lucrezia … One of your ancestors will marry into the Borgia family and father a child …'

Maria was silent for a while, stroking and patting me until I became calm once more.

'There is one more thing I need to show you.'

'What?'

'You are ready now, ready to face your future and I have no more excuses to keep you with me. I can't be selfish Lilly. I need to show you how to use the ley lines to find what you seek.'

'The door back to my world?'

'Maybe … but I think it more likely that you will find doorways to your destiny.'

'What then, Maria?'

She didn't answer. I reached for my cloak, throwing it over my shoulders as she took my hand and led me outside. We walked out of the boundaries of the *Castrum* and past the sentry, who bowed his head in terror as I strode beside Maria. We went out into the forest, my hunting ground. For the last few years I'd fed on animals alone. It wasn't as fulfilling as human blood but it helped to keep the savagery of the hunger at bay and protected the villagers from my vampiric needs.

As we drew farther away from the village Maria began to hum a familiar song. A song I'd heard before; it was the music of the ritual she used to give me the sight.

'Search for the ley,' she said but I was already seeing them by instinct. 'Cast out for the strongest one.'

'I see it.'

'Draw the power, as I taught you.'

I stopped walking as I reached the edge of the ley. It flowed directly under the river, fed the current with its power. I reached out with my mind, drew a circle around Maria and using the ley current I focused the energy up into my hands, eyes and mind.

'Excellent …' Maria gasped. 'You have such control …'

'Now what?'

'Send it out. It is the intention that counts remember. Tell it to search for your pathway home.'

I reached out again with my mind, focusing the ley power,

outwards, upwards, around us. It searched. The ley stretched out in countless directions all around the circle extending and elongating until it came across a solid wall of power.

'Bring it closer …' I told the ley, 'let me see it.'

I dragged it to me. My eyes were closed but I examined the object with my third eye. Purple light exploded at the back of my eyes as I scrutinised and prodded with my ley-charged psychic energy.

'It's a doorway!' I cried.

'Yes,' Maria confirmed. She was with me all the way.

'It's near. It's been there all the time; I just didn't know where to look!'

I opened my eyes and the doorway shimmered on the other side of the river. I closed the ley circle and turned my gaze on Maria.

'It won't stay forever,' she answered my unasked question. 'Once you cross there's no way back here.'

'I have to say goodbye to Angelina and Benedict.'

My heart hurt. The thought of leaving them, especially Benedict, was almost as painful as the thought of never seeing Gabi again. I could stay, wait the ages out. I wouldn't age after all and it would mean that I could see Benedict grow and live his life.

'You would also witness his death and mine,' Maria said, once more reading my thoughts. 'Can you live with that Lilly? Watching us age and die around you while you stay the same?'

I shook my head. Tears welled up in my eyes.

'No. I couldn't bear it. But how can I leave you?'

'You can. If you don't, something bad is going to happen. You need to follow your destiny as it arises. No matter what.'

The door shivered. Both of us turned to stare at it as it trembled precariously on the edge of the river.

'It's unstable!' Maria cried as an unnatural wind began to pick up.

'It's collapsing,' I confirmed. 'You're right; it won't be here much longer.'

Maria threw her arms around me. 'Go! Go now! Don't miss this chance. The past, present and future relies on you always leaving when it is time.'

'What about Benedict?' Tears leaked unchecked from my eyes. 'I don't want to leave him.'

'I know. But you must. I'll explain everything to my son when he's old enough to understand.'

The doorway shuddered again, lightening struck in the distance and a torrential downpour began, soaking us both in seconds.

'What's happening?' I asked. 'Why the storm?' But I already knew the answer. I was on the cusp of a paradox. If I didn't go through the door then maybe my whole family history would be completely changed. I couldn't risk that.

'Go!' Maria yelled above the thunder.

I leapt across the river, leaving Maria behind before I could change my mind. My heart was pounding in my ears, shutting out the noise of the storm. I looked back once, and then gazed deeply into the doorway, trying to see beyond it into the world behind. It was night time on the other side and almost impossible to see what lay there. The doorway was murky and dark. I could see nothing beyond but a dirt track road, lined with a forest of dense trees. I looked again at Maria.

Her hand was covering her mouth as she watched me, and her tears mingled with the rain. I turned swiftly, remembering that if this doorway was wrong then it would merely freeze me out and I wouldn't be able to enter. If it was correct, then I'd pass through and my next step and new life would reveal itself.

I hesitated, staring into that other world. It meant so many different things. I'd be starting all over again. Running blindly through a world that I didn't know and all to what purpose? I was scared, it was true. I had felt a measure of security in the *Castrum* and I really didn't want to leave.

Feeling torn I gazed around at this world which had been my home for seven long and happy years. The storm was reaching dangerous proportions. Lightning struck a tree some yards behind Maria and my heart lurched in fear. Maria glanced back at the oak's charred remains and turned back to me, yelling over the thunder.

'Go!' Somehow I think she understood that my delay was causing the storm.

The rain lashed down, whipping my skin, and Maria threw her arms over her face to protect herself from the stinging water. The sky lit up again and immediately a smash of thunder rumbled through the sky.

Tears rolled down my face but were invisible in the rain. I knew what I had to do. By staying I was putting everyone in danger. I turned away, closed my eyes and ran through the door.

Chapter 16 - Present

Loneliness

Loneliness is the hardest burden. I understand that now. Gabi's isolation sent him on a journey and I had found it hard to conceive how arduous that was until I found myself alone. Even now, I am alone with my magic and my fear of creating more of our kind. But it is an irrational phobia. What would it matter if there were a few more of our family when there is so much disease and death in this world?

Harry has been a companion of sorts but he will not leave his home unless I beg, and I'm too old and too proud for that. I should let him find love; let him make a mate that will travel through the centuries with him. I have punished him enough for all of his crimes. But I can't allow it. I am an obsessed and controlling parent. I still want him to suffer. At least until my own loneliness and pain is eased. So I can't release him.

I lie awake underneath the castle, soaking in the ley energy in the hope that I can raise my spirits and restore some of the peace I once had. *It is so easy to find calm when you are waiting, when destiny dictates your every move.*

But what now? Now, I am making it up as I go along. Since the day my younger self became trapped in the garden the world has changed. All this time I've been immobile. My hands were tied as the future was set. Now the future is unknown. I am as blind as everyone else and there have been no more doors opening for me for over three centuries. But of course the motivation has gone.

My time is now – I have finally come home and I will damn well enjoy it.

There is a shiver in the ley power, a vague and familiar tremor. 'No!' *Impossible!*

A door has opened nearby. But why here? Why now?

'I'm in my own time! God damn you! What more can you possibly want from me?'

The door shudders. My mind's eye scrutinises it. The velvet, liquid bulge quivers under my supernatural search, sucking at my mind. It feels glutinous; a cool gel.

There is no doubt then. A door. A fucking door! Great.

'No! I won't rise to the bait: I'm staying in my own time.' There is nothing more I can do. All that should happen has. 'So fuck you!'

But I am out of my bed. I rifle through my wardrobe, find a pair of black jeans, a black turtle-neck sweater and begin dressing. Gone are the days when I'll be caught unawares in a hostile environment. The door tugs and pulls as I slip on a pair of warm, fur lined, flat boots. I leave my room, run down the staircase and there in the hall, above the door, I notice the sword. It's hung there for years now, unused. I pull it down. My Viking sword is beautifully maintained, along with its scabbard and a belt properly made to measure. It fits snugly round my waist and thigh. I slip the sword back into the sheath. At the last minute I take my short leather jacket, lined with faux fur, from the cloakroom, throwing it over my shoulders and zipping it up to my chest.

Flying outwards across the River Clwyd I leave the grounds of Rhuddlan Castle. It is daylight and the remains of the fireworks display are being bagged up by two men wearing orange jackets. They can't see me of course, I'm too careful for that. The grounds are also being cleared following the Halloween party. What a mess these humans made of my beauty's tresses! The grass is trampled and dented, clumps of grass dug up by carelessly worn high heels are being pushed back by the caring hands of an old man, bent on hands and knees as though in worship.

And worship her you should.

I gaze back longingly at the castle. *Will I ever return?* Then turn to face the unknown once more.

The doorway is in Llanberis. That's an hour's drive away but only minutes for me to fly.

Even if it was farther I'd have no choice now; the doorway pulls me closer. I fly over mountains with frost-covered peaks. Ahead I see the interplay of the valleys and mountains. They are beautifully unique. Some look black, others green and there are even some blue tinged peaks. Of course it is all purely to do with how the morning sunlight catches them.

Soaring over vast and beautiful landscapes covered in mist, I pass over Snowdonia and glance down at the train as it makes its steady and slow ascent up the mountain. It is full of sightseers and there are flashes of light bouncing off the windows as the sun catches the lens of a camera. The train stops and the passengers exit onto the peak. Some move quickly away to take in the view while others merely stand around, uncertain of which direction to go in first.

I fly on unseen over their heads. Within minutes the people look like little more than ants foraging on the peak.

Ahead I see the myriad of colours reflected off the shale rocks from the low lying sun as I swoop into the pass. Their brightness is nothing compared to the shimmering doorway standing incongruously in amongst the boulders. I land ten feet away, resisting the magnetism of the door's blinking opening.

Llanberis Pass is a tourist spot. I look around to see a few cars parked along the road at the various stopping points. There is a family climbing up a short way onto the rocks. A dark-haired boy and girl, both in their teens, pose for photographs as their father snaps away. The wife is blonde; she's looking around the area, admiring the rocks and occasionally looking back at the children as they laugh and caper for the camera.

I see her breath steam as she laughs with them. The father tugs his red scarf up around his neck. It is then I realise how cold it is here. I rarely feel it these days. The pass is somewhat sheltered in parts from the sun and that creates a cavern of frosty air that might be hard to breathe if you are human.

I turn my attention away from the family as a group of six hikers walk by.

'There's a café with toilets jus' arund that bend,' says a woman in her fifties. She is sturdy-looking, a tough, salt-of-the-earth type. She has a broad Scottish accent.

'You said that an hour ago,' whinges a weedy man. 'It's getting desperate.'

'Weel if ya that desperate, you should pull doon ya kecks and d' it.'

'Oh Muriel! There's too many people about!'

'It wudnee stop me ...'

I pull my eyes away from the humans; people watching is a distraction, they are always a fascination to me.

I'm procrastinating. Not wanting to make a decision.

I draw closer to the door. The air is a white blur around the entrance though it probably isn't evident to the human eye. I stare through.

'What delights do you have in store for me now?'

The air in the doorway is blurred. I peer beyond the fog that intermittently covers the opening of each doorway.

'No! That's ... impossible. What earthly good would it do to enter there?'

I gaze into the centre of Manchester. It is Deansgate. I'd know it anywhere. After all, I spent most of my mortal life in that city. Why there, why at this time in history?

In the mist I see three faint images. A fourth figure appears. There is a battle ending with the fourth figure crumpled to the ground.

'I don't understand. Why torture me this way? I can't be there. It's too late. I can't do anything about that. I've always known it. Even though it broke my heart.'

But I walk forward nonetheless. I fall to my knees before the door, tears of rage pouring down my face. *I can't do this!* Surely this is the biggest paradox. If I return there and wait for my other self to disappear then I could see Gabi right away. But that's not what happened – I just know it isn't! I stretch out my hands, crawl over the rocks until I reach the portal. I gaze out at the devastation. There is chaos in the street surrounding the four.

I see Lucrezia, tears in her eyes, she's bending over the body and there is my Gabi, and me; the Lilly before the doors. Lilly comforts Lucrezia. They are all together in a sentimental group hug. I remember the emotion, the pity I felt for Lucrezia.

But the body interests me more now. He is a black and deformed shape – I can't think of *him* as *it!* He lies unheeded at their feet now. They aren't even looking my way. I see the destroyed, somewhat melted face, the twisted and distorted body. *I can't bear it anymore.* I'm insane with grief. Before I can stop myself I push my hands through the barrier reaching blindly as the scene before me distorts and blurs. The doorway ripples with the intrusion. My hands scramble, touch him and finally gain purchase. His clothing and skin is slick with a disgusting black gloop. My fingers slide away but I twist them into the fabric of his clothing gripping it as hard as I can. I begin to pull but I can only feel, not see if he is getting closer to the doorway. I push my head through and grab him to me – I haven't felt his touch in centuries! – pulling his shattered frame up to my chest. But I haven't time to languish. The door groans and creaks and I have no wish to be caught halfway through as it closes.

I yank him back, but the door resists. It doesn't want to allow me to return the way I came. Damn it, I will go back. I hurl myself back, clutching Caesare as close to me as possible. The gateway shudders and complains, but still we fall backwards and out into my own time. We roll briefly down the side of the mountain, our bodies intertwined until I throw out my hand and stop the freefall.

We're back in Llanberis.

I lift Caesare and carry him back to the anomaly. Glancing back through I can see that I have been totally unobserved by the three there. They break apart and glance down to where Caesare's corpse had been but the only sign of Caesare Borgia's remains is an ink black stain that is left on the road where his body fell.

The door crashes shut. I can see no more. There is an almighty rumble, like an isolated explosion. The closing of the door has started the rocks tumbling again.

I hold onto Caesare, lift him up in the air and fly away, back to the castle. I hear the young family screaming and running from the crashing rocks. I suspect that it is the first avalanche they've had here for years.

I glance at Caesare's silent body as I fly back over the mountains. He's barely recognisable as the man I once knew. Fate seems to have intervened once more. For now I can't understand the reason why he has been given back to me and, as I approach Rhuddlan, my mind flies back to the first time I saw him.

Chapter 17 - Lilly's Journal
A New Highway

My feet were protected by my sheepskin boots, but I could feel the coarseness of the ground through the soles as I landed on the rough road. I turned to gaze back through the gateway and there I saw Maria and Benedict. The child was screaming soundlessly and trying to get towards the door as Maria struggled to hold onto him. His slender arms outstretched to the doorway and tears were in his eyes as his mouth called my name. But the void gave me nothing but silence and the door froze over, paralysing their images for a split second before completely disappearing from the road.

I fell to my knees, my hands over my eyes. I knew I would never see Maria or Benedict again. No matter where I was there was no going back. I hugged my arms around my body, the cold outside was nothing compared to the chill in my heart. The thought of never seeing them again gave me excruciating pain but I knew I had to pull myself together and move on. There was nothing I could do but learn what destiny had in store for me.

There was a faint vibration in the ground, I lifted my head and stared along the track through watery eyes. In the distance I could make out the hurried advance of a team of horses pulling a carriage. I knuckled my eyes dry. Then I pulled myself up and hurried off the road and into the trees. Crouching down in the long brush and grass I waited as the carriage advanced.

'Pull over!' a male voice yelled in Italian, and the driver began to rein the horses in. The carriage pulled to a halt fifty yards or so past me and I slunk back deeper into the woods to make sure I wasn't seen.

The passenger threw open the door before the driver had time to clamber down from his seat.

'My lord ...?'

'I need some air, stay with the carriage.'

'But my Lord, this area is notorious for robbers and bandits ...'

'I know. Do you think anyone would dare tackle me?' he answered arrogantly.

The timbre of the passenger's voice was familiar, though I couldn't understand why. It had a musical quality that was seductive. His walk was proud and he strode confidently into the forest on the opposite side of the road from me giving me ample time to scrutinise him. He was wearing all black. Black frock coat and breeches, knee-length leather boots, and a black hat pushed down over his eyes. Very different clothing from the century I had just left. I could see a blond ponytail protruding underneath that trailed halfway down his back.

I was curious. There was a reason for my being here, there had to be. So, cloaking myself in invisibility, I followed him.

He walked a few yards into the trees before halting. Then he began to unbutton his breeches. Soon he was peeing against a tree. I was about to turn away when his voice rang out.

'Who's there?'

I became completely still, fearing my defences had actually failed me. He turned. I couldn't see his eyes but felt them land where I stood. His face was shadowed by the hat but his head turned as though he were looking around to see if anyone observed him. He tidied himself away, slowly buttoning his breeches again, but I felt that his eyes never stopped scanning the woods.

I suddenly realised that three men were also hidden amongst the grass and trees wearing camouflaged clothing. I resisted a giggle at the sight of their green breeches and jerkins. *Really, what is this? Will Scarlet, Little John and Friar Tuck?* Then they began to move, slowly creeping forward until the passenger's eyes found them stalking him. He drew his sword. I could hear his blood pounding in his chest, but he stood up to them bravely anyway.

They charged. The man's sword swung through the air cutting down one of the green-clad bandits immediately. The robber fell, hands grasping at his intestines as they spilled out onto the ground. The other two men ignored their dying comrade and threw themselves on the passenger. I saw his face clearly for the first time as his black hat was knocked sideways and he ducked beneath a swinging blade. My heart stopped. He looked like Gabriele! Surely it couldn't be?

I stepped forward instinctively as he rolled with the men. I thought he would be overpowered, but he threw them off easily, never once letting go of his sword. Within seconds he was back on his feet, quickly followed by his assailants. One of the thugs tried to edge behind him as the other rushed in, but the man was skilled, his reflexes were keen, and he swept the air around him with his sword forcing them to jump back. The shorter one grunted as he received a minor cut through the sleeve of his jerkin. But the wound was deep enough to send a splash of blood whipping through the air. It landed on my cheek. A slow trail rolled down my face like a bloody tear and I raised my hand to wipe it away.

The blood was on my fingers. I smelt it. It was like fresh coffee and chocolate cake. All the things I'd been denied since my exile from my own time. I licked it; savouring my first taste of human blood in ages.

Curiosity and a little blood lust made me draw even closer to the fight. I watched them tumble and roll; near enough to know for definite that the man wasn't Gabi. But who was it?

'My Lord! Are you all right?' called the coachman in a trembling voice from the road, but the coward never came into the forest to help with the fight.

In a wild rush the men overpowered the passenger, pushing him down on the muddy ground.

'You'll pay for killing my brother, you bastard!' yelled one of them, but the passenger kicked out and bucked, still trying to break free from his assailants. I was impressed by his courage and stamina. One punched him in the face, bloodying his nose, but for every punch they landed, he gave back two.

'I'll run you through!' he yelled. 'Do you know who I am?'

'You're a dead man,' said the other bandit, 'and we'll rob your corpse just the same.'

The heartbeats of the men were accelerated. My fangs began to extend in a primal reaction to the fight. I was hungry, starved. Only then did I realise I'd barely stayed alive on the animal blood I'd been consuming. There was nothing like the taste of human blood and I suddenly needed it. The small savour was enough to send me into uncontrollable desire. My stomach was cramping. I edged closer until I was almost in the fight. The man, though brave, was beginning to weaken under the onslaught.

Still unseen, I reached for the larger of the two assailants and yanked him back slamming his body into a huge oak tree. His breath huffed out from his lungs and I ripped out his throat cutting off his cry of fear before he could finish it. His blood gushed into my mouth, throat and stomach, rapidly rushing through my veins until I felt the familiar high. I guzzled him like a dehydrated nomad who has finally found an oasis. Behind me I was vaguely aware of the fight continuing, but all other sound diminished as I listened to the failing heart of my victim as his life extinguished. I fell away, gasping and sated like a wanton whore after a night of passion. I lay in the grass with my legs splayed out before me. I was panting, licking my lips and fingers.

The passenger and the other bandit were still fighting in desperation. Only one of them would come out of this alive. I sat up and watched, waiting for the moment to pluck the other mugger away. The hunger was rearing again. The fellow was scrawny, unlike his friend. I continued to lick my lips, feeling aroused again at the sight of them, but really it was the blood that was surging through my body with a fake lust that made this fight so interesting. That and curiosity. I had to see if this strange and familiar man would survive the attack on his own or whether I should finish the job, because something inside me said he had to survive.

The men rolled again and their clothing, one green, one black, flashed and merged as they tumbled and fought. I noticed that the passenger had finally lost his sword, but the fight was full-on hand-to-hand combat as a result, and he was better skilled than his assailant. He rolled the mugger over, putting his full weight on the other man's windpipe.

The mugger kicked and thrashed, but the other man was too strong for him. It wasn't long before he weakened and fell into unconsciousness. The passenger continued to squeeze until his fingers gave out and his whole body collapsed over the dead bandit. He rolled off the body and lay in the grass for a moment, taking harsh gulps of air into his lungs. Then he staggered to his feet. His limbs trembled from the exertion of the fight and he leaned for support against a tree. He was so close I could smell his perspiration. I couldn't resist it. I had to know who he was. So, I bent forward, licked outwards and tasted him.

His hand flew to his cheek. Then he saw the body of his second assailant. Fear came finally into his eyes. He looked around. Green eyes. Blond hair. So like Gabi but not him. But I knew who he was. That one taste had been enough to confirm it. I had seen the glowing strands of his life and heritage. He was Caesare Borgia and that meant I was in Italy still but this time in the sixteenth century. I had leapt forward by six hundred years. But why was I there? Why then?

I glanced down at the body of the bandit at my feet. Of course, the two of them would have killed him. It had been necessary to save Caesare. Was this the role I played in this time then; saving Caesare so that he would become a vampire and then turn his sister? I knew that this sequence of events had to happen, otherwise my own existence was in jeopardy.

I watched him stagger wearily towards the road. What part of his life was this? I had to find out more. I had to get to know him and learn where we were in his story, then maybe I could learn who had turned him. I was certain Lucrezia never knew that.

At that moment I was infinitely curious about this other vampire that must also have carried my gene. It had to be another family member. But who? With the exception of Lucrezia, Gabi and I had never come across another vampire during our travels.

I followed Caesare out onto the road and watched the spineless driver rush forward to help him.

'My Lord!'

He bundled his exhausted employer into the carriage, wrapping a heavy blanket around his legs. Within seconds he was back up on his seat and the carriage set off at break-neck speed. So intent on escape was he that he didn't register the slight thump as I threw myself onto the roof of the carriage.

Resting my head on the wood, I heard Caesare inside as he cleaned his wounds with a handkerchief, then wrapped himself in the blanket and promptly fell asleep. I listened to his breathing. He was bruised and battered but not seriously injured and I let the carriage lull me into a sort of meditative state as it rattled furiously along the road.

Within the space of an hour we were in Rome.

Chapter 18 - Lilly's Journal
Infiltrating Rome

'My Lord, we didn't know you were coming,' said the doorman as he stepped back, bowing.

'I wasn't aware I had to inform anyone of my movements, let alone my employees,' Caesare snapped, pulling off his gloves and hat and unceremoniously placing them in the hands of an old serving maid who ran forward to join the line.

The terrified servants stood at both sides of the huge entrance hall. I entered unnoticed behind Caesare who walked between them, barely acknowledging their presence. He was a frightening sight, covered in bruises and his clothing dirty and ripped. But even so, he examined the servants as though he were in his finest clothing. Once past them, he took the stairs two at a time and left the confused and nervous group to shamble away in different directions to do his bidding.

Caesare's home was only a few kilometres from Vatican City yet he shunned the church and his former life as one of the most notorious and influential men in Rome. The servants' fear of him was obvious and it gave credence to Lucrezia's story. Caesare's reputation was true then. He was brutal, arrogant and feared. I found him completely fascinating.

As Caesare left the hallway, an elderly woman, who I assumed to be the housekeeper came forward to talk to the driver as he deposited Caesare's bags in the hallway.

'Where has he been all this time? We thought maybe he wasn't coming back to Rome, with all the scandal. The things we've heard about him and his escapades. I'm amazed he can show his face.'

'He's been at his sister's house,' whispered the driver, glancing nervously at the stairs. 'Only don't ask me what he's been up to there, I'm too afraid to even think about it.'

'He's a *diavolo*.'

'Yes. But he pays our wages and besides he'd kill me if I talked.'

The housekeeper tutted as though she didn't believe Caesare capable of murder.

'You've been free of him for too long. You'll see. He just took on a band of ladri on the highway, and guess who won?'

The housekeeper glanced up at the staircase, her face pale. 'I can hardly believe it. I guess I had hoped he would never come back here. I'd better go and sort out something for his supper or there will be hell to pay. He'll have to make do with *montone* though; it's all we've got.'

'Get a good wine from the cellar and he'll be happy,' advised the driver, 'and send up a tub of water for him to bathe, he hates to be dirty. That will all help his mood, I'm certain.'

The housekeeper nodded.

'You!' she said, catching the arm of a male servant. 'Fetch his Lordship a bottle from the cellar and take it up to his room immediately.'

I stood by the doorway unsure of what to do. I felt that I needed more information about him but was almost certain I had arrived in the week when Caesare finally left Lucrezia, heavily pregnant, back in her country home while he returned to Rome to take care of business. That meant he was probably in his forties. I felt like a voyeur. I had stepped into his life, could stand back and watch him behave appallingly and see for myself that Lucrezia's story was true. I didn't want to be like a ghost watching the world unfold before me. I wanted to participate in it, just as I had in the *Castrum*. Besides it was becoming increasingly difficult to maintain my invisible state and the hunger was already resurfacing because of my expended energy.

The housekeeper gave orders for a bath to be drawn for the Lord and I waited for the servants to clear the hall before opening the door and slipping out of Caesare's house. I needed clothing suitable for the time, but first I needed blood and money.

Night was drawing in as I slipped down the street and began to look for a likely and suitably wealthy victim. Here more than ever, it was important to check my food and so I avoided anyone with a pale complexion or fair hair. There weren't many, Caesare and Lucrezia's fair colouring were quite exclusive, but there were few people around on this cold evening and certainly no one respectable on foot.

Tiredness made me drop my shields and I merged softly back into the world, but kept close to the shadows as I worked my way through the city. I needed a place to rest. An inn maybe, but I couldn't be seen like this. My disguise as a warrior female of gypsy origin would be too conspicuous. I had to become Lilly again and somehow the prospect both excited and scared me. I hadn't been myself for a long time.

I found myself wandering the docklands. I remembered Lucrezia's escapades here, yet to happen in this time. It made me feel strange, as though I were walking through the lands described in a novel I once read; only this story was real and I had been told it firsthand. This was the environment where Lucrezia had found a level of security for a time. I looked around for a likely victim. It was still early and the inns were barely busy. I noticed a young man walking holding a canvas, his clothing was worn and splattered with various colours of paint, yet he was dressed in the fashion of the time. He entered an inn called The Shuttered Door. The name and place were familiar, as though I'd seen it before. I suspected it was somewhere that Lucrezia had frequented, or maybe it had still existed in our time and Gabi and I had casually passed by. I didn't worry about it for long though. Instead, curiosity drove me to peer through the window at the man, and I saw him meeting with another man inside.

The second man was very interesting. He had dark curly hair, a pointy beard that reminded me of a bust I'd seen of William

Shakespeare at some time, as did his Venetian-style ruffles, hose and doublet. His clothing was made of satin or silk, I wasn't sure which, but it was in the most luxurious shade of green. Over his shoulders hung a dark velvet green cloak and around his waist was a belt holding a thin rapier.

The Venetian gentleman was admiring the painting, and his hand massaged the leg of the artist familiarly.

I watched their lips move and tuned into their words, zoning out all other noises around me.

'What do you think of this, Count? Is it worthy of your personal gallery?' asked the artist.

'Lorenzo, you have a lot of talent. I would like to see more of your … work. Maybe we should go to your rooms?'

The Count looked at Lorenzo, the artist, and his hand slid farther up the young man's leg.

'I can help you a lot, if you help me,' the Count said.

'You can help me sell my work?'

'Yes, my friends would love you. We could be very successful together.'

The innkeeper brought a bowl of steaming stew and a large flagon of ale for the Count. Lorenzo stared at the bowl. The Count began to eat as Lorenzo watched him consume every mouthful.

'Innkeeper, bring me more,' called the Count as he emptied the bowl.

The innkeeper returned rapidly with a replenished bowl and placed it down before the men. The Count didn't touch it. He left the bowl cooling in front of him as he sipped his ale. Lorenzo became hypnotised by the food.

'A long time since you ate?' asked the Count eventually.

Lorenzo glanced away, embarrassed. 'I've been working so hard on this piece, I forgot to eat today.'

'Mmmm. Try this. It's rather delicious.' The Count pushed the bowl towards Lorenzo. 'So we have a deal then?'

Lorenzo reached for the bowl, but the Count held it back.

Lorenzo looked up into his eyes. The Count smiled, his teeth were black and rotten stalks.

'Count? I'm not sure what you ...'

'We'll work out the details in your studio,' he answered letting go of the bowl and pushing it firmly into the boy's hands.

Lorenzo nodded, uncertainly taking the stew, but after the first mouthful began eating ravenously. The Count removed a full purse from his doublet and paid the innkeeper. Then placed his hand on the young man's leg once more, slowly drawing a circle with his index finger. The young artist barely noticed as he gulped down the food.

I followed them back to Lorenzo's impoverished rooms. The Count obviously had wealth and I was curious in that voyeuristic way I had adopted in this world. He may be a means for me to find the right clothing, the right lodging. Or at least some of that gold from his purse would be useful in obtaining those things.

God, I've turned into a thief these days as well as a monster.

I waited outside as they went up to Lorenzo's rooms, tuning into the excited chatter of the boy as he showed the Count his art. A few minutes later all went quiet and I knew the Count was coercing a different kind of service from the boy; he was an easy target after all. It was partly why I hadn't followed them in. I didn't particularly want that kind of voyeuristic kick.

A few moments later the Count came out. He was angry. Lorenzo followed shortly, his doublet was pulled open and he looked afraid.

'Please ... Count. You said you'd help me.'

'You haven't helped me though, have you boy?'

'I ... don't understand. I know some women who ...'

The Count stopped. 'It isn't a woman I want. That's easy to come by ...'

The Count turned away, anger oozing from every pore as he saw the disgust and horror on Lorenzo's face.

'Please ...' Lorenzo sobbed.

But the Count walked away.

I stepped in behind the Count as Lorenzo turned back to his door and wearily returned to his studio. The Count was unaware of my light tread behind him, and I didn't have to resort to invisibility as he was too consumed with his rage. I followed him from the docklands, out and down towards the city. The night grew colder and he pulled his cloak closer around himself as he cast around for a carriage to hire. The streets were quiet. On this cold night barely anyone was out. The Count and I were quite alone.

'Do you want something different?' I whispered next to his ear and he jerked around surprised.

He scrutinised my clothing. I was after all dressed as a boy. He had clearly liked the pretty Lorenzo and in the dark I was sure that to his human eyes I might appear male.

'You startled me. Where did you come from?'

'The docklands. I thought you needed some company.'

The Count smiled, his crooked and blackened teeth made me want to gag. I smiled back, trying to keep my expression boyish.

'Come into the light ...' the Count suggested.

I imagined Lorenzo's image, mixed with my own colouring and as the Count walked towards the lit garden of one of the expensive houses on the street, I used my power to change my aspect from gypsy to boy. I was truly becoming a chameleon. I stepped into the light.

The Count gasped. 'Beautiful.'

At that moment a hire carriage came by and quickly the Count hailed it.

'Inside boy, quickly,' he said as the carriage drew beside us. 'Do you have lodgings?'

'None that I would take a gentleman like you to.'

The Count turned to me in the light of the carriage and saw my face again. His expression was one of wonder.

'You are truly striking ...' he stuttered.

'Why thank you,' I opened the carriage door. 'Shall we?'

'Where to then gents?' asked the driver.

The Count gave his address and silently we rode through the city to his exclusive rooms on the outskirts of Rome.

It was quite a covert operation being sneaked into the respectable home of the Count. Obviously he didn't want anyone to know of his preference for boys and so he entered first and ensured that all of his serving staff were clear of the entrance way. Then he hurried me inside and up the stairs, which were covered in a plush, blue carpet, and into his private suite. Inside the room he locked the doors.

'How much do you charge boy?'

'Only what you can afford Count.'

The Count laughed. 'An ambiguous answer. I like that.'

He walked over to a small bureau on which stood a decanter and two glasses.

'I see you are used to entertaining.'

'Don't be impertinent boy. What's your name anyway?'

'Do you even care what my name is?' I answered.

The Count stalked towards me a lecherous smile on his lips, framing his awful teeth.

'I'm going to enjoy you,' he said.

I licked his cheek as his arms went around my boyish frame. Safe. No sign of my gene code anywhere.

'And I you,' I murmured.

My mouth found his throat and I teased the crucial vein with my tongue until the Count swooned against me. I led him to his luxurious bed. It was covered in silks and furs and as I pulled off my boots and lay down beside him it was the most comfortable place I'd lain in years. I sighed with pleasure, and fought the urge to just curl up where I was and sleep.

I pulled the Count to my chest, kissing and stroking him until his excitement frenzied in my arms. I felt his hardness press against me. He had no idea still that I was female, and even if he realised it was long past the point where it would matter. I stripped his doublet, bared his chest and ran my nails down him. As he tried to touch and caress me, I pushed his hands aside. I wanted his blood but not his death and so I would leave him with the illusion that he had slept with a boy he picked from the streets. Even though really, nothing like that would happen between us.

I bit him gently, determined to keep the bruising to a minimum and the Count spasmed and jerked into his breeches as I suckled his throat. His orgasm was real as was the eroticism of the moment to him. But not to me. He was food, and a useful tool. Before the night was out I'd know all about Roman high society and how to infiltrate it. I would be part of this world, and I would wait out my time until the door arrived for me to move on. At least I would make it fun and bearable.

As the Count slept I relieved him of his purse. In the morning he'd know he had been robbed, but would remember the passion and desire. He would recall the peculiar lovemaking with the mysterious boy in sheepskins and maybe he wouldn't mind losing his money so much after all.

Chapter 19 - Lilly's Journal
Il Salone di Piaceri

I picked information from the minds of the aristocracy with the same ease as stealing gold from their purses. All their frivolous thoughts led to one place. *Il Salone di Piaceri* was rumoured to be decadent. It was full of free speaking and free living people of wealth, who boasted of corrupt and debauched lives. Mostly this was just rumour. Little more went on in the public salon than an over-indulgence of wine and the occasional stolen kiss or caress behind the curtains in the great hall. Predominantly it was a place to have informal business gatherings.

The salon was run by a clever lady who made her living encouraging the aristocracy to visit her while arranging the right meeting. Sometimes that might be the introduction of a poor but titled Lord to a wealthy heiress from dubious origins. Or a merchant with a lucrative business venture to a group of wealthy aristocrats willing to gamble on something high-risk with a potential good return. Marnia Farnesse would willingly make the introductions for a fee. She was the person that most people would approach when they needed a little help in meeting the right people.

Having obtained clothing, money and a fake identity I visited the salon. It was the obvious place to learn more about this world and to understand if I had to remain here for any other purpose than I had already served by saving Caesare. After only a few days in Rome I had procured a small apartment, a driver and carriage and a wardrobe full of clothing, thanks to the money that I had taken so easily from several men, including the Count.

I arrived at the salon one evening with an envelope containing a letter explaining my needs and a large purse of gold. This was the fee necessary to employ Marnia and get her to aid my introduction into the right circles.

Once in my own place, I focussed all my attention on returning my image to my former self. Becoming the 'real Lilly' once more brought a rush of sad memories. I recalled my life in the twenty-first century with Gabi and those final days when I had foolishly let myself be attracted by the first door in the world of the Allucians. All that had happened since then was like a dream. When I looked back into my own green eyes though, I couldn't help but remember that everything so far had some significance. Even the garden, where Adonai had told me I could not merely return home. It was all a warning, all a sign. I was here for a reason which had yet to unfold. That undeniable pull into the first door had been crucial to the life of Maria and Benedict, and possibly even to Caesare Borgia. Although I wasn't superstitious by nature, I couldn't deny how things suddenly had a way of turning out like this.

'So, you are new in town?' asked Marnia.

'I heard you could help me,' I said holding out the gold. 'Will this be enough for now?'

Marnia Farnesse was a stunning woman. She had long black tresses, swept up at the sides to reveal small and pretty ears, while the fullness and beauty of her curls were left to cascade down her back and over her shoulders. She wore a dress of pale blue satin, off the shoulder. It revealed a pretty neck and her small perfect, firm breasts swelled above her low-cut neckline when she breathed, as the corset pushed them up into round globes. She was slender; her shape that of a teenage girl rather than a woman in her early thirties.

Marnia had never married. There was no question of her being 'left on the shelf' either. She had frequently turned down suitors of wealth, but she was in the rare position for a woman of her time: she had her own wealth and controlled her own money. She was not at the mercy of a father or brother who would marry her off for the best match or political gain. So, she reasoned, why would she marry anyone and give away her freedom and wealth? She had seen the results of such foolish trust so many times. The wife invariably became a slave and a brood mare, constantly at the mercy of the whims of her husband. He would then gamble away her wealth, or spend it on whores while she sat at home, helpless to prevent it. All because of love.

Marnia took my purse, weighing it gently in her hand. 'This will do nicely. Please take a seat.'

I sat down on a renaissance sofa of soft cushioned tapestry and Marnia sat opposite behind a desk, like a real business woman.

'What do you need?' she asked, cutting to the chase immediately.

'Acceptance in Roman society.'

'That's easy. A display of wealth makes questions of origins unnecessary. However, may I suggest a title? Calling yourself Countess for example or Marquise if you prefer will go a long way to securing a desired marriage.'

'I don't want to marry. I'm not looking for that.'

'Ah. A woman after my own heart. Men ruin beautiful women and child-birth does even more damage.'

'I won't be here long, I'm merely passing through. I just want to have fun.'

Marnia's gaze swept over me. 'You don't seem the sort to have "fun" but it's not for me to say. If you need help in avoiding unwanted motherhood, I have contacts.'

'That won't be necessary,' I laughed. 'I don't want that kind of fun. My heart lies elsewhere.'

'You are a most unusual girl. Let me clarify – you only want a legitimate status, one which allows you access to respectable homes and society?'

'Yes.'

'Why?'

'I want to observe Roman society. Meet the people, understand what they value.'

'I say again, why?'

'Distraction.' Looking up, I let Marnia see the sadness in my eyes. The pain of leaving Maria and Benedict, of being ripped from my home and time, of losing Gabriele all rushed forth as I stared back at her.

'Loss ...' she said and her instincts were right. 'Then distraction is precisely what you need.'

'But no complications ...' I reminded her.

With that, Marnia accepted me into her inner circle. Of course she needed information about me in order to make it work. I explained I was English and this made her job even easier. She would introduce me as an English cousin of hers, an heiress of title and fortune. This would make me desirable company for the kind of aristocracy I was hoping to meet. It was clear that Marnia didn't fully understand me. I was certainly an enigma and not her usual client, but she related to the emotions I'd shown.

'Of course, you are also a very beautiful woman,' she pointed out. 'There will be many suitors, but play with them or not. It is your choice.'

It was incredibly easy to become part of her world. I needed very few papers of identity, all of which I had already obtained. It was a moment so far removed from the Europe of my time. Wealth meant you were accepted. You could say you were any age, give yourself a title and create a lie of powerful friends in high places. Communication was far from easy with other countries, even other cities. Wealth made you believable. After all, who but the aristocracy had wealth? So what if you lie about who you really were? You were probably of noble birth anyway, but maybe illegitimate. After all, most people were.

'Have you any preference on name?' Marnia asked and I gave her the name of a character from one of my favourite books.

I would be the Countess De Winter; Alexandre Dumas would be proud ... And it was so appropriate that I would be the dark and dangerous beauty that betrayed D'Artagnan and the other musketeers.

On that first evening Marnia took me from her office into the main salon and began to introduce me to many of the 'right' people. I had dressed carefully for the evening, having spent the last few days scrutinising the fashion of the nobility whenever I could. I was dressed in fine silk of beige and cream and my hair had been put up by the servant girl I had hired to work for me.

'These are the nice ladies of the town,' Marnia whispered as she led me to a group of young women. 'Helpless gossips every last one of them. If you make the right impression on them you'll be talked about all over Rome. Then the invitations will flow ...'

'Of course the Marquis of Naples is a dear friend of mine ...' A young woman of no more than seventeen spoke with fluency and the others listened. 'His dear wife was ailing; it isn't a surprise at all that he is so soon widowed after his marriage.'

'What is he like, Agostina?' another girl asked. 'I heard he was handsome.'

'Oh yes, he is. Very. But a terrible philanderer.'

The women giggled as though outraged but were clearly titillated by the thought of the Marquis.

'Senorinas, may I introduce my cousin to you?' interrupted Marnia. 'All the way from London, in England.'

The introductions commenced and each of the women curtsied as Marnia told me their names.

'Lady Agostina Marano from Naples, *Signorina* Bella Peruch from Veneto, Vicenza Ferraro from Milan.'

The women asked questions about my family and my relationship to Marnia, a story which we had already worked out.

'Oh you really must come to my breakfast party tomorrow. My brother would adore you,' said Agostina Marano; who, Marnia informed me, was from a wealthy family in Naples.

'That would be very agreeable,' I answered.

'Oh no!' said Agostina suddenly. 'I cannot believe *he* would come here.'

'What is it?' I turned, but all I could see was a flurry of people bustling around someone who had recently entered the salon.

'Caesare Borgia,' Agostina answered. Her eyes were wide as she repeated the gossip she'd heard about him. 'They say he is in love with his own sister. His own sister! Can you believe it?'

'Yes, I can.'

Agostina gave me a very serious expression. 'I'd stay away from him if I were you. He has a terrible reputation and most women who come in contact with him usually end up ruined in one way or other.'

'What do you mean, ruined?'

'Agostina means that they are seduced, or left bereft of their inheritance ...' Marnia said. 'Borgia is definitely not for the faint hearted ... but then neither was his father.'

'You knew the Pope when he was alive?' I asked.

'My sister was his mistress, bore him children in fact. But she seemed happy enough with her lot and overall he was good to her. But Caesare – he's different.'

I took Marnia's arm and led her away from the small group of scandalised women as they whispered nervously to each other.

'I'm always interested in a little titillation,' I said smiling. 'Do tell me more. Why is he different?'

Marnia stared straight into my eyes, 'Do you know you bear a striking resemblance to his sister, only you are much younger?'

'I do?' I answered feigning surprise. 'In what way?'

'Your fair hair and your eyes. They are incredibly similar.'

I fell silent, but looked across the salon at Caesare. He was dressed in a Venetian style doublet and hose of dark burgundy. He was beautiful, despite his age and obvious debaucheries, and the bruises he'd sustained during his fight with the bandits a few days ago were barely noticeable under the faint dust of white powder on his face. He was every bit the fashionable and sophisticated gentleman as he bowed his head politely to listen to a woman standing beside him.

'If you crave such excitement I can introduce you ...' Marnia said.

'No! I'm just interested that's all. Tell me about his sister.'

Marnia proceeded to tell me all she knew of the rumours surrounding the Borgias. Firstly, of Caesare and Lucrezia's seemingly close relationship in their teens. Lucrezia's penchant for dressing as a boy and it was even rumoured that she shot at servants with a bow and arrow from her bedroom window when she was bored.

'Of course the most shocking of all is the accusations by her first husband ...'

'Yes. I'd heard something about that. He accused the family of incest?'

Marnia nodded. 'Politically it didn't do Pope Alexander any harm. Many believed him to be ruthless, he used his powerful position for personal gain and if this seeming "man of God" could do that then sexual deviance would not have been any worse.'

'I don't know; it seems worse to me. But then who knows? Lucrezia may have merely been a victim of her obsessive brother.' I answered vaguely.

'You speak as though you *know* that.'

I laughed. 'Of course not. I'm just willing to consider all sides. And, I knew of a similar situation, in London.'

'I see. Oh my dear. Look. Caesare has noticed me and he's making his way over here.'

'Oh no. I don't want to meet him. I'll go back to the girls.'

'But you must,' Marnia insisted. 'He's seen you also and it would be against propriety if I didn't introduce you.'

Caesare was indeed walking towards us. My heart began to pound in my chest. I had hoped to be merely an observer in his life, and had never planned to actually talk to the man. For a start, I knew from Lucrezia's account of him that he was completely without scruples. Our physical similarities may make him rather too interested in me and for that reason I had planned to remain outside of his personal social circle. I also thought that he wouldn't be in Rome for too long and the chances of us meeting again would be rather slim.

'Marnia,' Caesare stopped directly before us and I kept my eyes averted, afraid to meet his gaze. 'An interesting mix of people you have this evening.'

'Caesare, I only ever have interesting people at my parties. You know that. What brings you here this evening? I thought you had shunned my salon forever.'

'Of course not. I have business to attend in Rome. I couldn't possibly be here and not pay you a visit you divine creature.'

Caesare smiled and I glanced quickly at him only to notice again how like Gabriele he was. I swallowed, it was so hard to avoid looking directly at him, when all I wanted to do was openly scrutinise him in the brightly candle-lit room.

'But where have you been, you naughty boy?' Marnia asked. 'We haven't seen you since the funeral.'

'I retired to the country for a while.'

I felt his eyes on me, but kept mine deliberately averted, wondering, not for the first time if I should have created a different face for myself. I knew I was as much like Lucrezia as Caesare looked like Gabi. It had been foolish to appear as myself, but after years of hiding behind the gypsy face of Miranda, it had been a novelty to see my own reflection again and I had been loath to disguise myself. I wanted to be Lilly once more.

'Aren't you going to introduce me to this very charming and beautiful lady, Marnia?' Caesare asked finally.

Marnia glanced at me quickly, 'Er ... yes ... This is my cousin, from England. Lilly De Winter, Countess of Hampstead.'

'Really?'

Marnia touched my arm, her fingers squeezing slightly and it forced me to glance up. Caesare gasped but I kept my face as straight as possible, holding out my hand for him to kiss as I'd seen other woman in the room do. I hoped that my eyes gave no sign of recognition or knowledge of him. Caesare recovered his composure and took my hand, pressing my gloved fingers to his full, sensuous mouth.

'Countess. May I welcome you to Rome? Perhaps you would honour me with the next dance?'

I gazed around the salon, the musicians and the few dancers had been incidental to the atmosphere. I had barely taken in the moves. Stupid of me when I was trying so hard to be integrated into this world

'I ... don't know this one. We have different dances in England. Maybe in a few days when my cousin Marnia has shown me a few steps?' I knew my excuse was lame.

'You don't dance?' his eyes smiled with amusement. 'Then you must walk with me instead.'

'Walk? Walk where?'

To mine and Marnia's surprise Caesare took my arm and led me away. I saw the scandalised expressions of the women I'd met, but to pull away would cause a scene and perhaps create even more scandal. Caesare Borgia might not be averse to causing embarrassment in public from all that I heard about him but I didn't want to draw unnecessary attention to myself. Instead I let him escort me towards the open doorway which led into the main entrance hall.

I'd passed through the hall earlier. It was a huge expanse opening up onto a large central staircase. Caesare clearly knew his way around Marnia's fine rooms and he walked straight past her office and into a small, private drawing room at the other side of the reception. Inside a large fire roared in an imposing fireplace that was almost too large for the room. It was a beautiful room, plush and luxurious. I was still getting used to seeing striking furnishings and ornaments again after years of being surrounded by basic things. This world was a far cry from the poverty of Maria Serafina and the *Castrum*. I cast my eyes around, admiring vases, paintings and the beautiful rug before the fire which was thick and lavish with bright gold and red colours.

Two other couples sat opposite each other on sofas either side of the fireplace. Their polite conversation halted as we entered. Caesare nodded to them and then led me straight past towards the French windows. He threw open the heavy red drapes and outside I saw a huge garden. Without waiting, Caesare pulled open the doors and taking my hand once again, he placed it firmly in the crook of his arm and led me out into the immense landscape.

'You are very forceful,' I pointed out. 'I don't care to be frog-marched out of a party. What on earth do you think you're playing at?'

Caesare stopped and stared at me, his eyes wide and shocked as he examined my features. He really was very attractive. I even enjoyed the faint lines of age around his eyes.

'Who are you?'

'Marnia already told you ...'

'Marnia has many cousins – and not one of them is truly related to her. Who are you really?'

I threw back my head and laughed. 'If only you knew how many people regularly ask me that question, in many different situations!'

I pulled free of his grasp. He didn't try to stop me, which was fortunate because I would probably have broken his arm.

'You look more like my relative than hers.'

'Yes. I can see a resemblance. Strange isn't it?' I turned to admire a rose bush, bending slightly to smell one of the purple flowers.

'Don't you know who I am?' he asked suddenly. 'Aren't you afraid to be alone with me?'

'And I say again, Marnia did introduce us ... But yes. I do *know* who you are, your reputation preceded you. And why should I be afraid? We're at a public party.'

'Yes, my dear. But we are outside now and completely alone.'

Chapter 20 - Lilly's Journal

Caesare's Obsession

'I'm always alone,' I said as Caesare stalked me through the gardens. 'It holds no fear for me at all.'

'You are so like her …' Caesare murmured. 'Even down to that annoying arrogance.'

I felt his eyes examine my face as I studied the flowers and bushes in the garden.

'This really is beautiful. I've never seen a garden quite like it, even my parent's house. And Oakwood Lodge has magnificent grounds.'

I had forgotten fear and was totally confident. After all what could a mere mortal do to me? Even so, I knew I was rambling. The situation was more than a little uncomfortable. I wanted my moment of voyeurism. I wanted to see firsthand the society Lucrezia had tried to explain. The bigotry, the debauchery and the Machiavellian politics were all very intriguing and they would fill the time, take my mind away from all that I had lost; especially Benedict and Maria. But really, I hadn't planned on getting so close to the leading man of the story.

Caesare's hand circled my waist and he tried to pull me into his arms. He found me unmoveable. He pulled harder.

'You'll give yourself a hernia,' I warned. 'I'm heavier than I seem.'

He pulled again, his face flushed. Finding me impossible to budge, he stepped closer. Both arms surrounded me, his head bent down as he attempted to press his lips against mine. But I merely turned my head away.

'Don't touch me. And don't try to kiss me,' I warned, shrugging him off as easily as if I was swatting away a fly.

Caesare's arms fell to his sides. Then his raised his hands and stared down at them, observing the red dents on his fingers. His fingers looked as though he had been gripping something so hard and immobile that his hands were strained.

'Who are you? *What* are you?'

'I'm Marnia's cousin. And you, *Signor* are a sadistic, self-centred animal, no better than the infamous *Marquis de Sade*.'

Caesare was speechless, but then he said, 'Who?'

I sighed. *Wrong era?* My timelines were so confusing and history wasn't my strong point anyway!

'Good evening, *Signor*.'

I walked away from him; back through the French windows, passed the startled couples, and across the main reception back to the salon.

I rejoined the girls. They stared at me silently for a few moments seemingly at a loss for words. I had been gone for more than fifteen minutes, but not long enough for propriety to have been completely breached. Especially not in *Il Salone di Piaceri*.

'Outrageous,' Agostina burst out finally unable to contain herself.

I was rapidly learning that she was the most unconventional of the group.

'I know, the man thinks he's irresistible to women. I'm afraid I brought him down a peg or two.'

'You do have a very strange way of speaking,' Vicenza said. 'What do you mean, "brought him down a peg or two"?'

'Oh. I told him he's an arrogant and uncouth brute.'

The girls were scandalised but giggled, clearly enjoying themselves. Agostina laughed the loudest, until Vicenza tapped her arm lightly with her fan. It returned Agostina to her senses and she quickly glanced around to see if anyone had observed her outburst.

'I suspect he's never had a woman stand up to him before,'

Agostina said, her voice dropping to a whisper. 'Quiet! He's heading this way.'

All the girls' faces became serious and the chatter changed with practised skill to a mundane discussion of the weather.

Caesare stopped a few feet from the group and I watched him through the corner of my eye. His face was flushed and his fists clenched by his sides. If looks could kill ... His anger flowed from him in waves. Oh yes. He definitely didn't like women refusing him. But for all his fury he contained himself and he didn't advance towards us.

Marnia crossed the room, taking in the expression of fury on Caesare's face. She glanced at our small group talking innocently and back at Caesare. Then with practised skill she took Caesare's arm, leading him to the refreshments table.

'My dear friend,' she said. 'Come and taste this extraordinary wine I bought from a French merchant.'

'Who is she?' he asked.

'It's really quite delicious ...'

'She's a demon ...' Caesare ranted.

'No my dear, she's my cousin. From England. I told you.'

The girls were too afraid to return to our former conversation and so they began to point out all the relevant people I should meet while Agostina interspersed the formal information with gossip about each one.

'You really are shameful, Agostina!' Vicenza said.

'I know. But you love it, don't you my dear?'

The giggles expanded again, only to be interrupted by a Lord approaching to ask one of them to dance. I slipped away on the pretext of needing to 'freshen-up' and I fought my way through the crowd out into the next room. The second hall was crammed with people.

Merging with the shadows this time, I weaved in and out of the bodies, listening to snippets of gossip hoping to hear something that would be interesting or relevant.

'Borgia is reprehensible ...'

I stopped beside a well-dressed man in his late thirties as he bent down to whisper to an older gentleman sitting down at the side of the room. The old man was holding an ornate walking stick. His hands rolled over the silver and jewel covered hand grip.

'Yes,' the man nodded. 'They believe he murdered his father.'

'How?'

'Poison I suspect.'

'The Pope always had his food checked.'

The old man nodded, 'True. But would you check a glass of port handed to you by your own son?'

'What did he have to gain? Alexander's wealth went to the church and Borgia has his own money, long since settled on him by his father.'

'I know. But he wasn't permitted to see his sister was he? Who can stop him now?'

The first man looked the old man straight in the eye and instead of bending down once more he pulled up a chair and sat close beside him. 'I heard that he's been living there ever since the Pope's death.'

'At Lucrezia's, yes.'

Both men fell silent. I was leaning against the wall close by. Neither of them could see me, so I closed my eyes and focused on their conversation, but before they could say more another man approached. I glanced at the newcomer through my lashes as he bowed to the two men and exchanged a few polite words before moving on. I opened my eyes properly as he walked away, noticing his long blonde hair which was tied back in an attempt to mimic the local fashion. He was Nordic in colouring, with pale skin, very unlike the Italian locals.

'He's obsessed with her,' the old man continued as soon as the other man was out of earshot.

'Do you think ... she *wants* him to be?'

The old man shrugged, 'Who can say? The Borgias have never been normal. That Spanish blood I shouldn't wonder ...'

I walked away from them, merging deeper into the crowd and then I saw Caesare and Marnia talking to the tall man. I observed him fully then. He stood a good foot above most of the men in the room with the exception of Caesare, who was taller than average. The other man was foreign. I could hear snatches of conversation as Marnia introduced Caesare to him and although he spoke Italian his accent was slightly corrupted on some of the vowels.

'Harald, Count of Stockholm. He's a direct descendant of a king,' Marnia told Caesare.

'Really?' Caesare raised an eyebrow. 'Just like that bitch is your English cousin?'

'Caesare please. You know this is no way to behave.'

'I've interrupted something,' said Harald turning away.

'Not at all. Caesare is merely stamping his foot. He was refused by the most beautiful woman in the salon this evening. And he can't handle it.'

'If you were a man I would take you outside ...' Caesare said.

'If I were any other woman you'd take me outside ...' Marnia laughed. 'Stop taking yourself so seriously for once. Besides, the count has been hoping to meet you for a long time. He tells me he has a very attractive proposition for you.'

Harald bowed his head. 'I do. But when you are more in the mood perhaps.'

'No,' Caesare answered. 'I'm returning to the country tomorrow. My sister Lucrezia is expecting a child any day and as a dutiful brother I'd like to be there for her.'

Marnia's expression remained professionally still as he spoke.

'Then if this evening is good for you ...?' Harald prompted.

'Of course. May we use your office, Marnia?'

Marnia nodded, and both men left. She turned her head, looking around the salon to see where else she was needed and then slowly walked away to join a small group of men who were shyly scrutinising three young women on the other side of the room.

'Introductions for you gentlemen, I think ...'

Caesare and Harald walked through the crowd towards me, and I stepped aside at their approach, even though I knew I couldn't be seen.

'Thank you, *Signorina*,' Harald said nodding in my direction then he stopped, turned and stared at me. '*What are you doing here?*' he asked in English.

I shook my head, surprised but didn't answer.

'Count Harald?' Caesare said turning back. 'The office is this way.'

I gaped after him as he led Caesare away. Had Harald actually *seen* me? And if he had, he thought I was someone he knew.

Seconds passed and I followed at a safe distance, waiting in the main salon until I was sure that both men had entered Marnia's office. I went into the main reception and began to climb the staircase in the middle. Upstairs there were many unoccupied rooms. I turned left, searching for a room that may be above the office and quickly entered a small bedroom. Inside was a single size bed, and basic furniture, with several wardrobes. There was a large quantity of dresses scattered around the room. Maybe this was a courtesy room. Marnia had said if my clothing hadn't been suitable that she would have 'found me something to wear'. I looked beyond the dresses, quickly seeing what I was searching for. I crossed the room and opened the French window; as I hoped it led onto a balcony above the office. I stood on the balcony, then pulled up my wide dress and climbed onto the carved stone rail. I walked it like a circus performer, while briefly glancing down to see the best place to land. I had to be silent. Underneath the balcony lay a patch of thick grass and a pot of flowers directly below the office window.

I dropped down. The hem of my dress caught on a protruding piece of stone and despite my calculations I landed awkwardly on the grass and was forced to roll in order to avoid hurting myself. The grass was damp, and I could feel the wetness staining the silk of the dress. I ripped away more of its bulk. I wouldn't be able to return to the salon that evening, but at least I could move easier through the brush and up to the window. I had to see what was going on because I was very curious about Harald and his proposition. It might be important after all.

At that moment the curtain in the office fluttered and I bobbed down below the window ledge just in time to avoid being seen by Harald. I was still invisible but certain he'd seen me. By then I was wondering if he was one of those people with 'special gifts'. He may well have recognised that I was not human. After all if he could see me, what else could he do? My curiosity was even more aroused and I sat beside the window, tuning out all other sound but the talk of the two men inside.

Harald Of Sweden

Caesare poured Harald and himself a glass of port from a decanter in Marnia's office. Harald sat down on the sofa I had occupied just a few short hours ago. His long legs stretched out before him. He tugged at the Venetian clothing he was wearing. The doublet, although made to fit, was wrong on him. He was uncomfortable and restricted in this formal clothing. As I examined his face I began to see the strangest thing. His face and colouring were very familiar and he reminded me of someone. But who it was eluded me at that time.

I glanced at Caesare through the tiny gap in the curtains. He was also scrutinising the face of this stranger and his expression was serious as though he were in deep concentration. He held out the port to Harald, who took it politely but didn't sip.

'This has been a very strange night.'

Harald glanced over his shoulder at the door then back at Caesare.

'Has it?'

'I met a woman who was the very image of my sister, when she was all of twenty.'

'There are many beautiful women here, with physical similarities,' Harald observed.

'Yes, but not many with pale blonde hair and green eyes. Eyes like mine. Eyes like yours I might add.' Caesare tipped his glass towards Harald in a salute.

'I can see why that would be eventful,' the Swede said slowly. 'But not impossible.'

'How long have you been in Italy?' Caesare asked suddenly, as though this was the most important question in the world.

'Some time now.'

'And you have a business proposition?'

Harald stood and placed his untouched glass on a small round mahogany table beside an elaborate candelabrum. His body language was composed, but there was something about the subtly with which he moved, an elegant grace that seemed impossible for such a big man. I moved closer to the window. His posture was so memorable. It was one that Gabi and I would have adopted if we wanted a victim to feel safe.

Caesare leaned back against Marnia's desk, one arm resting on the polished wood, the other lifting his glass to his lips.

'I've heard a lot about you,' Harald was saying.

'I'm sure you have.'

'Interesting rumours. You have no respect for the weak.'

'The weak are meant to be exploited by their very nature,' Caesare laughed. 'So you know I have little scruples. Let's get that out of the way. There isn't much I wouldn't do if I could gain what I wanted from it.'

'So I've heard.'

'But what of you, Count? Are your morals intact?'

Harald laughed, throwing back his head. 'I should hope not.'

'Rape?'

Harald sat again, the conversation was becoming more interesting, and whatever his motives I suddenly realised that a crucial moment had passed. He appeared truly benign at that instant, unlike a few moments before.

'I see. We are to measure our manhood against each other by exploring our crimes? Yes, I've raped. And you?'

'Sometimes. But mostly women say that they were raped in order to avoid responsibility. They are all whores after all ... Murder?'

'Murder is the easy one. Of course everyone says you killed your father.'

'Do they? How peculiar: I'm completely innocent on that score. His doctor told me the old bastard drank and ate himself into an early grave.'

'Maybe the doctor was afraid of you.'

Caesare shrugged. 'Possibly ...'

Harald smiled. It was the worse smile I had ever seen, though he had unusually perfect teeth for the era: he was like a cat holding the tail of a mouse only the mouse hadn't realised it was caught yet.

Caesare caught Harald's expression though and on some primitive level I believe he knew there was something wrong with it.

'We could play this game all evening Count or you could just get to the point and tell me what you want.'

Harald placed his arms behind his head, stretching out his legs again. 'My proposition is most unusual. You see I am something of a collector. And I enjoy meeting notorious humans. When one has lived as long as I, one becomes bored of the normal things in life.'

'You are hardly even my age!' Caesare laughed indulgently. 'I could never get bored with life.'

'No? Not even after hundreds of years?'

'Ah the elusive immortality.'

Harald sipped his drink for the first time then licked his lips with a pointed tongue.

'Do you believe there are creatures that can live forever?' Harald asked casually.

'No more than I believe in the *Holy Grail*. But the question is, do you?' responded Caesare as he began to examine his finger nails.

By then my heart was pounding in my chest. There was much more to Harald than I had first guessed. Why hadn't I seen it? Why hadn't I *felt* his wrongness in the salon?

Harald stood again, stretching his huge arms out in a strangely warm gesture. He looked like the iconic image of Jesus with his palms upturned, giving a sermon. The gesture said "trust me". It also gave me the creeps and made me feel a pang of intense anxiety.

'I can see I am boring you. Therefore I shall be specific and get to the point.'

Caesare looked up, drank the rest of the port in his glass and then placed it on the desk beside him. He folded his arms across his chest.

'I do wish you would. There's a lady I'd like to find before the evening is done.'

'The beautiful blonde with the green eyes perhaps? I think I saw her.' Harald glanced over Caesare's shoulder at the window. His eyes bore into the gap as though he could see me peering through. 'She was very interested in you too, I think. I saw her watching you in the salon.'

Caesare met Harald's gaze, but remained quiet for a moment. Harald smiled faintly back at him, his expression benevolent.

'Well, if you have nothing else to say, I must be going,' Caesare said finally.

'Not yet. I haven't yet told you what I want from you.'

Caesare sighed. His heart rate was steady and he was calm and unafraid, but the slight tapping of his foot on the plush carpet showed me he was becoming irritated with Harald. And because of Lucrezia, I knew he was a very dangerous man when roused. He turned away from Harald and traversed the desk, seemingly searching for something. He picked up a fine feather quill, and tore a strip of parchment from a blank roll he found.

'When you decide to tell me you can send word to my house,' he said, rapidly scribbling an address on the paper.

He held out the paper. Harald glanced at it.

'I admit, you are more fascinating than most. Your crimes have been delicious to experience.'

'Count?' Caesare said continuing to hold out the paper. 'If you don't want this, then fine …'

'Even the situation with your sister is quite delicious.'

146

Caesare's back stiffened, he began to pull back his outstretched arm.

With speed faster than the human eye could detect, Harald took the paper, leaving Caesare staring at his suddenly empty hand.

'That isn't your address,' Harald said. 'Are you trying to get rid of me?'

'You have my word, *Signor*. That this is indeed *one* of my addresses. If I am not there, then your message will find its way to me nonetheless. Now, if you will excuse me, I am bored with this game and I have bigger fish to catch this evening.'

Harald stretched out his long arm and grabbed Caesare's ponytail long before he reached the office door. He yanked Caesare backwards, smashing him hard against the desk with one fluid movement. I heard bones fracture as Caesare's whole body fell against the furniture. He gasped for air, winded, and clung to the desk as it rocked back with the force, but didn't tip over, being made of strong and heavy oak. The glass Caesare had placed down so casually skittered across the surface and fell with a muffled thud onto the carpet by his feet. It didn't break.

I was on my feet and ready to enter the room as Caesare reached behind him, grabbing the first thing his hand fell on: a silver paperknife. He pulled it forward, pointing it at his manic attacker while his other arm hugged his damaged ribs.

'Who sent you?' he gasped, drawing in long pulls of air to re-inflate his lungs. 'I must admit I never expected an assassin *here*.'

Harald smiled. His huge hand flew out with blinding speed and he had Caesare's wrist. One tug and a disgusting crack echoed through the room. Caesare cried out, and the knife tumbled from his fingers, clattering across the desk. He pulled his damaged arm close to his chest, bone protruded through the skin. The wrist was ruined and blood poured down his arm, staining his cream and gold doublet a dark maroon.

I expected him to cry for help, but instead he stared furiously back at his assailant, anger fuelling his arrogance. He wasn't going to die easily. I had renewed respect for his inner strength, even though I knew his pride was unwise.

'You are a foolish creature to even attempt to fight me. I will enjoy adding you to my collection.'

Harald stared at the blood staining his fingers. His emerald eyes had darkened to jade and his teeth had grown long over his lip. My suspicions were finally confirmed, but I held back knowing that this was probably the moment and I mustn't interfere. Harald would feed on Caesare, and he would be reborn as a vampire. Instead of licking his fingers, Harald wiped them on Caesare's pale clothing in disgust.

Caesare glared back into the vampire's eyes as Harald reached behind him, picked up the paperknife. He showed it to Caesare. The silver edge gleamed, reflecting the candlelight but Caesare's expression was blank. Despite his bravery his body trembled as he started going into shock. Maybe Harald wanted fear, or maybe he'd expected Caesare to beg. He frowned as the man made no response to the open threat of the knife. Then as though it was the most natural thing in the world, Harald spun the blade, slashing Caesare's throat.

Caesare fell back against the desk. A horrible gurgling sound escaped from his lips as the blood poured from his throat. His one good hand flew up in an instinctive reflex to stop the flow. Harald picked up the empty wine glass from the floor. Taking Caesare by the hair, he pulled his prone body forward and over the glass, filling it rapidly with blood. Then he dropped Caesare to the floor.

Outside the room the commotion had been heard, several servants banged loudly on the door. I noticed the key in the lock. One of the men must have locked the door and I suspected it wasn't Caesare. Harald glanced at the window. I knew he could see me clearly and I made myself go very still, waiting for him to run towards me, trying to make his break for freedom. Instead he held up the glass as though in toast, before drinking down the cooling contents.

His eyes went black and he swooned like an addict taking a pure hit of heroin, then his eyes turned to me. I pressed my hands against the window and tugged at it. It was locked.

'Let me in!' I ordered, my voice cold, but I didn't feel calm. My heart pounded in my chest.

I threw back my arm ready to smash my way in.

Outside the room, the guards were rapidly throwing themselves against the door, but the lock and frame were sturdy and it wouldn't budge.

Harald remained composed. He walked forward throwing back the curtains fully and faced me. Then he reached up to the top of the frame and opened the window. I climbed in, running immediately to Caesare's inert frame. Harald closed the window behind me. I heard the lock slide back into place.

'He's dying!' I whispered. 'What have you done?'

'I'm a hunter and his head will be my trophy. You know that.'

'You fool!' I yelled. 'Not him, he can't die. Don't you see?'

Harald moved away from the window and into the room, he glanced briefly at the door. 'They are all ants to us. What can they do?'

'They would know we existed. We'd be hunted like animals. Don't you care about that at least?' I replied furiously.

'I didn't bite him. I thought you would be pleased.'

'Pleased? Are you crazy? That was exactly what you were supposed to do!'

'You confuse me,' he answered, shaking his head.

I grabbed Caesare's body, heaving him up over my shoulder.

'I'm not done with you,' I warned.

Harald looked back at me amusement lighting up his otherwise dead eyes. He clearly felt himself invulnerable.

'This is not a game ...'

'Of course it is,' he laughed.

I ran towards the window leaping up into the air and smashing through the glass and frame as though they were nothing but matchsticks and paper. Landing on my feet, I felt Caesare's body jerk and flop lifelessly but I could still feel his heart pumping, albeit weakly. I ran as fast as I could away from *Il Salone di Piaceri* and the cold-blooded Harald.

My carriage and driver weren't far and I threw the body of Caesare into the coach, screaming for the man to drive. Already under my influence, he cracked his whip without question, sending the horses galloping forward and away from the grounds.

Inside the rocking carriage I kneeled on the floor beside the body of Caesare. What would it mean to me if he died right then? Harald had not bitten him. He hadn't been planning to. He wanted to make 'a trophy' of him. Mount his head on some obscure wall no doubt. Yes and in the process drink his blood, but why hadn't he bitten him? I couldn't understand it. His fangs had grown, he wanted his blood but he hadn't let his mouth touch Caesare at all.

Maybe Harald could recognise the vampire gene just as I did and had not wanted to make another of our kind. But that was damn inconvenient!

Caesare's breathing became shallow. I looked down at him, his skin was pale. His life's blood was slipping away. Caesare Borgia was dying. And that meant ... what? Would I die too? Would I cease to exist? Or would Lucrezia still be bitten by someone else?

I couldn't risk it. I had to ensure my own survival. I loved immortality and I was damned if I'd give up on it so soon.

I shook Caesare. His eyes fluttered open and gazed into mine.

'I'm going to save you? Do you want to live?'

'What are you ...?'

'I'm a demon! You said it yourself and you were right.'

My fangs began to slip forward out over my lip. Caesare's eyes glazed over.

'Look at me! I'm going to save you, but you'll be selling your soul to me. Do you understand? You'll come when I call! You'll do what I need you to do, no matter what I ask of you.'

Caesare's eyes blazed into mine. His life-force, so strong, didn't want to go without a fight.

'Yes ...' he murmured.

'Is that what you want? To be reborn as my demon child ...'

'Yes ... Mother ...' His head fell back. Blood splashed upwards onto my lips and the flavour of him drove me insane.

It was the best human blood I'd ever tasted. Sweetness filled my stomach and his blood was comforting as it pounded through my veins. I bit down on his throat, ensuring my saliva merged with his blood. Hoping that this was the way, this would change him. It's what Gabi had told me he'd done after all.

But his blood, oh his blood ...

'You're one of my own ...' I swooned. 'You taste so good.'

For the first time in years sexual passion flooded my skin, my loins. I burned. It was ecstasy. I wanted him. Desired him. My breasts ached for his touch. I pressed myself into him. Felt his body respond to my touch and my bite in that involuntary way all my victims did. And he hardened. The bite was seduction.

But his heart was slowing and his consciousness slipping away.

'No!' I didn't want him to die. I had to have him. 'Wake, damn you!' I cried.

But he was out cold, falling into oblivion. I continued to guzzle him, his bloodlines stretched out before me, even behind my closed lids. It told me the story of the future, reaffirming my very existence. Despite all of this, despite the incestuous nature of my relationship to him, his blood still tasted so, so sweet and I wondered if I could ever get enough of it.

Chapter 22 - Lilly's Journal
A Witch's Child

The colour was gone completely from his face as I tucked him into my bed. His face sagged without its natural expression and the cheeks were hollow. His lips had the blue hue of a corpse and if he slept, it was as though in the grave. I watched his eyes glaze over with the faint white film of death and then closed his lids, shutting out the emptiness of his sight.

Was this how it happened for me? I didn't remember and all I could do was wait. I recalled Gabi's tale of his wife Amanda, as they sailed to Alexandria. Gabi had waited for days hoping she would live, while her body rotted away. Tears sprang to my eyes. Oh, how he'd suffered. I didn't think I could bear to wait so long. But then, I didn't love Caesare. He was a means to an end and he carried the vampire gene. He had to live. It was that simple. It was also terrifying.

His blood had given me a renewed vigour unlike any blood I'd consumed. It had a magic; a witch's brew I'd never before experienced. And I felt wired. I paced the room, partly anxious, but mostly to burn off some of the excess energy.

I'd bandaged his neck wound, but left the broken wrist, unsure what to do for the best. Even so, I'd tried to prod the bone back through the skin, straightening his fingers and wrist as it lay on top of the sheet. His hands were icy. Long before we reached my home the blood had stopped flowing, though most of what had remained in his veins flowed in mine by then. If his hand had still been bleeding, there would have been nothing left to push around his body.

I'd done a mental number on the driver. He probably wouldn't be the same again. After cleaning up the blood in his carriage I'd made him forget everything. His memory of the evening was completely wiped clean, a blank. I hadn't had time to refill it with some dubious story of merely collecting me and returning me home. He would never recall seeing my five- foot-six frame carrying over my shoulder a man of six feet or more, covered in blood.

The dress I'd been wearing lay in a heap by the window. It was utterly destroyed. But blood, grass and mud were the least of my worries. Thank God I'd ripped away the hem earlier! I'd never have been able to run in that damn thing otherwise.

My eyes fell on Caesare. Did I see the faintest movement of his chest? Was he breathing? I walked to the bed only to find him completely still, his condition unchanged. What on earth was I thinking bringing him here? What would I do with him if he did wake? It was all so foolish. After all he probably would have survived Harald's attack without my intervention; otherwise I wouldn't be alive, would I?

Therein lay the crux.

How would I ever know? But I had believed that Harald was going to kill him and that was all that mattered. I'd done what I had to. Worrying about it wasn't going to solve anything.

But if Caesare was dead, Lucrezia's account of him turning her would never happen. And then the future would definitely be changed. Fuck! It was such a curse being smart. Why did I have to worry so much about the future? It was already done: I'd lived it, so surely it couldn't change anyway. But I couldn't be certain.

How long does the change take?

I sat down in a cushioned rocking chair by the window. My newly acquired servants had been left instructions not to disturb me, that I would call if I needed anything, but I could hear them moving around the small house. It was early morning. The maid was humming as she tidied the parlour. I could hear the dull clang of fire tools as she swept the hearth. In the kitchen a knife scraped the skin from vegetables as the cook prepared food for me for later. Not that I would need it. I felt fuller than ever but the normal things had to be observed if I wished to avoid suspicion.

There would be scandal in *Il Salone di Piaceri* for certain after the night's shocking events. My actions may not have been observed by human eyes, but my absence would have been noted. Marnia's office was covered in blood, some of which would be found in the glass used by Harald. Also the hem of my dress lay conspicuously on the lawn. There would be cries of murder at the very least. Caesare's body would be nowhere to be found. And what of Harald? Had he left after I'd taken away his prize, or did he stay behind and continue his sickening murder spree? But more importantly – who the hell was he anyway?

I rocked harder in the chair, chewing on my thumb nail as I gazed out over the street. When I got my hands on that bastard I'd –

I glanced back at the silent body then closed my eyes. The phobia of paradox threatened to consume me in a panic-attack of supernatural proportions. My chest heaved and I felt as though I were being suffocated. Maybe this was it. The end. Borgia was dead and that meant me and my entire family were wiped out all in one easy step.

I took a deep breath.

'But then, I always was a drama queen,' I murmured, suppressing a hysterical giggle. 'Calm down girl, you're still here. All. Is. Not. Lost.'

A strange noise, like the snapping of a lead pencil, called my attention back to the bed. I jumped out of the chair. At first I thought nothing had changed, Caesare was still blue and motionless. I examined him closely looking for anything that would give me hope. His hand jerked up and I stepped back startled. The cracking sound grew louder. It was coming from his wrist! His body was repairing itself!

'Oh my God!'

I pulled up the chair and sat facing him, watching the changes as they rippled through his body. The wrist straightened out, the jutting bones retracted into his flesh like a film being rewound on fast. The torn skin meshed together, became a faint scar line and then faded away as though someone had used a magic eraser to rub away the marks. I leaned forward and removed the bandaged from his throat in time to see the knife wound and bite mark disappear completely as the skin healed.

His face warmed up. By that I mean the colour returned to his skin. The blueness around the lips disappeared, leaving them plum and pink. Healthier looking than before his unnatural death. His cheeks filled out, the sallow sagging was replaced with the full bloom of youth. Caesare had been in his forties, and I could see evidence of his debaucheries slowly being eradicated from his flesh. The fine lines around the eyes and lips shrank and faded, leaving the skin smooth and almost line free.

His chest rose, taking a ragged but full breath. Caesare was undoubtedly alive. I had saved him, God help me. And God help Lucrezia when she faced all that was to come because of my actions.

Sensuous, full, black lashes parted to reveal eyes much greener than before, much more like mine than they had been. Blond hair, which had been thinning slightly with age, was full and shiny, thicker and longer. I was sure of it! I had remade him in my own image. It was true. As a carrier of my gene he was a perfect specimen and so beautiful that I was mesmerised by him. Egotistical though it was, I felt like Baron Frankenstein when he first looked at the man he'd brought back from the dead. This was my creature. My child!

'Can ... you ... sp ... speak?' I stammered as his eyes scrutinised me.

'Yes.'

'How do you feel?'

He raised his hand to his face, examining his wrist. Hours before had been the source of crippling agony.

'Wonderful. What ... did you do?'

'Don't you remember?'

Caesare closed his eyes, his brow wrinkling as he struggled to recall. His healed hand massaged his head.

'A business proposition ...'

I waited.

'At Marnia's.' His eyes flew open and met mine. 'Oh my God!'

I leaned forward, carefully taking his other hand, 'You're okay now. It's all fine.'

'Witch!' he hissed pulling back his hand.

'The more appropriate term is "vampire" actually. But I do happen to be a witch. I was taught about magic by the best there is – six centuries ago now ...'

Caesare shook his head. His mind refusing to take in all that I said.

'You need to sleep some more I think,' I told him, reaching over and stroking his brow whilst calling on the ley line power nearby to sooth and calm him, just as if he were a child. 'Later we'll go out and I'll show you the ropes. You'll need blood. I drank all yours and you'll feel pretty empty sometime soon.'

Chapter 23 - Lilly's Journal

Weaning

'You came to turn me, is that it?'

'No,' I answered shaking my head. 'Observe only. I wanted to know *who* turned you.'

'But how did you know I was going to be turned?'

'This is very hard to explain. And I haven't been around one of my kind for maybe nine or ten years now.'

'Are there many of us?'

I looked away, 'I didn't know about Harald until last night. And then it was almost too late.'

'Start from the beginning,' he suggested. 'I need to know everything.'

I studied his face and body language. Caesare was ecstatic. He loved his new found power and strength which didn't surprise me at all after Lucrezia's story. But his calm cheerfulness did. I had expected arrogance, brutality and perhaps even a crazed killing spree. Not this restrained, controlled and dignified attitude to his rebirth.

'You're not what I expected.'

He turned to me. The sensuous smile dropped as his face became serious.

'I've been a fool my entire life. This feels like a second chance.'

'I see that. And it is. Don't screw it up.'

His smile returned, flirty and free. He was gorgeous. And so like Gabi my heart ached. I frowned.

He'd been a vampire for a few days by then and he was a fast learner. Under my direction his feeding was controlled and the victims were rarely killed.

I'd shown him how to move across the city unseen by bounding over the rooftops of Rome. And so we gazed over the city from the steeple of St Peter's. It was an irony not lost on me, but Caesare made no comment about the former church of his father as he surveyed the city like an emperor studying his kingdom. He perched on the edge of a tower like a beautiful gargoyle. Yes, I know that's an oxymoron, but it was the strangest sight even to me. His stillness and perfection were completely captivating. I fought with myself constantly to try not to stare at him.

I pointed down to the people below, travelling through the evening, in various ways, as I tried to distract myself from Caesare's magnificence. An old woman was struggling along the street carrying a heavy bundle. The wheels of an ornate private carriage, splashed mud on her already dirty rags as the livery-clad driver cracked his whip on the horse's rump. Two urchin children were being chased by a local merchant as they hid bread under their ragged coats. A few members of the clergy stood on the steps of the church; more terrifying than welcoming to the small band of church goers that entered the doors with bowed pious heads. They were all blissfully unaware that two monsters stood above them.

'If they are evil, then do what you like,' I advised. 'But otherwise small feeds. Little but often: it's the best way to go undetected in the world. Death brings unwanted attention. There will be cries of witches and demons all over the place, and that means trouble from humans.'

'But you said they can't kill us.'

'A human can't kill our kind by any means I know of. But I wouldn't want to test that too much, would you?'

'No. Discretion. I understand.'

He was like a tame puppy: excited to indulge in this wonderful life, but all the time I knew the clock was ticking. I had to teach him enough, so that he'd return to Lucrezia and turn her, just as he had in the story she'd told Gabi and I. And that was going to be soon.

'You need to leave. Go to your sister's again. Try to resume a normal life.'

'I'm not going back,' he said.

'What?'

'I've been so cruel, Lilly. My crimes against Lucrezia are the worst you can imagine. I'm loath to justify it. But once I loved her with all my heart. She deserves to be left to live her life without my further destruction of it. If anything, I'd like to make amends for my cruelty to her. And I'm sure my absence from her life is the best gift I can give.'

'Oh my God. You've gone … soft.'

Caesare laughed and reached for my hand, he pulled it down towards his breeches, and pressed against me. He was hard and aroused.

'I want you. I want to travel the world with you.'

He pulled me into his embrace and I allowed the hug. It was so easy to be affectionate with another of my kind. I'd missed this so much. He kissed my mouth gently and then more urgently. Lust coursed through me in response to his vampire aura. It had been so long since I had enjoyed any sexual intimacy, especially with an equal, but I pulled away shaking my head. My intervention couldn't change the course of events, so I babbled a feeble excuse.

'No. Not you and I. That can never be, Caesare. I'm your creator, it would be like …'

'Incest?'

He turned to stare out over the horizon, his eyes were cloudy with what I suspected was unshed tears.

We immortals are far from monsters despite the myth. Our strength, agility and speed are all enhanced but so too are our emotions. We feel deeply. Caesare, in the early days of his weaning, was feeling the world. Knowing he had the power to crush it, he clung to his humanity more than he did as a mortal.

He was nothing like I expected and not at all as Lucrezia had led us to believe. Not for the first time I began to worry about the story she'd told. Everything that I'd done, everything that had happened had all been because I was trying to follow some format that made her tale happen. But what if it wasn't entirely the truth?

I was afraid. Afraid that he wouldn't shake off this new found conscience. Afraid that he wouldn't fulfil his destiny and seduce his much loved sister one final time, turning her into a blood-sucking, cold and heartless monster. Because I needed her to be everything she had become. She had to change Gabi. She had to turn my beautiful lover and then he could turn me.

Chapter 24 - Lilly's Journal
Blood And Desire

'You need closure on your old life then,' I told Caesare. 'We'll travel together and you can see Lucrezia one final time. Tell her you are sorry.'

'She'll notice I've changed.'

'Yes. But maybe she will forgive you and then you will have your atonement.'

Caesare nodded. He wanted his fresh start more than anything. And it gave me hope for him.

'What then?' he asked. 'What about ... us?

I stroked his thigh, my fingers drawing provocative circles close to his groin. He groaned under my hands. I pushed him back on my bed. I'd been playing him, teasing him, for the last few hours all because I had to get him to agree to see Lucrezia. Once he had, I felt reassured that my past and future would remain unaltered.

'Then, I'll give you what you need. That is, if you don't still want her when you see her.'

He grabbed me, pulled me to him and I permitted the kiss, keeping my own sexual attraction to him tightly bottled up. I couldn't let myself want him. He became persistent, but I pushed him away. I was so much stronger than him. The power of the ley lines was my advantage. He'd learnt the hard way not to try to force himself on me. A bloody nose and a busted leg, no matter how quickly they heal, are enough to deter any rapist, even a supernatural one. It also made me even more intrigued about Lucrezia's tale. Clearly, taking what he wanted was a natural instinct for him, but he had backed down quickly once I fought him off. Instead, he changed his tactics to seduction, quite clearly used to getting all of his own way.

'I have you; you are perfect,' he said. 'I'm sure that Lucrezia's charms will seem somewhat lacking now.'

I smiled, but didn't answer. Love is a powerful thing. His crazy obsession could surely not have dispersed so easily?

'I feel sane for the first time in years,' he said as though picking the thought right from my mind. 'Looking back, my life seems to have been all for this moment. I was meant to meet you, meant to love you.'

I laughed, slapping away his groping hands. 'You lust after me. That's not the same thing as love, Caesare.'

Hadn't I said almost exactly those words to Gabi? The truth was I'd learnt that we were all made for this. At least every carrier of the vampire gene was. Being with Caesare constantly reminded me how crucial it was that things occurred in the right order.

Despite my first fear that my intervention was a problem, I trusted to fate to make the events happen. Everything was going well. I'd arrived in this time to save him, once from mortal robbers and the second time from an immortal murderer. Since that night I'd searched for the Swedish vampire, but he was nowhere to be found in the city. It had been odd that I hadn't sensed him. But then, I hadn't known what I was searching for. Harald, if that was really his name, would not escape me for long though. I resolved to find him as soon as possible and find out where the hell he'd come from and why he'd targeted Caesare that night.

'Please, Lilly,' Caesare whispered, his hands stroking up my arms, circling my body.

I let him draw close again, revelling in his touch as his aura brushed me. My nipples stood up, along with the hairs on the back of my neck. He felt wonderful. I wanted. Needed ... I kissed him, plunging my tongue deep into his mouth and feeling the response of his pressing back at me, as he tried to prove his dominance once more. I let his tongue rake my mouth. The lust surged up my body. My face flushed with excitement and desire drove me. I let him roll me back this time. His mouth left mine, swept down over my throat and kissed a trail over my half exposed breasts.

He tugged urgently at my skirt, lifting it up, so that his fingers could explore the soft skin on my legs. I felt his sharp nails tear through and shred the fine silk stockings, finding my bare skin. He groaned against me, moving downwards. But I stopped him, pulled him up on top of me and savoured the pressure, the delightful thrill of his hardness pressed against me.

'Yes ...' he gasped and he ground against me, the dress fabric and his breeches the only barrier between us.

I rolled him on his back, changing our positions. His arms hugged me close. I wanted him so badly but knew it would be a mistake to give in. Perhaps he'd need to be desperate in order to seduce Lucrezia again. I was concerned that if I made love to him then he'd completely abandon his promise to see her one final time. Holding back was the only way I could ensure he would, even if it was because he thought I'd give in afterwards.

I pushed his arms away, rising up. I was sitting fully clothed on top of him. I pressed his arms down above his head and he chuckled, a deep throated, sensual sound that reverberated through my very being. Then I kissed a line down his body, peeling back his breeches.

He came out of his clothing big and hard. He was beautifully formed and my mouth ached to be around him. I wanted to taste him so much but resisted. His hips heaved upwards in a subconscious offer and I licked the top of him until he groaned and begged for more.

I slid up his body, fingers finding his nipples and learnt he was sensitive there too. He squirmed beneath me his chest arching, small sighs escaping his lips.

'There are other pleasures I can give you,' I said, shaking my hair aside to expose my throat.

He stared at me, surprised. 'You're no victim ...'

'Neither are you,' I answered, fangs bared. I bent, offering my throat again. 'Exchange is no robbery ...'

A gasp exploded from his lips as I bit him. Then I turned enough to allow him proximity to the bare flesh around my throat. His fangs found me, excited and needing. The pain of his bite was delicious. I rocked my body over him as his blood gushed down my throat. He tasted every bit as delicious as when I had bitten him for the first time. His blood was nectar to me and his grunts of pleasure, the pressure of his heated body, told me that I tasted every bit as good to him.

It wasn't long before I brought him to a shuddering climax as his blood, and mine, flowed round our bodies in perfect union. The flow continued, bringing waves of pleasure to us both and I cried against his throat as I came, leaving me jerking and twisting in his arms. I shuddered. My whole body jolted against him as he rolled me over onto my back, positioning himself above me. He stared into my eyes.

'I've never experienced anything like this,' he said. 'Sex but not sex.'

'Yes,' I gasped.

His lips found mine, our fangs still out, still needing, and I ran my tongue between those sharp points until he hardened again and pressed his cock violently against me.

'Please ...' he begged and he began to tug at my clothing again. 'Let me see you at least ...'

I laughed again, slapping away his hands and throwing him off me.

'No. But nice try. Later, when we return. We'll travel to the country tomorrow. You must see your sister. Then I'll tell you everything there is to know about me. And why your survival was so important.'

'Tease.'

'Yes I am. Get used to it. Being around me is never going to be the easy option.'

He lay back on the bed eyes closed, sated but not convinced he was. He didn't understand at all the implications of what we'd done.

I stood up, walked to the window and pulling back the thick velvet drapes gazed out into the Roman street. I needed to put some distance between us because, God help me I wanted him still. But the sex was only part of it.

His breathing told me he was already mostly asleep. Caesare was under my influence as surely as my mortal servants. He would do as I said. After all, that was the pact he made with me on his death-bed. Like any witch, vampire or demon I would hold him to his contract until all that was meant to be had happened. Then I could move on out of this time and hopefully return to my darling Gabi. Or so I tried to convince myself. But how would Gabi feel about my infidelity with Caesare? After all the sharing of blood was a far more intimate practice than sex would ever be.

As I lay beside him listening to his breathing, Caesare was unaware of the turmoil I felt. Right then, I felt as much of a slave to him as he was to me, and the guilt and pain of wanting and needing anyone other than Gabi was almost too much to bear. Tears slipped from my eyes. My emotions were hyped, wrung out and I felt so drained.

I left him sleeping and went outside. Forcing anger back into my heart, I searched the city once again for any sign of Harald. Beating the shit out of that degenerate Swede would ease my pain and frustration a little I was sure. But as with all my previous searches of Rome, he was nowhere to be found.

Instead I found a hapless mortal staggering around the streets in a drunken stupor. I drank his blood and beat him until his legs and arms were broken, bloody masses of pulp. Then I snapped his neck – I'd never leave anyone suffering like that and anyway he might tell of the demon blood-drinker that tortured him.

Licking my lips I felt glutted on blood and not the least bit happy with my loss of control. But I don't make excuses for myself. I don't sparkle in the sunlight. I'm the real deal. I'm a vampire. I drink blood. I kill. And sometimes I really get off on it.

Returning before morning, I woke my household, and told the coachman to prepare the carriage. We were leaving Rome that morning.

I roused Caesare, 'Let's get this show on the road.'

Corrupted Corpse

For love, I have survived the centuries. For fear of paradox I made sure that all that Lucrezia told me would happen, did happen. But what if Lucrezia had lied? How were we to know if her story was the truth? Yet she had been vivid in her description of the day she was turned.

In the early days Caesare had never been the monster she portrayed him to be. Yet Lucrezia had been adamant that he was such a creature, had described in detail the sadistic ceremony during which he turned her. Was it possible that two people could tell the same story in so different a way, yet each still be telling the truth?

Caesare's body is in the castle. I feel her shudder as I bring his deformed and crippled corpse down into her belly. The poison that covers him wrenches at my beautiful home and his presence makes the castle groan and complain. The very bowels of my stronghold reverberate with her discontent as she tries so hard to make it known that she is rejecting him.

'Please ...' I beg. 'I needed to do something. Otherwise the doorway wouldn't have opened would it?'

I pull the ley power out and around him, shielding his cadaver until I can figure out exactly what to do with it. The castle sighs. She is protected now from the evil, black gloop that covers him.

'I'm sorry,' I say. 'But I can't help myself. I wish I could explain this intense feeling I have for him. But I'm not sure you'd understand.'

Rhuddlan shudders once more but I feel her power surround and hold me like a friend and I cry softly on her incorporeal shoulder while all the time I stare at the mutilated body of Caesare. I have no idea what is going to happen. But the castle understands me as she always has. She is a reflection of all my strength and power and now she holds me up at my weakest moment.

I've broken the rules and won. I've refused to play fate's game for once. But what would have happened if I had materialised fully on the high-street before Gabi, Lucrezia and my 'younger' self? It was the age-old impossible dilemma.

I've cheated the door, by reaching through, not passing through. It may have an effect on the present, but what do I care about a future I know nothing of? I've spent enough time worrying. This is my time. I will make my own decisions from now on. Neither fate nor Adonai will force me to do anything I don't want to do.

I lie back on my bed once more, but my mind is on Caesare in the next room. Another quandary: can the vampire die, even when his sister rips out his heart and burns it in supernatural fire? Or are we truly immortal?

I close my eyes and turn my head into my soft pillow as the tears continue to leak out, staining the red silk. I think about the last time I saw Caesare alive. This was an entry I had been avoiding making in my journal, but writing has been known to be therapeutic.

I sit up and look around my room. The laptop is on my dressing table where I left it the day before. I'd stopped writing, struggling to carry on, because ... because I didn't want to tell Gabi everything, but fought with myself against omitting this one truth. It was an important truth, one which had changed everything for me.

Now I have to write it. There is nothing else to do, and rest will not come until this story is told. The story about how I fell in love with Caesare Borgia, and was happier than I'd ever been in my entire life.

Chapter 26 - Lilly's Journal
Lucrezia's Rebirth

It was early evening when the coach clattered into the grounds of Lucrezia's home and Caesare and I found the servants gathered in the crescent-shaped driveway in a state of terrified panic.

'What is going on?' Caesare asked, leaving the carriage and facing the crowd.

Some of the grooms were mounted on horses and several of the footmen were carrying torches and pitchforks.

'My Lord!' one cried. 'It's her Ladyship ... she ...'

'Speak up man! Tell me what's happened to my sister!'

'Lord,' answered another maid, her voice trembling. 'We thought ...'

'What did you think?' I asked, exiting the carriage with my glamour in place: I had taken on the dark and sensual colouring of Miranda once more. I didn't wish to be mistaken for Lucrezia in the panic. Although it had briefly freaked Caesare to watch me change, he had soon become very curious of this amazing power I had.

'Calm yourselves,' I said. 'What has happened here?'

I took the servant girl's arm, staring persuasively into her eyes.

'Signora,' she said, more confidently. 'The Lord came back late in the evening yesterday. He instructed us all to go to our beds.'

'What Lord?'

The girl looked at Caesare, a slight frown on her face.

'That's impossible. We only left Rome this morning. Last night *Senor* Borgia was dining with my household.

'An impostor then,' Caesare said. 'Did you see his face?'

'No Lord. He was wearing a large black hat, just like yours. It was pulled down over his face, but he stared into my eyes and I thought ...'

Caesare glanced back at the crowd as they fell eerily quiet. I could hear their random fears projecting out like beacons into the night air. They thought him a devil. So why would it be impossible that he was capable of being in two places at once.

'What happened then? Where did this impostor go?'

'He went to her Ladyship's room, Sir ... as you always do.'

'Lilly, what's happening?' His hand reached for me and his fingers trembled in my grip.

'Then what?' I asked the girl, looking deeply into her eyes once again.

'I found her this afternoon,' she said in a trance-like monotone. 'The cook made me take in soup and bread. She hadn't stirred: we'd heard nothing from her room all day. But that ... wasn't too unusual.' The girl blinked and awareness came back to her eyes as I eased my power back slightly. She glanced down again and briefly back at Caesare. 'I knocked, but there was still no answer. Then I opened the door a little, calling out to her to say I was bringing in a tray and she needed to keep her strength up. Having just had a baby and all ...'

'The baby is born?' Caesare asked.

'Yes, Sir. Almost as soon as you left the labour began.'

From Lucrezia's story I knew that the baby had been sent away to her husband, in hiding with their other children, but I didn't want Caesare to become distracted by this fact. I recalled how Lucrezia had lied, saying the child was dead, for fear of her safety.

'What's your name?' I asked the girl, distracting her and Caesare. She began to cast terrified glances towards the other servants. All remained quiet, listening to her tale.

'Talayla, my Lady.'

'What happened next, Talayla?' I let my power flow into her again, and felt arousal flood her body. I smiled to myself despite the situation. Sometimes it was hard to resist playing with the humans. I relaxed her a little, and then released her mind to continue with her story. She was no longer afraid, but totally willing to tell me everything.

'The Lady was in her bed and so was ... Lena ...Only the mistress ... She was so different and Lena ... There was blood everywhere. I dropped the tray. I screamed.'

Then the footman came forward and revealed to us how Lucrezia had been like a crazed and angry monster. She had run to the windows, thrown herself down three storeys. Yet she had stood up and run away as though nothing had happened.

'She was a demon!' the footman finished. 'And she killed Lena.'

'When did this happen?' Caesare asked.

'Hours ago.'

'What are you all doing then?' Caesare wanted to know. 'Where are you going now?' He looked around at the men. The mounted servants had dismounted as Talayla and the footman spoke, but they clung to the reins of the horses as though at any moment they would re-mount and sped away.

'They were going to hunt her down ...' said Talayla.

Caesare glanced at me and I knew he wanted to go after her.

'No, we need to find out what really happened. You see, I already know the script Caesare, and this isn't how it was supposed to play out.'

He stared at me long and hard. Then took my hand and led me assertively through the crowd. 'All of you are to stay here. There will be no more deaths this night. Anyone who disobeys me will live to regret their disrespect.'

He stood amongst the servants and not one of them dared to stare him down, all bowed their heads for fear of being noticed.

We went inside the house. Caesare led me through the long and ostentatious hallway, up a wide and imposing staircase. The house was richly furnished and I glanced briefly at the family portraits that lined the staircase and walls of the long landing as Caesare took me to the west wing. He knew his way around and didn't hesitate in his urgency to get to Lucrezia's rooms.

The door to the bedroom had been left slightly ajar. Inside was the luxurious bed, the dressing table with her personal effects, her clothing strewn over a chair. All the finery and luxury of a Lady of her social standing.

The room, however, reeked of blood. It covered the carpet, near the dresser and there was a blood stained paperknife placed before the mirror.

'She slashed her own wrists with this,' I told him. 'She wanted to die, but it was too late, she was already immortal.'

Caesare said nothing, but his eyes were as cold as winter.

There was a body in the bed, but someone had covered it with a sheet. Caesare lifted the cover. 'Lena. They'd better move her; the weather is warming up and she'll begin to stink before long.'

There was a splash of blood on the bed, but not much, just as I'd expect from a new and inexperienced vampire.

'Any chance she'll rise?' he asked me.

I shook my head. 'No.'

Caesare walked the length of the room.

'This wasn't supposed to happen ...' I said again. 'Not like this I'm sure. It's not what she told us ...'

'Then what was, Lilly? All along you've known the future. Is this your witchcraft side? Are you a prophet then also?'

I shook my head. 'Not here, we may be overheard. But I will explain. I promise.'

'What's that smell?' he said suddenly.

I followed him as he pushed open the door to an adjoining chamber. Inside was another room as large as Lucrezia's and scattered on the floor were half open trunks of male clothing. I sniffed the air and the strange odour we'd detected was stronger in here.

It was incense. Mingled with the blood I hadn't recognised it at first. I followed the scent and found a black robe draped over the bed. It looked like a monk's habit. I lifted it to my nose. Blood and this powerful scent. Herbs and witchery.

'These are my clothes ...' Caesare said.

'Even this?' I held up the robe.

'No. I've never seen that before. What's happening Lilly?'

'I don't know. I really don't. It can't be a paradox ...'

'What is a "paradox"?'

I shook my head, 'It's hard to explain.'

'Just try. Because somebody came here last night. And that somebody turned my sister and the servants thought he was me, even down to him having my trunk and clothing. How can that be, Lilly?'

I asked him where these possessions had been the last time he saw them.

'My house near St Peter's ...'

Caesare had never been there in all the days he had been with me. He hadn't left my side. Instead he'd retrieved clothing from a small apartment he owned because there were no servants or prying eyes there. It was a small place near the docks. I hadn't asked but I'd assumed it was where he entertained his lovers. So, I knew for certain he hadn't been to St Peter's, but someone had. And that someone had probably masqueraded as Caesare.

'Come, show me the cellar.'

He looked at me surprised, 'I don't know where it is. I've never been down there.'

'Then we ask someone.'

I took his hand and this time I did the leading, back down the stairs and into the hallway, where we found the footman lighting the candles with his torch.

Caesare went outside and instructed the servants there to move Lena's body, saying that she must be interred in the family crypt for the time being. At least there it would be cool and airless and the smell of decay wouldn't taint the air of the house.

The housekeeper, an elderly Italian woman, matronly in shape and stature showed us to the cellar, searching through a large bundle of keys until she found the one that fitted the lock. The footman led the way, carrying the torch as he went down the slippery steps ahead of us.

The cellar had an old damp smell. It reminded me of the house

I'd lived in as a child and the ancient cellar we had that my parents used for storage. It was a smell I'd always liked. Musty damp earth. This cellar was used for storing the wine. It was cool but not excessively cold and stretched for most of the length of the house itself, though divided into many large rooms.

Several wine racks lined the walls of the first room and stood in rows like the aisles of a library. I went over to one of the racks, observing a varied collection of wines and champagnes. The rack was undisturbed.

'What are we looking for?' Caesare asked.

'A room that nobody uses.'

The footman rushed around the room lighting all the torches and the dark gloom lit up into a bright and luminous space.

We moved on through the room, preceded by the footman as he continued to light up the way. I didn't tell him that we could see perfectly well in the dark. After all we were trying to avoid suspicion.

'Here!' said the footman as we entered the vintage cellar. 'Look. This rack of wine bottles has been moved.'

We examined the scraped and disturbed dust on the floor. An entire wine rack had been moved away from the wall. Caesare and I looked behind the rack and there we discovered a hidden doorway. Caesare and I exchanged glances. No human could have moved it, not without emptying the rack of the bottles of port first, yet the undisturbed dust on each bottle showed that none of them had been touched. Despite that, it was curious that the impostor had known to use this room, or of its existence. It would have taken research, and maybe many months of exploration to know that the room was even there.

The door was stiff but the footman pushed his shoulder against it and it gave with a hideous groan. It was pitch black inside, but I could see everything, as could Caesare. The footman lit the torches lining the walls and then turned around to take in the room.

A large blood-filled pentagram was carved into the cold stone ground. Huge metal rungs had been hammered into the rock, and bits of ragged rope, torn like cotton threads, were tied to the rungs. It had clearly been used to restrain someone. Around the pentagram were the crumpled waxy remains of five black candles, each placed on one of the points of the star.

'Mother of Satan,' gasped the footman crossing himself. 'It's witchcraft.'

'Yes, it would seem so wouldn't it?' I murmured.

There was a makeshift altar. A black box covered with red cloth, and on it still laid the tools of the ceremony. I bent down to examine a small bowl which had clearly been used to extract blood from the victim. I picked up a blood stained knife, it was sharpened so much that I involuntarily pricked myself as I tested the edge.

'Leave us,' I told the footman and willingly he hurried away. 'Recognise this?' I asked, holding up the paperknife that had once been on Marnia's desk and had been used to slash Caesare's throat in her office.

'Harald?'

'It's the only explanation I can find.'

'How did he know to come here? Why Lucrezia?'

'Harald has been stalking you, Caesare. As weird as that seems. He saw you as some kind of prize lion to hunt down and destroy. When he couldn't have you he came here after Lucrezia. He could have been watching you for a very long time before he made his move.'

'He didn't kill her … She's turned.'

'Yes. That's a certainty. And he disguised himself as you too. But maybe he didn't know she'd turn. From the bragging he did to me, I'd say his usual MO I mean … modus operandi,' I explained, 'is to kill his victims. Let's get out of here. I've seen enough.'

By the time we reached the upper floor, the footman had told his co-workers of the room below. The servants were in a state of panic once more.

'It's evil. We need a priest.'

'I think that's an excellent idea,' I answered. 'Send two men to fetch one. The house will have to be purified. Then there will be no evil left here.'

'You don't believe in that, do you?' Caesare sneered once we were alone.

'No. But they do and they have to sleep here tonight. And the last thing we need is a load of panicked peasants screaming "witchcraft". Come on. We're leaving.'

'We have to find Lucrezia.'

I shook my head. 'That's the last thing we can do. But we need to get out of here before this witch-hunt really gets underway. I'm going to find that Swedish bastard, even if I have to cross the ocean to do it. He's dead meat.'

Immortal Enemy

'I'm from the future. I know that is hard to believe. But it's the truth.'

My carriage rattled back towards the city at break-neck speed. Caesare sat opposite me. His eyes were dulled and he was tired and more than a little scared. We'd left a few seconds before the priest arrived. Somehow I thought it important that we didn't come in contact with the superstitious clergy.

'It doesn't matter. I need to find Lucrezia.'

'No. She won't want to see you, don't you understand?'

I told him then of her story of the events of the night, describing in detail the ceremony with which the vampire played his game. She had said it was Caesare. But it wasn't. It was Harald.

'So he used black magic to seduce her? Is that what you are saying?'

'I don't know. But Lucrezia described being tied up by you. She said you cut her wrists and the blood leaked into the pentagram. We saw that was true today.'

'But why did she say it was me?'

I shrugged. 'He fooled her as he did the servants, maybe. He's obviously a very powerful vampire. He may well have used mind tricks, just as you've seen me do.'

'But he didn't kill her ...'

'Harald may actually think he killed her. That was probably the plan. Then he got all lust-filled and excited and bit her instead. I don't think he knew she carried the gene. If he even understands about that at all. Although I never understood why he didn't just bite you in the first place if he didn't understand the vampire gene. It's like he has some inside knowledge but not enough. It's weird.'

'The servants said they found her in bed, so how did she get from the cellar to her room without being seen? She must have been covered in blood.' Caesare wondered.

I speculated that Lucrezia may have been left tied up as her attacker thought her dead.

'She could have awakened, disorientated, and yanked herself free. Those ropes were torn, not untied and so that would make sense. And with her new found strength, freeing herself would have been as easy as ... jumping down three storeys and being able to run straight after!'

Caesare was thoughtful. The implications of what had happened were slowly dawning on him, but he didn't want this to happen any more than I did. He wanted to know where she was.

'She's safe. I know that and you're going to have to believe me when I tell you.'

'Where?' he asked again.

'Caesare, she doesn't want to see you. She thinks you raped her again and turned her into a blood-sucking monster. Right now, you're the last person she needs.'

'I'm finding this incredibly difficult to take in.'

He fell silent. His face turned away, he couldn't meet my eyes. Perhaps it was guilt for the many times he'd raped his sister in the past. But I didn't hate him, neither did he disgust me. Instead I pitied him. It didn't matter to me that he had been a vile human monster. He'd seen the error of his ways, which was all that mattered then. And as a vampire he was more humane than he had ever been as a human.

'It's all in the past now and you can't change a thing. The way I see it, there are things that don't have to happen from this point on. Whatever Lucrezia told me, I'm not that convinced her version of the facts was wholly accurate. There's only one thing that has to happen now; she needs to turn Gabriele. That's another reason you must stay away from her.'

'I won't prevent it. I could guide.'

'No. If she knows that her bite will turn him, she may decide not to. And that means we're all dead. Sorry to be so melodramatic about it, but that's the facts.'

'This ... paradox?'

I nodded, but this strange turn of events had thrown me a curve and I was more in the dark than I had ever been.

We reached Rome early the next morning and I sent the coach driver away; he hadn't slept for over thirty six hours. I was certain he needed some rest, and we'd have use for him soon. I began to disband my briefly employed household. I gave the servants letters of recommendation and two months' salary to tide them over, then sent them all away. Within two days the house was completely empty of everyone but Caesare and I.

I was in a state of dilemma. What more could I do here?

Caesare went to make enquiries at the docks and any other points of entry or exit in the city. We had to learn if Harald had been back. In the empty house I reached out, searching for ley line power and quickly tapped into a line that I knew was in the next street. I pulled the power to me, drew a circle around my body and focused the power up and outwards.

I searched for Harald.

I had been relying too much on my vampiric powers to find him, and the bastard still remained hidden. But the ley power was my strongest asset; it stretched out as far as needed. I sent it out in a power surge, a huge circle that engulfed the city with one purpose: to find the other vampire, Harald.

A faint trail fed back through the circle. I found his presence at *Il Salone di Piaceri*, but it was old; it traced back to the night he attacked Caesare. Then where? The trail was all over the city. Harald had no doubt watched me teach Caesare how to survive his new life, while we thought we were looking for him in turn. How foolish we'd been. Harald probably had been hiding in plain sight all the time. At least until he decided to kill Lucrezia.

I found his trail focused around the docks however.

I pushed the power out from me farther. A ship! He'd returned to Rome and boarded a ship. I should have known.

I tried to follow, tried to work out the direction he'd gone, but across the water the trail went cold. It was too obscure and this ley line power would only stretch as far as its own limits. I was furious with myself for not thinking of using this sooner.

I cast around briefly for a doorway, it was a habit and part of me hoped that one would suddenly appear and take me out of this confusing situation. I had never wanted to become so completely embroiled in Caesare and Lucrezia's past. It was bizarre that I was even there.

Caesare returned to the house. He was exhausted and hadn't changed his clothing since the night we found Lucrezia gone.

'I found a merchant who sold a ticket on a ship bound for the Netherlands. It seems our enemy has flown the nest.'

'I assume he's making his way back to his own soil,' I said.

We both fell into a state of profound depression. I knew that the best thing we could do was leave Rome and perhaps go somewhere where Caesare was unknown, but his reluctance to leave surprised me.

'I have to get my affairs in order and check that everyone is unharmed in my household at St Peter's. I need to contact Marnia, find out all she knows about Harald. It may give us a lead at least.'

Once again Caesare surprised me, especially with his concern for his employees. It gave me an unpleasant feeling in the back of my skull. A half-formed terror and suspicion lurked there, but I couldn't put my finger on it. One thing for certain, he wasn't the hateful arrogant creature Lucrezia had made him out to be.

'Marnia will have many questions,' I pointed out.

But I knew that Marnia responded to money and her silence

and loyalty could be bought and paid for without too much trouble. I allowed Caesare to see her alone. I thought there might be less scandal if Caesare and I weren't seen out together publicly and I had for all intents and purposes disappeared from the social scene as quickly as I had arrived. I was sure that this wouldn't cause too much concern, after all I had no history here, and Marnia would be told to make up a story of me having to suddenly return to England. My flippant attempt to mix once more with humans had left me feeling exposed. It was a mistake I wouldn't repeat again anytime soon.

A few hours after Caesare left a young boy knocked on the door. Having sent all the servants away I opened the door myself and peered out at the urchin child as he held out a letter to me.

'For the Countess,' he said.

'I'm the Countess. Who gave you this?'

'Some gentleman. He said I had to wait an hour first and then you'd give me an extra coin for a job well done.'

'Did he now?'

I handed the boy a coin. He examined it, and then bit into it to see if it was real. Then without another word he turned and ran away.

I stared at the letter in my hand. It was on parchment and sealed with a wax emblem that I recognised as Marnia's seal.

I closed the door and snapped open the seal. The night was drawing in and the handwriting was scrawling across the page as though the writer had been in a hurry. I went into the drawing room and over to a bureau where I lit a candle. I held the letter close to the light.

Lilly,

Forgive me. I had to leave but rest assured that I will return. I know I owe you my life and I have not forgotten my pledge to you.

Marnia told me there have been sightings of Lucrezia. I have to see her and make sure that she is well and safe. She has not had the benefit of a caring mentor as I have and I fear for her sanity.

I've left Rome on horseback and I am riding alone because I wanted to save time.

The rumours are bad Lilly. They talk of her as though she is some mindless revenant.

Another young girl has been murdered. She's the daughter of a Justice and that makes it all worse. Mamia's contacts say they have a woman in custody fitting Lucrezia's description.

Lilly, they plan to burn her as a witch!

Forgive me again for suddenly leaving you, but there is so little time and I have to hurry. I have to try and save her.

Please understand.

Yours in blood and honour,
Caesare.

I placed the parchment down. Caesare! No! *I should have stopped you! I should have known you'd do this.*

Again I was in fate's hands. Once more I had to wait to see how events would turn out. Caesare had gone and there was nothing I could do. Perhaps this was my time to leave also. I couldn't control what would happen could I? I was the living proof that it had already occurred.

I sat down at my bureau. I would pen a letter for Caesare. I would wish him well for the future. Hope his life would be exciting and free, and warn him of the consequences of careless feeding. I would release him from his pledge, giving him the tools to survive. Just as a mother raises her child to face the world.

But my feelings towards him were not at all motherly.

I stared at the blank page.

He was gone. I doubted he'd come back. What did it matter anyway? I was meant to move through this life alone. I didn't need Caesare Borgia tagging along, complicating things. After all, what would happen when the next doorway arrived? Attachments meant pain. I'd learnt that with my love for Maria and Benedict.

I was supposed to be heading home and back to Gabi anyway. Wasn't that the plan?

A strange feeling overwhelmed me. I wanted to scream. Anger surged through my head and limbs and I threw myself down on the sofa. I fought the urge to kick and thrash in a childish tantrum. It was some form of hysteria but I wouldn't, couldn't, give in to it. I sucked the frustration down inside me instead. Then I lay in a stupor. Numb. Cold. Alone. My thoughts zoned out.

I stayed there all night until I drifted into a tortured and fitful sleep in which I constantly searched for Gabi, then Caesare, without success.

Chapter 28 - Lilly's Journal

Dreams

I dreamt of the complexities of paradox.

Once more I saw Benedict, his small hands outstretched to me as I disappeared before his eyes. As the door closed my mind's eye saw his life unfold. He grew. He lived. He loved. He married and then the children were born.

Benedict's world merged with the stories of Gabi and Lucrezia and they haunted my dreams as well as my waking hours. I lived in a state of perpetual fear, and it was only in Caesare's absence that I realised that for those few fleeting days we'd spent together I hadn't been afraid. Cautious, yes, but afraid, no. Teaching him had absorbed my world, taken away all of the loneliness and pain. He'd been the distraction I needed, but once he was gone all of my phobias returned.

I began to worry once more about Benedict. Had his life been fulfilled as it should? Had Maria been happy when I left, or were they tainted by my presence forever? I tortured myself about Lucrezia and her hold on Caesare. I knew his future after all. In the twenty first century I'd been there at his death.

He'd turned up, calling me 'Mother', only I hadn't understood it, not then. He'd attacked Gabi using some form of mind-control to suffocate him. His incredible power had been a threat, his death a necessity. Had I known at that time what was going to happen, would I have been able to avoid it?

But I hated knowing. I wanted to rip it from my brain along with these confused emotions I had for him.

'He's a bastard,' I told myself. 'He'll turn bad – you know he's going to turn bad. And you can't save him.'

Part of me was struggling to believe it. Lucrezia, I realised, had never said what happened to Caesare once he went through the door in the Allucian corridor. She had brushed it off, saying she never saw him again. Maybe that was true but we only had her word for it that he actually did disappear. So far her narrative wasn't proving to be so accurate.

'I hope you were wrong about this,' I whispered to her dream figure as it floated behind my closed lids.

But the fact remained that Caesare died in my past and his future. And I did see that with my own eyes.

'Why am I still here then?' I asked the empty walls of the house. 'Why hasn't a new door appeared?'

I understood that in the *Castrum* it had been imperative for me to study with Maria. She had shown me the way to move forward, but I'd been in her world for seven years. I'd learnt patience at the time and the door had arrived when the moment to leave became important. But what was so important to learn here? Why couldn't I just leave?

The days passed in silence. Cocooned in self-pity I didn't go out. As surely as the loneliness consumed my soul, the bloodlust and hunger began to bite deeply into my stomach. It had to be fed, there was no way I could starve it. Especially when the pain became too much to bear and the fever of starvation set in.

Eventually, I stumbled out into the night, combing the city for a likely and worthy victim. Although I still checked my food, I was more brutal and deadly than ever before. Even though I'm not proud of the vicious torture I placed on each and every unsuspecting victim in those horrible, dark and lonely days, I still make no apologies for behaving as nature intended.

Blood Lovers

A short hysterical laugh escaped my lips as I found Caesare in my doorway. His dead eyes stared past me. I rushed forward to catch his weak and drained body as his legs crumpled beneath him, and reaching past him I unlocked the door. My heart was pounding as I supported him inside. A sense of unreality came over me as I wondered briefly if this was a dream. My arm tightened around him, a reaction to the memory of the last nightmare when he'd dissolved in my arms. I helped him into the lounge and sat him down on the sofa.

His clothes were dirty. He'd been on the road for days, and as predicted, his search for Lucrezia had ended disastrously.

'They burnt her before I got there,' he said dully as I pressed a glass containing brandy into his hands.

Caesare stared at the glass as though it contained poison, but I raised it up to his lips, knowing the warm liquid would help dispel the chill from his bones.

'Have you fed?' I asked, and he shook his head.

'Not for a few nights.'

I fetched a blanket whilst he began stripping away the damp clothes from his body. I wrapped it round him and pulled him back down onto the sofa beside the fire. I threw a new log on the dulling embers, and blew softly on the flames until they caught. The room lit up as the fire burst back to life as it greedily consumed the wood.

As Caesare drank the brandy the colour slowly returned to his face.

'Why do I feel so weak?' he asked.

'You need to feed regularly. Especially as you are such a new vampire.'

I knew the weakness was not solely caused by his supernatural body being starved. He was heart-sick and I couldn't tell him the truth. I knew Lucrezia had survived the fire, but she had seen him and fled. Telling him the truth might send him once again on another fool's errand.

I held his hand, 'I'm sorry.'

'You said she was safe. That I shouldn't go after her.'

I didn't answer. I curled up beside him and nestled my body close to his.

'What ...?' he murmured surprised at my sudden display of affection.

'For body heat.'

I lied. I was so pleased to see him, and I didn't want him to see the smile in my eyes, the hope in my face. By curling up like this all he could see was the top of my head. I could feel his aura pressing with sensual familiarity against mine. Caesare wrapped his arm around me and we fell into a companionable silence, in which I knew that my aura, lapping his by our sheer proximity, was soothing and calming him.

'It seems that your "paradox" didn't happen after all,' he murmured. 'Lucrezia is dead and you're still here.'

I said nothing. His lips pressed into my temple and he began to shower slow kisses all over my hair. I pressed closer, subconsciously encouraging him.

'I was afraid I wouldn't find you when I returned.'

I turned my face to him, finally meeting his eyes, 'You thought I'd just magically disappear?'

'Yes.'

I stared into the flames as the log crackled in the fire. 'I wanted to leave, but couldn't bring myself to.'

He took a sharp intake of breath, 'No?'

The kissing began again, this time more demanding and I raised my face up, eyes closed and let him kiss every part of my face. But not my lips. I wanted this innocent intimacy to last. I knew he wanted me. He'd be grateful for any love and affection I showed him. His life had changed so dramatically in the space of ten days, but then, so had mine.

Even though I was afraid to admit, and afraid to fall into his seductive Borgia traps, I wanted Caesare just as much as he wanted me.

'You need to feed,' I said again.

'I need you ...'

His lips found mine. I let him kiss me as he pulled me closer up and onto his lap. Then I nuzzled his neck.

'You're right about the body heat,' he murmured. 'I'm much warmer now.'

I turned my neck to him. 'Feed. I ate well tonight.'

He stared at the vein that pulsed in my throat and then hugged me to him again.

'No blood share then?' he asked.

'I think we can share so much more than that.'

My lips found his again, and this time, despite all of my misgivings, I gave him everything. Hang the future, I was in my present and I had to live and love. So I gave him passion and I gave him blood and our joining was better than anything I'd ever experienced. Even with Gabriele. It felt like the last time either of us would ever love.

Caesare's Body

I walk around the body, subconsciously outside of the ley circle I've drawn around him. The corpse is in stasis levitating in the centre of the room. There is no sign at all of rot or deterioration. He is frozen, but this is only temporary; I have not as yet set any permanent ward around him.

His remains are still hideous though. A warped and twisted face, dark poisonous ichor covers his hands and grows from his flesh like black oozing sores. In the ley field it is held motionless as it drips down and away from his skin. What if I remove this tainted oil? What then would I find?

It is an interesting idea and so I focus the ley power inwards and begin to clean him. In centuries past, loved ones of the dead cleansed their remains before dressing them in their finest clothing for burial. Didn't Caesare too deserve a final and dignified send off?

'Let's see what's under there.'

His body lights up with blue light. A cold flame sweeps the length of him, searching out skin and flesh and bone under my direction. The glow follows his body like a sparking fuse wending its way towards a keg of gunpowder. I step back as though waiting for the explosion. A dark gaseous cloud begins to build up around the edges of the circle as the air inside becomes speckled with dark bursts of exploding oil. I send a surge of power in to dispel the venom. The circle is now visible to the naked eye and the edges glow and blister as the toxin tries to escape its prison. The black cloud becomes liquid again and crackles round the edges, before setting alight in a huge whoosh that burns away the remnants in an ultimate rush of power. Caesare is obscured briefly but the fire around him remains cold as his body is cleansed of all signs of the dark poison.

I step into the circle as the flames die. Then stare down at his face, his once so beautiful face!

One eye stares back at me. I take a sharp intake of breath. Can there possibly be some life left in there? The other eye seems to have been burnt out of its socket.

I look down at his open chest. The heart is gone, ripped out by Lucrezia and maybe that was always what she had done to him in her own way. Yes. She destroyed his heart and created this hideous monster that reflected on the surface all the sins he'd committed like some reverse Dorian Gray. It is an emotional emasculation.

His face is blistered. Impossibly wounded and scarred.

'You're immortal and self-healing. Disfigurement is impossible. What happened Caesare?'

But his lifeless body can't answer me and I reach forward, closing his single remaining eye so that his dead and lifeless pupil can no longer reflect the sadness on my face.

I step out of the circle, but cleanse myself first in the ley power. Just in case. After all I still don't know what has happened to him. As I glance back over my shoulder, examining this crippled and deformed shape, I can't help but wonder where that black and vile substance originated.

I sit beside him for a while. Even immortals need to mourn their dead. My enduring heart, so heavy that I can barely lift my chest to breathe, keeps beating and pumping, beating and pumping.

I wait until the sun sets when I feel the call of bloodlust. Then I leave his side once more to take flight, soaring over the sea, screaming like a wounded albatross, until all sailors bow their heads and hide from my siren's wail.

Chapter 31 - Lilly's Journal

Hope

My love had found an outlet in Caesare. My life had new meaning and the thought of eternal loneliness was banished. We became inseparable, hunting together as we had in those first few days. He was truly my companion and my lover. I pushed away my fears for the future and we stopped talking of paradox, never worrying about what would happen beyond the immediate. I had hope for the first time in years.

Love changed everything. After all why would he feel the need to go searching for his sister now? Caesare thought Lucrezia dead and there was no reason why they ever had to meet again.

I persuaded him to leave Rome. We were constantly hiding from people we knew, so it made sense to start a life elsewhere. By encouraging him to leave I thought I might change the course of events in the future. After all what did it matter if Caesare never became embroiled with the Allucians? The only event that had to happen was that Lucrezia needed to bite Gabi and that wasn't for another hundred years. During which time, it would be best if Caesare and I left Italy.

'Where do we go?' he asked as he listened to my plan, accepted my rationale.

'I have a craving for home.'

We took a ship to England and as we arrived in Portsmouth in the early sixteenth century I saw a Britain that was as alien to me as all the centuries I'd traversed so far. Gone were the modern docklands with electronic machinery to lift luggage and cargo from the decks. We were in a world of carriages and cheap labour. Children were employed to carry heavy loads for lazy merchants. The docks were filthy and swarming with urchins, beggars and suspicious looking rogues. The streets were covered in excrement and piss because of a lack of toilet facilities. But I glanced around, breathing in the tainted air and I felt a strange sense of peace on returning to my homeland.

Caesare and I had boarded the ship under new names. We were honeymooners and we behaved like it. A fresh start gave both of us a bright outlook on life and I enjoyed every moment and every new experience of the journey, even though the quarters were cramped and uncomfortable. No matter what, to us the journey was blissful, and the blood of sailors had been rich. Of course, none of the victims we took from would ever remember our vampire's kiss; they would merely put it down to the dreams generated by the rocking of the ship. But we had enjoyed their subtle seductions and they were all left unharmed. It was almost a shame to reach our destination.

We disembarked on a warm spring morning. I walked down the gangplank onto the dock while Caesare was supervising the removal of our trunks into a waiting carriage. Money wasn't a problem for us. Caesare had accrued a large capital under the papal rule of his father and I didn't ask how. I had my suspicions, but if he had behaved in any way criminal in his old life, none of that mattered anymore, and his wealth was certainly a benefit to us.

I glanced back at the ship. Caesare pushed back a stray lock of his lavish hair with a sensuous hand as he calmly talked to the ship's captain. He felt my eyes on him and smiled at me. I loved him. I was so happy that I thought it would never end.

The docks were bustling. A small band of dock-workers lifted and humped boxes and crates onto waiting transport. A finely dressed merchant was over-seeing the loading of his shipment An off duty sailor hefted his rucksack over his shoulders and headed out towards the taverns, A preacher, wearing all black and a white collar, stood on a wooden crate and quoted scriptures to anyone who would listen ... What was wrong with this wonderful day?

That's not right!

My head swivelled back to where the preacher had stood.

There was no crate, or man-of-God, and that was just as well, because it was incredibly unlikely there would be one, although I didn't know my history well enough to be sure. I glanced around the dock, trying to make sense of what I'd seen. Perhaps it was merely a trader selling his wares? But there was no one around that was even remotely like the man.

I walked away from the ship and out into the docklands and found myself close to the spot where I'd thought he'd stood, but there was no sign of anyone.

A soft white flake fell on my cheek and melted. I looked up. It was snowing. *Impossible!*

'We're ready, darling,' Caesare called.

I went to him and he was smiling, gazing up at the white sky with wonder.

'This is snow,' I said. 'Have you ever seen it before?'

'Never.'

He was thrilled and excited.

'Come let's get to our hotel before it begins to settle, and the carriage won't be able to move through the streets.'

I glanced back briefly as we walked away and the air quivered. An anomaly was appearing in the docklands. I knew exactly what it was. A doorway, and there was no way I was going through it. I wasn't ready to leave. So I turned away taking Caesare's arm. The warm spring day rapidly descended into a cold and wintry blizzard. I felt, not for the first time, that someone somewhere was showing their displeasure at my refusal to play their game. I wasn't going to be a pawn anymore. No fucking way!

Our carriage drew away, pausing briefly beside the doorway. I glanced through, vaguely making out the shape of a barrel-like carriage being pulled along a rough road by a sturdy horse.

I turned my head away. 'No!'

'Darling? What's wrong?' Caesare took my hand. 'You're freezing.'

A shiver ran up my spine.

'Yes. Somebody walked over my grave ...'

'What a strange expression.'

I buried my head in his chest, hiding the fear I felt. 'I love you.'

He cuddled me close. 'I'm so happy Lilly. My life has never been so right.'

The snow fell in a flurry of large flakes that rapidly covered the roads and streets, driving people back indoors. As the carriage clattered through Portsmouth towards our hotel, I stole a frightened glance outside. The streets were empty. It felt like we had entered the world of a film I'd seen with friends when I was a student at Manchester University. The abandoned streets reminded me of the road into Silent Hill. The grey snowflakes could quite easily have been ash. It felt as though I had just entered hell.

Echoes

'Lilly, no ...!'

I jerk awake. The echoes of a voice I once knew ripple through my sleep, disturbing my rest.

I walk down the hallway and into the spare room. His body lies in wait, like some sleeping beauty in a politically correct fairy story. I can't bear to look at him like this. Since I removed the black poison, Caesare's corpse has begun to heal. He now lies in perfect form, floating within my ley circle, safe and preserved. He is as beautiful now as the first day of his rebirth.

Even the cavity in his chest has closed. Is there a new heart growing inside?

But what does this mean? Is the vampire gene so strong that the body will live on when the soul has gone?

'I wish sometimes I hadn't saved you. Then none of this would be happening. The gene would have died, and I would never even have been born.'

Caesare's perfect body doesn't respond. It's an empty shell, and time is drifting on. My eyes blur with unshed tears as I walk around the ley, examining every line and curve, and feature of his face. He's absolutely perfect.

The week I promised Gabi is almost over. I will keep my word and meet him.

My phone begins to ring in my pocket. I lift it out, glancing at the number that flashes on the screen, but my bleary vision can't make out the tiny numbers and I never bother to add names and numbers to the contacts list. I've no need, I always remember them.

'Lilly. I thought you'd have contacted me by now.'

'Oh Harry. It's *you*.'

'Yes. Of course it is. Where are you?'

'Rhuddlan.'

'So, how did it go?'

'How did what go?'

'You are making me work for this aren't you?' Harry laughs. 'How did your meeting with Gabriele go?'

'Oh!' I take a breath, unsure how to explain all that's happened in the last few days. 'I haven't seen him yet.'

The phone becomes silent, yet I know the connection hasn't been lost and Harry is still there.

'A lot's happened,' I say when the stillness becomes unbearable. 'There's too much to explain now.'

A loud crack echoes from the ley circle. I glance at Caesare, but see nothing altered.

'I have to go,' I tell Harry. 'I'll call when I have something to tell you.'

'Lilly, wait! I've been having dreams.'

'There's nothing unusual in that ...'

'While I'm awake. And I've been seeing some strange things ...'

I grow silent and let him talk.

'I keep getting flashes of memory. I think it is related to when I vanished.'

I say nothing but my heart grows cold with an irrational fear.

'In the dream I'm cold Lilly, so very cold. And there's this black oily liquid. Lilly are you there ...?

'I'm listening.'

'Lilly what happened? Where did I go?'

'I don't know, Harry. I wish I did. But ...' I tell him about Caesare and the black ichor.

'There's some connection,' he says. 'There always is.'

'I know.'

'I'll come to Rhuddlan,' Harry says.

'No. Not yet. Let me figure this out for myself for now.'

Harry says, 'Okay.' But he sounds relieved that I don't need him. He's never been good with angst.

'Keep me posted. And if you need me, you know I'll be there.'

I hang up the phone and stare at Caesare. I don't need Harry, I never have, but I stare at my lover wondering what it is that I do need.

Chapter 33 - Lilly's Journal
The Preacher

'Why do you resist my call, Lilly? You know what you have to do, what must be done.'

'I don't want to leave! He needs me. I have to change the future this time. I have to go against all that was meant to happen.'

An old gypsy stared into my eyes as she stroked the head of a chestnut horse. I had never seen anyone so old before. She seemed ancient, wizened and crone-like but her aura gave off a mix of colours and sparks that were most peculiar. It was raw power.

She walked towards a camp fire. Behind her was a multicoloured barrel-shaped caravan with a horse grazing quietly beside it.

'Who are you?'

'Carmelita is my name.'

'But what are you?'

The old woman chuckled then threw some herbs into the fire. The flames burst upwards, turning purple and green. It was like a miniature fireworks display. I couldn't help gazing into the mesmerising colours as they crackled and burnt, spitting out cold sparks in all directions.

'I'm waiting for you,' Carmelita said. *'And I'm tired.'*

'I don't know you ...'

Carmelita smiled at me, a toothless but warm grin. *'No, but you will.'*

I woke with a feverish sweat beading on my naked body. Caesare slept soundly beside me. England proved to be a fertile hunting ground and we'd fed well for days, but the over-indulgence of blood had made us both sluggish and sleepy. Early that evening we'd fallen into bed, made love frantically and then slept.

I pressed myself against Caesare's cool flesh, but he stirred, rolling aside. My body was too hot. I was burning up as though I had a fever.

I slid from the bed. The room was cool and the night air on my naked flesh helped to take this strange temperature down. I pulled aside the curtain, gazing out onto the street at the snowy scene below. It was around three in the morning and the road was understandably empty. Moonlight reflected in the snow, making the morning already seem light.

Behind me Caesare rolled over in the bed. I looked back at him. He was over on my side, wrapping his arm around the pillow. Light from the window fell on his face and bare chest. I admired him for a while, a smile playing on my lips.

There was a small but imperceptible movement in the corner of my eye and I turned back to the window to see what it was. The preacher stood below. His hat was pulled down over his face, and he wore the same clothing I'd seen at the docks. His soapbox under his feet, arms waving, he preached silently to an invisible audience. It wasn't possible! It had to be my imagination. I was probably still dreaming. I yawned and stretched letting the curtain drop back as I did. Then tried to turn away, determined to climb back in bed beside my lover.

Outside the wind howled. I lifted the curtain back once more. The snow fell heavier. The preacher hadn't disappeared as I'd hoped he would. He stayed on his box, untouched by the elements.

I dropped the curtain and, on impulse, raised it again. The preacher remained.

Turning I reached for Caesare's discarded breeches and pulled on his clothing. I opened the wardrobe, it creaked loudly, but Caesare didn't stir. I pulled my cloak free from its hanger and slipped it around my shoulders. I paused. I considered gazing outside again, but I knew the preacher would still be there. I had to go outside and get a closer look at this strange ghost. After all, it appeared to be haunting me.

I slithered from the hotel like a silent shadow and into a blizzard. I could barely see, relying on instinct to find my way to the spot where the preacher stood. As I crossed the road I could just make out the blurred black shape standing oblivious to the storm. I stumbled towards him, curiosity throwing away all caution.

The preacher was in a globe-shaped bubble, like a reverse snow globe. He thumped on his bible, holding it up to the air, while somehow managing to keep his face covered by the wide brimmed hat. I reached forward and placed my hands on the bubble. It felt solid. I pressed harder on its resistant surface.

The preacher waved his hands, his mouth moving silently. I pressed my ear to the globe, attempting to hear his words. He seemed totally unaware of me.

I slammed my fists against the surface sending a painful vibration up my arms. I walked around it. A unique and perfect cocoon of power was holding in this anomaly, or perhaps it was designed to hold something out.

I felt eyes on me, and looked up to find the preacher's face turned in my direction.

I squinted through the snow, trying to see under the hat, but there was a dark space where the face should have been.

'Who are you?' I called, but the wind whipped away my voice.

Even so, the preacher stopped waving his arms. Then the light of the moon bounced onto the globe, illuminating his face.

'Adonai!' I yelled. 'Damn you, what do you want?'

Innocent eyes smiled back at me, but his face was inscrutable.

'And ye will burn in hellfire ...'

'Go to hell!' I cried. 'You have no power here.'

'You know what you must do,' he said.

'I won't! You can't make me! I'm happy damn you! I won't leave him.'

'You have to follow the route of destiny, Lillith. You can't go back, you have to move forward.'

'I am moving forward. I'm living my life. I deserve this!'

'You can't stay in this time. You can't stay with him.'

Adonai stared up at the hotel. I glanced back at the window half expecting to see Caesare gazing back at me, but the curtains remained closed.

'I love him.'

'He has his own destiny to fulfil.'

I shook my head. 'No! The future isn't set for him. It can still be changed. I don't want him to go bad. I don't want him to die!'

I covered my face with my hands: my tears freezing on my cheeks, like long thin icicles. 'What happens then? Tell me that? What happens if I break the rules and don't go through that fucking door?'

The globe was gone, along with Adonai. I stared at the empty space for a few moments. Bemused and confused. There was a huge round circle where the snow hadn't touched the ground, but it began to fill rapidly as I stared.

I turned and trudged back through the snow to the hotel where I sneaked quietly inside. It was still calm, all staff abed. I stood in the lobby as snow fell from my cloak onto the plush carpet. Panic swept me. It was an irrational fear that I would be forced to leave Caesare. I couldn't bear the thought.

'No. I won't leave him. Do your fucking worst Adonai. I'm staying here.'

The wind howled against the closed door of the hotel. It sounded like mocking laughter.

I climbed the stairs like a convicted villain walking up the steps to meet the hangman's noose.

In the room Caesare slept soundly, completely unaware of my brief absence. I removed my clothes: my skin was no longer feverish but deathly cold. I slid into the bed, wrapping my arms around Caesare. I held onto him all night, afraid he'd vanish as easily as Adonai had. My seemingly secure world had suddenly become precarious. I didn't sleep at all.

Chapter 34 - Lilly's Journal

Incrimination

I had to make a decision. I realised that. Adonai had never interfered before. And other than the occasional glimpses I'd thought I might have had of him in other times and places, he had been out of my life since the day I left the garden.

'He has no right to interfere now,' I seethed.

As the weather worsened the villagers began to panic. There had never been such terrible and extreme weather this late on in the year before. It was almost the end of March and crops could be affected.

The sky darkened as I stared from the balcony window of our room. Caesare and I could leave. We wouldn't starve, but I wondered if this freak storm was all because of me. There had been similar freak weather when I almost missed the door from the *Castrum*. I'd been torn then. I loved Maria and Benedict, hadn't wanted to leave them, just as I didn't want to leave Caesare. Every new future would bring trials. I'd have to start again wherever I went, trying to figure out what purpose I had there.

I had begun to believe that my purpose was to save Caesare, but Adonai said it was a hopeless cause. Yet how could I leave him to his own horrible fate?

Caesare re-entered our room, smiling at me. His cloak and hat were covered with snow. He was like a little puppy.

'This isn't usual weather for this time of year,' I pointed out.

'No?'

'It's freak. And it is frightening the people.'

'I know. But why are they so afraid?'

'A late or spoilt harvest could mean starvation.'

'Nature will have its way,' he answered. 'There's nothing that can be done about it.'

We'd been there a week. The snow was several feet thick, and villagers were digging themselves out of their homes. The hotel was rapidly running out of supplies, and new provisions couldn't be brought in as the port and village had become completely cut off from the rest of the country.

Caesare kicked off his boots and spread himself on the bed. 'Come here.'

Lying down beside him I let him open my taffeta robe. And then I made love to him as though it was for the last time.

'You're just being selfish. You'll let others suffer and die because you keep fighting your destiny,' the Gypsy Carmelita said.

'Fuck you. I won't leave him.'

'Then things will get worse. And he will suffer along with the rest.'

'Your extremes of weather can't hurt us,' I laughed.

'Don't be foolish, girl. There are many ways we can hurt you and all you love. You'll do as your destiny dictates or know the worst of it.'

I sat up in bed as I heard the scream from below. A servant girl was crying and yelling.

'What the hell ...?'

Caesare pulled on his breeches and ran to the door.

'What's happening?' he called

'Murder!' yelled another servant and the cry went up all over the hotel.

'What on earth is going on?' Caesare asked as the innkeeper came upstairs holding out his cloak.

'This is yours isn't it?' asked the innkeeper.

'Yes,' Caesare answered. 'I don't understand ...'

'There's blood on this, Sir. We'll have to call the local guard in to see this.'

The servants gathered around the door of our room. Their expressions went from fear to curiosity.

'I wore that cloak last,' I said. 'I left it downstairs to dry off after my walk outside. There was no blood on it then.'

The eyes of the servants turned to me. I didn't appear fragile, but I certainly didn't seem as though I could have dragged the body of a dead man into the hotel.

'Whoever did this,' I continued, 'wanted to place the blame somewhere else. It's not that hard to believe that we, as strangers here, would be used as scapegoats.' I projected waves of persuasion through my voice and the servants became calm and docile until all thoughts of blame left their weak minds. 'But think about it. We couldn't possibly have committed such a crime. And if we had, why would we have brought the body here to be found?'

'Of course the lady couldn't possibly have done 'im,' said a male servant. 'I found the body. No lady could 'a done that.'

'And my husband was here in our room,' I explained, and heads nodded as though they could personally recall seeing him.

'I came in to light the fire,' said a young maid. 'He was in here.'

And that ended the suspicion and the enquiry. I closed the door as the innkeeper and servants walked away.

'That was close,' Caesare murmured. 'What the hell happened though? How on earth did the merchant's body get there?'

It *had* been our kill, but the body had been left a long way from this location.

I shook my head but a voice rang in my ears: a left over residue of my dream.

'There are many ways we can hurt you, girl ...'

Cold, icy dread clutched my heart and turned my stomach to 'udge. This wouldn't be the end of it.

'We'd better dress for dinner and go downstairs like the seemingly innocent customers we portray,' Caesare said, reaching for his doublet.

'This is insane,' I murmured.

'Peasants are always worried about foreigners,' he shrugged. 'The suspicion is gone, but maybe we need to move on soon, whatever the weather continues to do.'

I nodded. Moving on was probably a good idea. The farther I went away from the door the better, but my mind wouldn't let go of the thought that ultimately I'd have no other choice but to leave. Carmelita had said Caesare had his own destiny to fulfil and I knew better than anyone what that was.

I can't leave you, I thought as I watched him dress, glorying in the way the brush ran through his thick blond hair. He tied back his hair with a black thong, his long slender fingers rapidly twisting the leather until his thick hair was totally controlled. Then he turned to look at me and my breath caught in my throat. He was so beautiful. So perfect. How the hell did he become that black mutilated monster that died at the hands of his own sister?

'What's wrong?' he asked as I closed my eyes trying to push back the horrible memory of my past and his future.

'Nothing. Just a bit concerned about the whole "body" thing.'

Leaving Caesare

Several more mysterious bodies turned up, all of them somehow incriminating Caesare, before I accepted that Adonai and Carmelita were not going to give in. The threat was real.

We had to leave the Inn when two more of our kills were found. A posse of peasants and soldiers followed rapidly on our heels. No amount of mind control could make the villagers forget the strangeness of the kills. It was like a witch hunt with lit torches and screaming women; just plain weird considering all the movies I'd seen featuring those very scenes.

'We'll have to split up,' I told Caesare eventually. In some strange way I was trying to tell him I had to leave him.

'Why? They'll never catch us.'

'I know,' I said. 'But if the rumours spread they'll be looking for a couple fitting our descriptions. We need to get farther away from here and then meet up again.'

'I don't like it. I don't want to leave you alone.'

'I'll be fine. But I don't like how you keep being implicated. I'm stronger than you, darling. I've been around a lot longer; I know how to deal with this. You just have to trust me.'

It nearly choked me to tell him to 'trust me', especially when I knew we'd never meet again, at least not for five hundred years in his time. My betrayal of him then, kind of explained his behaviour a little in the future. He'd made kills and thrown them at my feet like a cat bringing home mice to its master. It also explained why Caesare's angst had been so focused on Gabi. In the future he'd tried to kill Gabi. Perhaps that was some form of jealousy manifesting in his insane brain.

These considerations made the parting even harder. I felt so responsible for Caesare. All that happened to him from this moment on would be completely out of my control, but that still didn't mean I wasn't somehow responsible. Even so, I had to send him away. There was no telling what would happen if I continued to fight my destiny.

It was hard to persuade him but eventually Caesare listened to my reasoning and I sent him off in the opposite direction from the port, heading inland towards London, where I believed he would make a life for himself among the aristocracy.

Soon he'd forget about me, and his life would be as it had been destined. At least, that is what I told myself but it didn't make it any easier.

'Never forget that everything I do is to protect you.' I told him.

'Yes, *Mother*,' he laughed, kissing my mouth. 'We'll meet up in London then?'

I nodded, but then glanced away. I was too choked to speak. Then I pulled him to me, holding him for too long as I revelled in the smell of his hair and the touch of his hand as he stroked my spine.

I watched him lumber away through the thick snow until well after he was a distant dot on the landscape, and then I still stared after him, hoping for some final glimpse. Someone was going to pay for this, even though right then I felt I had no choice. Maybe it would be the first person who greeted me on the other side of the portal. Carmelita's image floated before my eyes. It was strange how I *knew* she existed, even though I only saw her in a dream. But I was certainly going to get answers from that old witch when I got there and then maybe I'd strangle her anyway.

Hours after he left, I turned back towards the port and under the cover of invisibility I re-entered the town to find the snow was rapidly thawing.

I saw a scullery maid rushing through the streets with a basket full of food from the newly reopened market. Two young urchin boys were playing on the street, throwing rocks along the road to see how far they could make them skitter. A carriage travelled rapidly up the rough road, quickly followed by another. The port was getting back to normal.

I could only assume it was because we had left the town.

I hardened my heart, forcing steel back into my spine as I made my way back to the doorway. The people here could continue their lives as though nothing had happened, despite the murders, while all the time, I, a supernatural creature with seemingly limitless strength and psychic ability, couldn't even gain mastery of my own destiny. There was something wrong with this picture and I was damn well going to find out what. I certainly didn't like being bossed around like this. Although I couldn't fight on this occasion I would bide my time. An opportunity for revenge would present itself and I had eternity to wait for that moment.

I stood before the door. The air shivered and I felt something akin to satisfaction flowing out from the opening towards me. Destiny felt like a real person just then, and it pissed me off big style.

I glanced back at the hotel, gazing up at the window to the room Caesare and I had occupied.

'I hope to God we meet again before it's too late for you,' I said.

But Caesare would never hear my words, and I never would see him again on my travels. As I walked through the portal I felt like the biggest failure in the entire world and it wasn't a nice feeling. Not. At. All.

Chapter 36 - Lilly's Journal
The Gypsy Life

Carmelita was waiting for me by the camp fire as I stepped through the doorway. She was dressed in multicoloured clothing, which had faded with wear and age. They suited her worn and tired face. She was both aged and ageless in a somewhat mysterious 'wise woman' way.

As I walked towards the fire she waved to me as if she was an old friend and this wasn't our first meeting. She had invaded my dreams to talk to me, so maybe those moments counted as an introduction in her eyes. Whatever she felt, it was certain that we were to behave like old friends. I hated her. I wanted to kill her in the most extreme way I could imagine, and my imagination was pretty vivid.

She indicated the stool beside her, so I sat down pulling my rich velvet cloak around my body though I wasn't cold. It felt like summer, quite unlike the weather in Portsmouth, but the cold seeped out from my soul nonetheless and my hands trembled as I held them out towards the flames.

I felt the door quiver and close. I didn't look at it. I was feeling completely and utterly miserable. The control I thought I had on my own life had been a tentative illusion. Someone else was calling the shots and I really didn't like it.

'You took your own sweet time,' Carmelita said.

'I didn't want to come.'

'I know it. And you nearly caused a serious problem.'

'Don't piss me off,' I answered. 'I'm really very angry right now. And I'm dangerous when roused.'

Carmelita laughed, 'There's no point in your anger. Destiny

says jump, you jump. No matter how immortal you are. Your powers mean nothing to the universe.'

I scrutinised the old woman's face as she prodded the fire with a stick, making it burn hotter. She was very small, almost dwarf-like, except all of her features were in perfect proportion. Her hair was white, but I imagined that it would have been jet black in her youth. Her skin was a weather-worn brown and her eyes were the blackest orbs I had ever seen. My eyes saw 'helpless little old woman', but some primitive part of my brain told me she was dangerous. Curious.

'Why won't it leave me alone? I've done everything that was needed. My staying with Caesare wouldn't have changed the final outcome. My vampire gene will still find its hosts. I'm living proof of that.'

Carmelita continued to stoke the fire, throwing on the occasional twig and branch until she raised it up to a roaring flame.

'You can't change time, Miranda. Fighting destiny will only cause you and those around you pain.'

'My name's Lilly ... and do you think that my sudden disappearance hasn't caused Caesare pain?'

'Miranda,' Carmelita replied stubbornly. 'You cannot change his fate. All that happens must happen in the way it is meant. You can't pick and choose your own future.'

'So everyone keeps telling me. What about freedom of choice? And I'm called *Lilly*.'

'That isn't a luxury you have. Miranda.'

'Okay! I get it. I'm Miranda now. This is all becoming very predictable.' I sighed wiping my hand across my forehead. 'I guess I go and save Lucrezia from Caesare then?'

Carmelita nodded, 'But first there are some things you need to learn.'

'And you're going to teach me?' I raised an eyebrow in what I hoped would be a cynical expression.

'Yes.'

'What if I decide to just kill you and go and find Caesare? What's to stop me?'

Carmelita laughed harshly and then reached for the pot on the fire, stirring the contents rapidly. Her frail hand shook as she withdrew it.

'There are forces at work which you don't understand, girl. And I have no doubt in my mind that they will deal with you if you attempt to change the course of things. I'm here for a reason. There are skills you need for this next phase in your life.'

I sighed. 'Okay. Knock yourself out. But tell me this ... once you've taught me these "skills" what's to stop me from going to Caesare instead of Lucrezia? After all I'll know exactly where he is.'

Carmelita patted my arm and smiled, 'All will be clear when the time is right. What you lack is faith, child.'

'Faith? That's absurd. Faith in what?'

'Faith in yourself. That's the only kind worth having. You'll do the right thing and eventually your efforts will be rewarded.'

'That's the kind of mind-fuck my mother does on the pupils at the school in order to get them to behave ...' I muttered. 'It won't work on me. It's manipulative bullshit.'

But Carmelita smiled and said nothing.

I sulked as Carmelita stood up and put a feeding bag over the horse's head. I missed Caesare and I worried how it had felt for him to realise I was never coming to meet him. He must have been so worried, then so hurt, then perhaps he was even angry.

'This is Bellina,' Carmelita said as she stroked the horses head. 'She is a special creature.'

Sulking isn't really in my nature and curiosity soon pulled me out of my bad mood. I walked towards the horse. 'She doesn't look special.'

'She's a sturdy animal. She will see you through all that must be.'

I found myself patting the horse as Carmelita spoke. It was soothing touching her.

'She's nice.'

'Look after her and she will look after you.'

I watched Carmelita as she hitched the horse back up to the caravan. The horse was calm and serene, displaying no sign of agitation. Once hitched, Carmelita patted and praised her. Then she sang a lilting folk song and the horse whinnied in pleasure. I couldn't believe the youthful voice that came from the old woman. It was the voice of a young girl rather than an old crone. The horse nuzzled her as her voice rose and fell in a beautiful melody.

'Now it is your turn,' Carmelita said and she began to undo the leather straps that held Bellina to the wagon. 'Hitch her.'

I did as I was told, genuinely curious about the horse and Carmelita. Once hitched, I patted and praised the horse. I felt an immediate affinity with the animal, and it was strange. I had never had much interest in them before. Through my travels horses had been a means of transport, but I'd never learnt to ride nor thought about them other than as being part of the current world I inhabited. Then I found myself intrigued by one. It was almost as if Bellina was something special and different.

Carmelita doused the fire, then picked up the stools and stowed them in the back of the caravan. She took my arm. Then led me to the front and made me climb up on the driving seat.

'I don't know anything about driving a caravan, or horses for that matter.'

'Time to learn,' cackled Carmelita. 'Up you go now; I'll be by your side.'

We spent several days practicing driving and hitching Bellina. Carmelita made me do this so often that it became second nature. Soon I became the full-time carer of the horse. Bellina was fed and groomed by me alone. Carmelita no longer sang to the horse but insisted that I learn to instead. I practiced the songs she taught me, and the horse whinnied and nuzzled me. Bellina became mine and somehow it made everything feel better.

In the evenings we camped out beside a fire. Carmelita made

soups and breads with practised skill, and sometimes I'd slip away into the woods or the nearest village to hunt for blood. All this time she never let me see inside the caravan; it was off limits. But I was curious about it.

'Soon it will all be yours. But for now, that is my domain,' Carmelita explained.

Despite the rough ground and grubby bedroll on which I slept I didn't mind being outside. The air was so warm and comforting. It was the middle of summer, and it was easy to drift to sleep looking up at the stars. This whole world of Carmelita's, the gypsy life, was so at peace with the world that I felt its calming effects sooth the pain of loss from my heart. It lulled me. I could think about Caesare, but the pain had vanished. It was almost as if I'd dreamed the whole thing. I never realised at the time but it was a similar sensation to the time spent in Adonai's garden. I felt hypnotised and my senses were dulled.

'Where are we anyway?' I asked on the first day.

'Italy.'

'Figures. How long have I been missing from Caesare's life?'

'Two years.'

Two years! But of course it stood to reason. Carmelita told me Caesare had returned from England and was residing once more in Rome.

'Did he search for me?' I wanted to know. 'Or did he just return and resume his obsession with Lucrezia?'

'It doesn't matter,' Carmelita answered. 'What will be *must* be.'

'Can't you give me any hope at all?' I asked.

'You forget *faith*, child.'

Carmelita was the most frustrating woman I'd ever met. I'd been with her for two weeks and I felt that she was some kind of miniature gaoler, which was of course ridiculous. I could leave whenever I wanted. Or could I?

In the evenings, when everything else was done, she taught me to dance. They were sensuous rhythmic moves used in a variety of ways. The clothing she gave me, bright and colourful

214

gypsy costumes with beads and coins sown into the fabric, was designed to create music when I moved.

I had taken to wearing the face of Miranda again. It had become an old safety net whenever I was in new and uncertain territory. Somehow by being her again, it made the pain of my losses so much easier to bear. By wearing another face I could almost forget Lilly's feelings. I could almost convince myself that I was a gypsy living the carefree nomadic existence that Miranda would have.

But after two weeks I became impatient again. Why was my life being so controlled by others? I was determined to find the answers.

'What is your connection to Adonai?' I asked Carmelita as she prepared her bed for the night.

Carmelita shrugged but didn't answer.

'Only, I know there is a connection. So you might as well explain it.'

I followed her around the camp until she turned to face me.

'All will become clear when the time is right,' she said.

'Don't screw with me old woman. I'm sick of being messed with. I want answers.'

'Tomorrow.'

'Tomorrow?'

'Yes. I will give you answers tomorrow.'

Briefly pacified, but very suspicious, I went about my evening routine as usual. This consisted of seeing to the horse, practising my dances and helping Carmelita tidy up. Carmelita would then climb into her bedroll and I would go out into the woods to feed. But there was something hypnotic about the way she nodded, 'See you in the morning.' It was almost as if I had no other option but to return to her, and the urge to do so would become intense as soon as I fed.

But that night things felt different.

'Goodbye, Miranda,' Carmelita said.

I looked at her confused. 'I'll be back before morning.'

'I know,' she said.

I left the camp, running like a lioness set free onto a prairie. There was a town nearby and I'd fed there successfully a few nights before. That night I planned to find some deserving victim because I had the urge to kill rather than just to take a small amount as I usually did.

It was a bigger village than most, having its own tavern and guest house. This made it all the easier as the tavern played host to many travellers on route to Rome. Strangers to the villagers were the ideal victims. Their disappearance would not be questioned by the locals and would barely be noticed.

I saw my prey holding a glass of brandy in his hand as he sat alone in the tavern. His clothing suggested 'foreigner'. I recognised the Tudor fashion period of doublet and hose, covered by a short cape that was actually attached to his shoulders. He had a white, stiff ruffle around his neck that resembled a neck brace. It looked very uncomfortable.

I was sitting at his table before I let him see me.

'Can I read your fortune, *Signor*?' I asked in my contrived Gypsy English.

The man stared at me and blinked. 'Where did you ...?'

'I'm Romany, *Signor*. Most people try not to see me.'

The Englishman stared at the full round skirt I was wearing and my crop top that showed a flat brown stomach. I wore a scarf over my hair –then jet black, as were my eyes. I looked every bit the gypsy.

'You're a very pretty girl,' the man said. 'I can't imagine anyone ignoring you.'

'No? But you are too kind.'

I reached across the table and took his hand. His palms were sweating, he was slightly over-weight, but I still quite fancied removing that stiff collar and chewing on his neck in full vampire bloodlust. I raised his palm to my lips, flicked my tongue over his skin and tasted him out of habit. His eyes bulged slightly and he squirmed a little in his seat.

'Perhaps you'd like to give me a private reading? I have a room here.'

'What makes you think I'm that kind of girl?'

I teased him for a while before capitulation making him apologise and then beg.

'I'll pay you well ...' he said.

I laughed. Men are so easily manipulated. I took his hand and led him upstairs, deliberately rocking my hips as he followed me.

'Shall I pay now?' he asked as he closed the door to his room behind us.

'I don't want money,' I said removing the collar from his throat.

I took him swiftly. He barely had time to blink as I ripped into his jugular. His blood gushed all over his fancy clothing as he hit the ground. I fell on his prone body, squirming above him, gulping him down as his blood ejaculated into my throat. Predictably he soiled his hose ... But at least he enjoyed dying.

It was daybreak when I returned to the camp. Carmelita was still tucked up in her bedroll. The fire was out which was strange because the old gypsy was normally awake and making breakfast at this time.

'Carmelita?' I said.

She didn't respond. I stepped closer. She was lying on her side and I reached out a hand to her shoulder, turned her over onto her back. Her eyes met mine.

'Thank God! You gave me a scare.' I said. 'What's happening today then?'

But Carmelita didn't reply. I looked at her closely. The old witch never stirred, and when I realised she *was* dead I felt strangely bereft despite having only known her for two weeks and in spite of so wanting to kill her when I arrived. Oddly, this was the first time I had gone through a door and had someone on the other side to welcome me. Even though I'd been furious with her and Adonai, it had made the passing into this world so much easier.

But the old gypsy had tricked me. She'd promised me answers. It was almost as if she knew she was going to die and so she'd kept her secrets until the end.

Return To Rome

Carmelita's tiny body felt like that of a child as I lifted her. She was dressed in her finest clothing. An outfit covered in beads and coins, brilliantly colourful in purple and pink. It was a young girl's dress, but it still fitted her with room to spare.

Carmelita had left me a note. I owned the caravan and her job was done. She left instructions for her burial and I followed them to the letter, saying an obscure and strange rhyme over her corpse, before interring her under a large oak tree.

'It was my time to go,' her note said. 'Do me just this small favour and then I can enter the heaven of my faith.'

She'd deliberately led us to this clearing, and specified the tree and the clothing she was to wear. So it was that I entered the caravan interior for the first time.

It wasn't as I expected.

Inside was a comfortable divan, a small table (partly attached to the wall of the caravan) and two stools. There were a couple of chests, one was full of clothing, but the dress she wanted to wear to her grave was left out on the divan.

'It was my wedding dress,' she'd explained. 'I go now to meet my husband. We knew eternal and ultimate love. Death can't separate real lovers, Miranda.'

I washed her body, changed her clothing and wrapped her carefully in an off-white sheet I found in the other chest. Then I dug the hole, made sure it measured exactly six feet deep. Carmelita was quite specific about that. Afterwards I said the prayers and set a ley circle around the area to deter animals from digging up her remains.

I felt somewhat aggrieved though. Her words about 'real lovers' left a hole in my heart. I doubted my own feelings then, for either Gabi or Caesare. Perhaps I didn't know what real love was. After all, I had so quickly fallen for Caesare, even after all the years of pining for Gabi. I shook myself. No. I did love Caesare. I did love Gabi. Who is to say you can't love two people in such a long lifetime?

I packed up the camp. I didn't want to spend the night in the clearing, I needed to move on and leave Carmelita to her rest. As I collected the pots and pans, stowing them in the huge wicker sack, I picked up her note once more.

'Be there for Lucrezia. You must teach her some of what you learnt from Maria Serafina. Teach her herbwifery, and the basic spells that can be made from herbs. Don't give her the ley-sight. I'm sure you have many questions, but all will be revealed. Trust what I tell you, and above all, trust yourself.

'Have faith, Miranda, and you will once again become Lilly.'

I tucked the note away in the chest and hitched Bellina to the caravan. The time had come to go back to Rome, and I had to use all of my strength to avoid breaking the rules by running to Caesare. Instead I would steal Lucrezia away from him and take her on a personal journey.

'Carmelita,' I whispered over her grave. 'I'm a woman when it comes down to it all. But instead you expect me to act like an unfeeling monster. You've promised me answers, yet always you give me riddles. I love Caesare and my loss is so fresh.'

It was so unfair. But the only response I had was the moaning of the wind through the branches of the oak tree.

'Destiny expects too much of me.'

I climbed up on the driver's seat and clicked my tongue. Bellina moved away slowly. Even the horse was reluctant to move on and leave her previous owner. I sang to her as we left the clearing and she picked up pace as we drew onto the main road, heading back towards Rome.

I didn't question how I knew the way there. I just trusted to fate and pointed the caravan in the direction that was reasonable. Bellina trotted happily as I sang. We drove through the night and the next day until we saw Rome on the horizon. By then my thoughts had settled. I realised that there was no point fighting it. I had a job to do and no matter what, I couldn't get out of it.

The rest, as they say, is history.

Chapter 38 - Lilly's Journal
Another Departure

I did as I was told and 'rescued' Lucrezia from Caesare. But I lied to her about his motives, because the truth was I didn't know them. True, I am many things: vampire; witch; herbwife, but I am not a seer and I do not prophesy the future. All that I knew, all that I revealed to her, had come from my direct knowledge of her future. And this was the biggest and most insane paradox of all. Lucrezia had already told Gabi and me what Miranda taught her. I was Miranda and I therefore knew what I had to teach Lucrezia. I tried not to think too deeply about it though, because I couldn't really make any sense of how this was all happening to me. All I knew was that it had taken tremendous strength to turn the caravan away from Rome and to leave Caesare behind, especially when I'd been so close to him.

I kept Carmelita's final words close by and whenever I was tempted to reveal more to Lucrezia than I should, I pulled out her letter from the chest. This urge to re-read it was as though Carmelita was sending me a warning from the grave: I'd see her dark gaze flash behind my eyes and I'd bite my tongue. Then go and read her letter. It was exhausting living the lie but I didn't tell Lucrezia about the ley power. Somehow I knew that it was really important to keep this power to myself.

I could not even reveal that I too was a vampire. When Lucrezia went out alone to hunt, I went in the opposite direction, but I always made sure I was back before she returned. I grew to like her, even love her a little, but I didn't always like the way she behaved. Being with her became a routine, but I held back with my emotions. I could never truly be myself with her. I always felt that to grow too attached to anyone meant that one day I'd be ripped out of my safe and secure world. I'd find myself alone again in another time and place. It wasn't worth the pain.

So I grew colder. My emotions withdrew. I avoided relationships with men and my relationship and attitude towards Lucrezia was mostly business.

'Let's go out and have some fun, Miranda,' she said. 'You're never any fun – it's all about work with you!'

Seven years passed, I had exhausted all of the herbwife knowledge, and Lucrezia was a proficient witch, especially good at cloaking her presence. This was the most important spell I could give as it would ensure that Caesare couldn't find her. And that, after all, was how the tale was supposed to go.

We returned through the lonely and deserted roads to Rome. By then we had travelled the length and breadth of Europe, both of us playing at being Gypsies. I was lulled into the mind-state that made me believe there was no point in changing anything or trying to shape my own destiny. For a time my lot was to keep Lucrezia out of trouble. After years of travelling with her I had almost forgotten that one day another door may appear to take me away from this world.

'There's a village nearby,' Lucrezia said. 'I can smell it. And I want a man tonight.'

I nodded. She was as promiscuous as I was celibate. We were like two opposite sides of a coin, each anticipating the other's mood.

'I'm going to dance like a demon whore and then take my pick from the one whose heart pounds hardest at the sight of me.'

'Yes,' I said. 'Have fun then. We'll find somewhere to rest the horse and you go into town.'

'Why not come with me, Miranda?'

I shook my head. 'You know I don't have any interest in such things.'

'You're a woman aren't you? You're flesh and blood. Why not take a lover some time? I don't believe you when you say you aren't interested.'

'Here is a suitable place,' I said changing the subject.

'Maybe you prefer women ...'

'Shut up.' I said before an argument could erupt. She constantly tried to bait me.

I pulled the horse over into a clearing and rapidly jumped down. As I unhitched Bellina I looked around. The area was vaguely familiar, but then most roads and woods and clearings were alike. Bellina whinnied under my hands as I pulled the bit from her mouth, setting her free. She scurried around the edge of the clearing.

'What's the matter with her?' asked Lucrezia irritably.

'Nothing,' I said. 'She's just a little highly strung tonight.'

Bellina recognised the clearing before I did. It was the final resting place of Carmelita and Bellina couldn't settle.

'I'm going to move us,' I said as soon as I realised, catching Bellina and fastening her back to the caravan. There's another clearing about five miles down the road.'

'Why?'

'Bellina doesn't like it here. And it will bring you nearer to that village.

Lucrezia smiled, 'Alright. I forget you are human and distance means something. Let's move closer.'

I resisted the urge to smile at her misguided words and climbed up on the front of the caravan. Clicking my tongue I steered Bellina back onto the road. It took a while to encourage the horse to drive away. She turned her head and reared up until I sang her favourite song. Then we were on our way once more.

Lucrezia sat beside me. I could feel her anticipation as we neared the village.

We arrived at our new resting place and once again I freed the horse. She was much calmer then and found a patch of sweet grass to graze. I patted and groomed her, making sure that she was as comfortable and calm as she could be. And as I soothed Bellina I also began to feel better. It had been strangely unnerving arriving at Carmelita's grave.

'Go to the village then. Have fun.' I said, turning away to begin building the camp fire.

'Anyone would think you wanted to be alone.'

I laughed and shrugged.

Lucrezia giggled as she left, 'I'll tell you all about my escapades when I return. And then you'll be sorry that you didn't join me.'

'Get on with you,' I answered. 'Your escapades don't interest me.'

A few hours later Lucrezia returned and she was not alone. There were two men with her.

'Miranda, I brought you a present,' she called.

I climbed inside the caravan, threw out a bedroll and then closed and locked the door.

'Aw. Doesn't she want to play ...?' one of the peasants asked.

'Come out, come out, wherever you are,' the other chuckled.

'Don't worry about her, boys,' Lucrezia laughed. 'There's enough of me for both of you.'

I lay on the divan and listened to their grunts and moans as the men took her over and over. Lucrezia made sure I heard her enjoyment and she laughed and giggled, calling out instructions for them to take her this way, or 'bend her over'. When they finished, and the men collapsed in a heap either side of her, she leaned over the first and fed from him. The second slept soundly as his friend was killed, only waking when Lucrezia curled up beside him.

'What? You want some more, you insatiable whore?' the man said as she reached for him.

'Oh yes,' she said. 'I want you.'

I pulled a pillow over my head but it was no use. I could hear the trickle of blood as his heart was bled dry. My fangs extended in response to the smell and the sound of death.

'Don't worry, Miranda,' Lucrezia said outside the caravan. 'I'll get rid of the bodies. I don't want to offend your virginal sensibilities.'

When she left, a slight figure carrying a man effortlessly over each shoulder, I hitched Bellina to the caravan and drove away into the night.

I wanted to teach her a lesson, but I never saw Lucrezia again.

Chapter 39 - Present

The Pain Of Centuries

'Why do you torture me like this, Lilly?' Gabriele begs. 'I can't bear this. You said we'd meet. You said you'd let me know where you are.'

I listen silently to his tears but I remain cold. I'm willing to consider a reunion, although I believe my heart can no longer love. Maybe that will change when I see him. But I am afraid to even meet. Gabi hopes for a return to our old relationship, but I've experienced so many things that maybe it won't be possible.

'I don't know what to say,' I answer finally. 'It isn't out of cruelty that I do this, but more ... I need to be certain of how I feel. I'm sorry.'

'But a week ago you loved me. How can that change?'

I sigh. How much do I tell him on the phone?

'The last time you saw me was only a week ago, but for me much more time has passed. I don't really want to get into this over the phone. It's much too complicated. You must understand that things *have* changed.'

'Then talk to me, share it. I love you, Lilly.'

'The problem is, I've been alone a long time now. Sharing isn't something I do easily anymore.'

'You never have to be alone again,' Gabi says and somehow it really annoys me that he can be so accepting and desperate all at once.

I feel misunderstood, and despite the fact that I'm probably doing a really shitty job of explaining myself I take it out on him.

'I like being alone,' I say. 'And I'm only around others on my terms. I'll be in touch if I want to see you. Okay?'

I hang up the phone feeling like the cruellest bitch in the entire world. How can I explain that things have changed even since last week when I made that first phone call? The fact that a door re-opened in *my* time was a complete confusion to me. I hadn't been through one for centuries. I had been left instead by fate to stumble blindly forward, never knowing when and if the next portal would arrive for me. It was the ultimate uncertainty and I could not allow myself to be lulled into any sense of security.

On the day that my former self left the present I had thought myself safe at last. I had hopes that my life would become meaningful again. That was why I called Gabi. I wanted to be with him again. Wanted his love. I was ready to take risks again. But now, I don't know what to do anymore.

Caesare's body lies in my spare room fully restored but his essence is absent. I broke the rules in pulling him back through the gateway. So what consequences now await me?

'Caesare. Darling ...? I actually have no idea what to do. I've spent centuries knowing of a sure future. Seeing Gabi again was the singularly most important thing in the world. I had almost forgotten how much I loved *you*. And here you are again. Whole but incomplete.'

The body breathes. It has been doing that for a few hours. But the hope in my heart is fearful. Caesare's vampiric body is indestructible, but not his soul. Surely he isn't in there anymore?

He is like a coma victim and my ley circle is his life support. What will happen if I remove the circle? I am afraid. While I have this beautiful reminder of a love I lost, I fear losing it more than anything.

My heart hurts. It pounds in my chest and screams with the pain and grief of centuries. The cruelty of this world is often too hard to shut out.

I scream. Hard and loud. The howl of an animal in pain.

'Damn you! Damn you, Fate, Destiny or whatever the hell you

are that put me here. I want this to end. I can't endure this anymore.'

I fall to the ground beside Caesare and cry until the tears become blood, and still I weep on.

Maria Serafina strokes my fevered brow as I lie on my pallet in the herbwife's hut. She sings a lullaby that is hauntingly familiar.

I open my eyes and look up at her.

'You've been on an arduous journey. What did you see?'

'I saw a life of endless emptiness. Loves lost and then regained but untouchable. What does it all mean?'

'Oh, Lilly. We search our whole lives for happiness, security and love. But how do we know when it is real?'

'It felt real, Maria. It felt like a premonition of the future. I will find Gabi again and I won't want him. I'll still want something unattainable.'

'Destiny is cruel,' Maria said.

She stroked my head again and I closed my eyes letting her soothe me.

'Being a mother means responsibility,' Maria murmured. 'It is never easy. You are the mother, but you have such power in you, Lilly. You have the power to solve all of these problems.'

'But how? The ley power?'

'It's more than that. You need to visit another past. This time you can't cheat ...'

I shook my head, my eyes flying open to scrutinise her calm visage once more.

'Another door, Maria?'

'Another door. But this one will lead you to an important truth.'

I opened my eyes to find myself on the floor. Beside me the ley circle glowed as Caesare hovered above the ground like a magician's assistant. This was no freak magic show but the real deal. I knew how to use it but not how to raise the dead, or how to return a lost soul to an empty body. Could I call the doors to do my bidding? Maybe that's just what I needed to learn.

Raising The Dead

Bellina led me back to Carmelita's resting place. I pulled up the caravan in the clearing and set a ley circle to hide us from Lucrezia.

I'd had enough. I was sick of being Lucrezia's nursemaid and with the increasing familiarity with which she behaved. I didn't want men around the camp. Humans were food to me, nothing more, and I knew, if I stayed, my true self would soon be revealed. I couldn't risk that. I'd planned to return to Lucrezia in a few days, but for a while I wanted to show her I was annoyed.

I went to Carmelita's grave and felt around the ley circle. Nothing had been disturbed in the last seven years and Carmelita rested as she had before.

I unhitched Bellina and the horse trotted immediately to the circle and began pawing at the edge of it with her hoof.

'You haven't forgotten her have you old girl?' I said. 'But if you keep doing that you'll disturb her sleep.'

I sang to Bellina, patting and stroking her mane until she calmed and would let me lead her away.

I set up the camp and for the first time in seven years I didn't sleep inside the caravan, but pulled out a bed roll and stretched it out beside the campfire. Bellina grazed, but stayed nearby, occasionally turning to glance back at where Carmelita was buried.

I drifted back to sleep, feeling a sense of freedom that being only responsible for yourself can give. I dreamed of travelling the roads with Bellina, living a hermetic life, no more Lucrezia: it was my ideal heaven.

A loud rumbling rolled through the clearing. I jumped from my bed, immediately alert, and looked around.

Bellina was kneeling before the ley circle that protected Carmelita's grave and she whinnied gently as though afraid to make too much noise. I went to her.

'What is it old girl?'

The ground where Carmelita lay was undisturbed but beneath us the soil shivered. It was as though the earth had indigestion and was trying to cough up something it found unpleasant. The circle lit up with a pale yellow light. The earth inside began to crack and break up. The ground lurched.

Bellina was hurled to her feet and bolted to the side of the caravan in open terror, foaming at the mouth. I followed her and began to sing, trying to calm her, but I didn't feel calm myself, so my mood was reflected in the music. My voice wavered and the purity of the sound was compromised. Bellina became increasingly frantic.

Behind me there was a loud snap. I grabbed Bellina's rein as she reared. I pulled her to the back of the caravan and tied her securely.

I returned to the grave. The ley circle held, but something wanted out of that pit and I didn't like the idea of that at all. A fissure had appeared and soil bubbled up through the ground. I watched in horror as a frail, dirt encrusted hand reached up and out, followed by another. It was like an old horror movie I'd seen in my own century. Stick-thin arms tugged and pulled. Claw-like fingers flexed and dug into the ground. Then Carmelita's head emerge from the grave.

I stepped back from the circle in astonishment and fear. The old crone cackled as her pitch black eyes fixed on me. I realised I was hiding behind a power that she too could easily control.

'Your job is done, Miranda.' Her voice was cracked and broken.

'Carmelita?'

'It's time to move on.'

I sensed a familiar vibration behind me. I turned. Another door arrived and was hanging in the air around twenty feet away.

I turned back to Carmelita who was still clawing her way out of the fissure in the earth. My anger flared. 'So that's it? You rise from the grave and I just meekly go through that door. The fuck I will!'

I glanced at the caravan. It had been my home, and Bellina had become a trusted companion. I didn't want to leave them. Once more I realised I'd failed to avoid emotional attachments despite my resolve, and grown to love an animal and the nomadic life I led.

The wind picked up. Lightning flashed and thunder exploded in the sky. The ground rocked and raged, splitting beneath my feet as I was pushed closer to the door.

'I won't be bullied this time.'

Carmelita smiled. A wicked, toothless grin, and dry earth tumbled from her mouth. She raised her hand. A surge of energy hit me full in the chest and hurled me backwards towards the gateway.

'You'll do as you are told, bitch!' said the old witch.

My feet stumbled against the flexing earth beneath me and I fell hard to the ground. I clawed at the earth, reaching for and grabbing hold of one of the protruding roots of the oak tree Carmelita had been buried beneath. The rapacious wind whipped and tore at my hair, clothes and legs as an invisible force dragged me closer to the door.

'Damn you! I won't go this time!'

But Carmelita laughed, and her laughter had power. My vampiric strength gave out, and even though my fingers scrambled for a purchase I didn't have the stamina to hold on. The root ripped from my grasp, shredding the skin on my fingers and, still screaming my anger, I was tumbled towards the shivering opening.

'Next time I see you, I'll fucking kill you!' I yelled into the wind.

I slid farther, still scrambling at the dirt, and as I passed the caravan I stretched out my hands towards my sword. I called up the ley power, and dragged the sword and belt to me. There was a moment's resistance as my body hit the doorway and then sudden silence as I slipped through into another time ... another place ... and my sword and belt came tumbling through the void with me.

On the other side, the door froze over, leaving me with a snapshot image of the old woman, white hair streaming out from her head, insane laughter on her filthy lips and her once-black eyes had become golden orbs.

What the fuck was going on?

Norse King

As the door faded from sight I glanced down at my injured hands. The blood had already been reabsorbed back into my skin and the wounds were almost healed. Being immortal, and self-healing, had its advantages. I stood, brushing myself down, and found myself in the courtyard of a huge castle. Looking up at the expanse of walls I could see four large turrets, one for each corner, and a parapet along the top, manned by guards wearing armour that seemed to be straight from a Robin Hood movie, particularly the helmets which were oval with a flat metal plate to protect their noses.

I had landed in the middle of the courtyard beside the well.

'You! Girl! You can't sit there.' I turned round to see a guard staring at me. 'Dancers are supposed to be in the servant's quarters until the feast. You shouldn't be here.'

The guard had a faint accent, though he spoke in English.

'Where am ... where do I go?' I answered quickly.

'That way.'

Grabbing my sword and belt, and following the direction of his outstretched arm, I saw a huge oak door leading into the castle. I walked slowly but confidently towards it, the coins on my dress jingling. I pressed my hand against the smoothly planed surface and the door gave easily on freshly greased hinges. I glanced back at the guard who had been joined by another, and they stared at me with blank, unreadable expressions. I had no choice but to continue the way I had been sent. Inside a stone staircase led down into the depths of the castle.

I couldn't figure out why I was here. I had fulfilled everything that I knew of Lucrezia's history so surely there was nothing more I could do to ensure that her history remained the same. It was pointless to send me to yet another time; why hadn't I just been returned to my own?

Halfway down the stairs I stopped. *What the fuck was going on?* I felt like a pawn in some game that a supernatural force was playing. I didn't like it one bit. All control was being taken from me. I even began to question every decision I'd made in the last few years. Was there nothing I could do that wasn't already decided by someone else?

I thought back to Adonai and the garden. It couldn't be a coincidence that I'd begun my journey there, nor that Adonai had reappeared on occasion to make me take a new route. Although I hadn't seen him during my time as Miranda, Carmelita had turned up to make me do what I was supposed to do instead. Different person, same intent. So how were they connected? So far, I'd played their game, but no more. No matter what, I wasn't going through another doorway.

I heard the clatter of armoured feet climbing the stairs from below and by instinct I cloaked myself. I moved close to the wall as the soldier passed, but he shivered as though he felt my presence.

Okay. Let's see what this is all about.

I descended the torch-lit stairs feeling irritated at the thought of starting a new life again, but as I neared the core of the castle I felt a huge surge of ley power. I searched it out, and found one of the most powerful ley sources I'd ever felt. It resonated from a river that ran alongside the castle, and the vibrations rippled along the foundations of the stone.

At the bottom of the stairs I touched the walls. The castle sent out a lick of power, which travelled through my arm and over my body. I felt like I had been tasted and I wondered if my lineage was being projected somewhere for some unusual being to read. The vibrations echoed under my feet as I walked forward. It felt like a welcome.

In the bowels of the castle I could hear music, and the familiar jingle of coins and beads. Gypsies? Bright light poured from a room off a corridor at the bottom of the stairs. There was the sense of many people filling the room and the din of their chatter echoed through the corridor. I followed the sound to its source.

At the door I uncloaked myself, attached my sword around my waist and walked in confidently to find a crowd of entertainers. There was a man dressed in a harlequin costume, a troubadour playing a lyre. The tune sounded like *Greensleeves* or some such melody, but that would make the era much later than it appeared to be, so I knew it couldn't have been that song. A group of dancing girls practised in brightly coloured skirts and tops. Each of them had bells on their wrists and ankles. In the far corner of the room was a cage containing a huge black bear and his trainer was feeding him scraps through the bars. A group of minstrels sung together in harmony, their voices filling the air with a natural beauty that complimented all of the other sounds.

The troubadour stopped playing and stared at me as though I had two heads, then, like a slow ripple as I moved through the room, the rest of the people stopped what they were doing to appraise the newcomer.

The dancing girls glared at me.

'Who are you?' asked one of them, her head held up in arrogant inquisition.

I turned to look at her and caught sight of my reflection in a large mirror positioned against one of the walls. Somehow I had subconsciously dropped the image of Miranda and I looked like myself again. My hands flew to my face as I experienced a momentary confusion. Perhaps the force of being thrown through the portal had ruptured the glamour spell. It was strange that I would just lapse after being Miranda for seven years.

'Lilly,' I told them. 'My name is Lilly.'

I felt like I had been in a coma and had almost forgotten my identity, but within moments the sensation evaporated and I felt completely and utterly myself again.

'Lilly ...' repeated the troubadour who then began to recite a poem about flowers. 'And a beautiful flower you are too,' he said when he finished.

'What do you do then?' asked another of the girls, hostility lighting her eyes.

'I ... dance.'

All of the dancers crossed their arms.

'And, I sing folk songs ...'

The minstrels stared at me.

'But mostly I read palms.'

The silence broke, and with a sudden rush the girls clustered around me.

'Read our future,' they begged, 'and maybe we'll let you dance with us.'

I sat down cross-legged on the straw-covered floor and began to demonstrate my palmistry skills. It was so easy to deceive humans. I merely read their body language and their metabolic responses to things I said, changing my story to suit their desires. I'd practised it long enough in Italy and the words spilled from my lips with undeniable ease. Plus, the ley power was strong in this large underground room and the thoughts of the girls floated around me like some bizarre ethereal monologue. I knew their names, ages, thoughts and feelings and above all I could figure out what it was they wanted to see in their future.

'Ariadne ...' I said. 'You will find love.'

'Love?' replied the girl giggling and glanced around at what she found to be a disappointing array of men. 'Not in this castle.'

'You're not staying here though are you? You'll move on to the next town ...'

'Yes. Will I find him there then? Will he have dark hair?'

I nodded. 'Yes and he'll be tall.'

One of the girls, Marya, wanted her sick brother to get well. 'He had some kind of ailment. It makes him sneeze and cough and his chest makes this horrible wheezing sound.'

All in the room fidgeted when she mentioned the illness.

'When did you last see him?' I asked, examining her face closely.

It was Ariadne who answered, 'Last week. We passed by her village so she detoured and went home for a few hours.'

I sniffed the air around Marya, but she was healthy enough. 'At least you are well and I see hope of a speedy recovery for your brother.'

The other girls offered their hands and their thoughts and they returned happily to their friends believing that I was truly gifted as a palm-reader.

'So, you sing?' asked the troubadour, whose name turned out to be Francis. 'May we hear you?'

I sang a few of the folk songs Carmelita had taught me and Francis clapped with pleasure as did the minstrels.

'We also do a juggling act,' they told me, 'and over there is Bernie. He's a fire-eater.'

The group welcomed me slowly and I became part of the show without even having to ask.

'We'll put Lilly on in the second half ...' suggested Francis. The court ladies will love you telling them their fortune. You're of a strange colouring for a gypsy though. Maybe we should cover your hair and paint your skin? You'll need to take the sword off too.'

'No. I don't need a disguise. I want to look like myself. And my sword stays on my hips.'

Francis shrugged. 'Whatever you say, milady.'

It was unanimous that I joined the show, even though I wasn't part of this troupe. I went along with it. What choice did I have? It would have been strange if I'd refused and, as always, I was trying to discover why I was here in this time. It wasn't clear at all.

'We're performing in front of the King,' Francis told me.

'Which King?'

Francis gave me a long hard stare, 'King Edward of course. He had this castle built and it's newly occupied. Didn't you see all the guards around the place?'

I nodded, 'Yes, but I thought that was normal for a castle like this.'

'Where've you been girl?' Francis shook his head. 'No head for politics then?'

'Not really, but I'm sure you can explain it to me.'

'Edward I of England set about a full campaign to conquer Wales. And since he won that campaign he had this castle built.'

So I was in Wales. That was a first.

'That would explain why his guards are so serious and suspicious then.' I answered. 'Obviously they are concerned with the King's safety.'

Francis nodded. 'And why none of us is going in there wearing weapons.'

'I'm not taking off my sword,' I said again, but I didn't know why I felt it so important to hold onto it.

The show began in the great hall and the dancing girls went on to perform, while Francis played the lyre. The bells on their wrists and ankles jingled in time with the lyre music and it created a beautiful echo throughout the castle walls. I waited as the other performers did their acts. Mostly they were applauded, but sometimes a 'boo' went up from the crowd and guards removed the act in question back to the holding room downstairs.

'It's a hard life we live,' said the bear trainer as he led his docile bear back to the cage. 'They wanted me to prod him with a hot poker.'

'That's awful,' I said.

'And now, for your delight! Your Royal highnesses, ladies and gentlemen, we give you the blonde gypsy, Lilly and her unique magic,' Francis announced, and I was hurried out into the grand hall.

I was facing the King as he sat at the top of a huge 'U' shaped banquet table on an ornate throne. He was wearing black and gold finery. His crown was made of gold and covered with diamonds, rubies and sapphires. It stood precariously on a small head, only held on by his huge ears that even his mop of curly hair didn't hide. He was incredibly thin, with a pinched and mean-looking face. I didn't like him.

'What entertainment do you bring girl?' asked the King.

'I read palms, your highness,' I answered, bowing low.

Performing was no stranger to me; Lucrezia and I had done this many times as we made our way across Europe.

'Come. Read this palm,' he said holding up the hand of the woman on his left. 'Eleanor, you'd like your palm read wouldn't you, my dear?'

The woman wore a small tiara that was studded with similar jewels to the King. She was also heavily pregnant. She stared at me terrified.

'Your highness,' I said. 'With your permission I need to see your palm. Please do not be afraid this will not harm you or your child in any way.'

Queen Eleanor held out her hand and I took it carefully. Her palm was hot and she shivered at my touch. I glanced back up at her, briefly meeting her eyes. Eleanor had reason to be afraid. The child she carried was not the son of the King. Quickly I averted my gaze back down to her hand.

'I see much happiness and health in your future, highness. You will give birth to a strong and healthy boy.'

'Thank you,' she answered pulling back her hand quickly.

I met her eyes once more and the fear in them had dissipated. The King reached out over the table and deposited a gold coin in my hand. I bowed and backed away, carefully avoiding glancing at either him or the Queen.

'Who else would like to hear their future?' Francis called.

A few hands raised and I found myself drawn to a man on the right of the King. He had his head down, even though he raised his hand. I held out my hand and met his eyes. They were eyes as green as my own. He wore a long and unruly beard and his hair hung over his shoulders with two thin plaits either side of his face.

It took a moment for me to recognise him.

'Oh!' I gasped.

Sat in the chair behind the huge table was Harald of Sweden; the vampire who had tried to kill Caesare and had turned Lucrezia. I noted the surprise in his face at my reaction, but there was no recognition of me at all.

'Girl?' he asked.

'My name is Lilly,' I said as though I thought it would mean something to him.

'Do you want to read my palm?'

I stared at the King and back at Harald. I could feel buried rage rising. The murdering vampire bastard was parading himself before English royalty! Was he there to hunt as well? I looked into his cold green eyes, and saw nothing. No remorse. The anger was gripping me, and I swallowed as I felt my teeth start to prick against my lower lip. I've never been one to keep a level head, and so I did the first thing that came to mind, something that any insulted and abused woman might do to their enemy.

I spat at him. I know. It's a dirty habit, but I'd spent seven years with Lucrezia, and she taught me some new tricks. Some of which I wasn't proud of.

'Gypsy!' roared the King. 'Show my guest some respect. This is a King you see before you. King Harald of Sweden.'

'Yeah. Right. I'll just bet he's a King. You murdering son-of-a-bitch!'

But by then the rage and fury in my head had done its work. Fangs bared, all reason fled, I launched myself across the table at Harald ready to tear his throat out.

I landed on the other side in a clatter of flagons and food, hitting his chair and toppling it over backwards. Harald had gone. His supernatural speed exposed him to the King and courtiers as the fake and the monster he was.

'Seize her!' shouted the King as he sidestepped behind Queen Eleanor in fright.

I glanced around, snarling.

'Where's that damn impostor. Get back here you cowardly bastard!' I yelled.

The ladies of the court were screaming and cowering. The guards were terrified but began to slowly surround me as I looked left and right, my fangs bared and crazy for blood. The fury rose even higher.

'You honestly think your puny men can stop me?'

I leapt into the air and somersaulted over the heads of the guards. They turned around; spears and swords pointing at me. I ignored them, searching instead for my enemy. I'd sworn I'd kill him but Harald was nowhere to be seen. Of course he was exposed; seconds before he fled from my grasp I'd seen his fangs and so had the King.

'I won't harm you,' I said, turning back to the King. 'But don't trust that bastard, he's a murderer. He hunts in high places. And I suspect that you were going to be his next meal.'

I glanced quickly around the room, plotting my escape route, and my eyes fell on Francis as he stared at me, paralysed with fear. I felt a momentary pang of sadness. I had quite liked him. It was unfortunate that he and the troupe now knew I was a monster. I ran for the exit, pushing my way through the guards that came running in when they heard the din. I swatted them aside as though they were nothing but toy soldiers.

They picked themselves up and chased me. I climbed up to the top turrets; not that I felt they could capture or harm me, but more to avoid hurting them. The only person I wanted to kill was Harald, and he wasn't human so that didn't count. At the top of the castle I gazed down at the sheer drop on the other side of the walls. I hadn't really fallen that far before, but I had to risk it. As the guards approached me, ready to skewer me with their lances, I launched myself off and then something unique happened. I felt the ley line reach up to me. It held and supported me and I felt a surge of knowledge that this power could allow me to fly. Gabi had been able to, but he'd implied it took over a hundred years before he could. I grasped and welcomed the ley and surged up into the air, my mind shaping my direction and speed, and flew over the river and away from the castle.

Once a safe distance away, I gazed back at the castle's splendid beauty and I knew then that I'd return. My heart had found a home and it was Rhuddlan Castle. She, in her turn, recognised a kindred spirit and saved me in my hour of need.

I stopped flying and, floating in the air, looked back at the guards scurrying on the turrets. I was too far away, and the night too dark for them to see me hovering there, but my eyes could easily make out the activity in the castle.

Down below I saw a dark shape leap from one of the lower floors. Harald! He landed with a thump, but jumped up immediately and ran down the side of the hill towards the river. At the bank he hurled himself over the water. He was heading my way, but clearly didn't realise it. Good. He wouldn't escape me this time.

I hovered in the air like a swimmer treading water, watching him cross fields and wastelands, stopping for breath only when he was almost directly below me. The poor fool thought he had escaped.

I dropped down on him before he knew what hit him, knocking him to the ground. He quickly threw me off, he was strong, but I reached for my sword. I doubted any vampire could survive having their head lopped off, and I was in the mood to do him some serious damage.

Viking Vampire

We circled each other. My sword was firmly in my hand but I had not expected him to recover so quickly after knocking him to the ground. He made a lunge for the sword, his hand sweeping towards my wrist in a chopping motion. I pulled back, slicing his hand, then swung the sword at his head. Harald leapt into the air and somersaulted over my head. I turned, keeping the sword pointed upwards, and then threw myself at him. Harald sped away at the last moment, tumbling to the ground with only a small scratch across his stomach. He rolled and was on his feet again facing me.

'I know you. I remember ...' he said, glancing down at his cut hand. It was already healing.

'You murdering son of a bitch!' I lunged at him but he ducked away with lightning speed.

I swung again, Harald jumped inhumanly high to avoid the sword which hummed through the air below him.

'You can't kill me,' he said. 'Many have tried ...'

'I'm a vampire though, and I'm going to have a bloody good attempt.'

Harald laughed, taunting me as though I were nothing more than a stupid and inadequate female. I went inhumanly still and watched him caper around like a court jester. I was patient and could wait for my chance to cut off his foolish head.

Suddenly he vamped out. He threw himself at me, all teeth and fangs and with fury in his eyes. I swept the air with the sword as he landed in front of me, skimming his throat with the sharp edge of the blade. He froze.

'Don't move or your head will part company with your body,' I said. 'Let's see you recover from that.'

Harald's eyes followed the sword right down to the hilt.

'It's you! You're the one who made me what I am.' His eyes were wide as he met my gaze. 'That is my sword.'

'What?'

His laugh was nervous. 'Don't you remember?'

I shook my head and pressed the sword closer to his throat. The skin broke and a sliver of blood dribbled down the blade.

'It was two hundred years ago ...'

I shook my head again, 'No. I'm careful.'

'A raid. On the coast of Italy. A stupid little village which seemed such an easy target. Little did we know that it was under the protection of a witch and a demon.'

And then I recalled where I had first seen him. A flash memory of a battle. Decapitation of a Viking. The bloodlust raging through my starved veins. Tearing out the throat of a rapist. Maria Serafina straightening her clothing as the dead Viking's body fell to the ground. I'd left him for dead. *Oh my God! He's Benedict's father.*

'I killed you ...'

'Yes. But then I rose again.'

'Shit!'

That was in the days when I hadn't thought to check my food. It made sense. Benedict carried the gene, so why hadn't I realised that his Viking father had been the original source?

We stood facing each other for a moment. I was absorbing this new information, and slowly the rage left me.

I sheathed my sword and the Viking lost his defensive stance as we stood and stared at each other.

'There's no point in me trying to kill you,' I said. 'We're indestructible.'

'I know,' he answered. 'I ... I always wanted to find you. I wanted to ask you how this happened. I didn't expect to find you like this ... with my sword.'

'That's a common theme in our vampire stories,' I answered,

remembering how Gabriele had been seduced, turned and deserted. Lucrezia also. 'Damn!' I'd inadvertently done the same – minus the seduction of course. In fact, I couldn't even remember if Harald had enjoyed himself at the end. I had been so starved and strung out after leaving the garden.

'I have questions ...' Harald said.

'I bet you do. And you've had no one to talk to about all this either,' I realised how lucky I'd been to have had that year with Gabi. It had been a good grounding and at the end of it I knew and understood my nature, even though I had been cruelly ripped from my own world into his.

'I guess you need to talk,' I said, relaxing slightly and sitting down on the hillside. 'And I'd better listen because it's the least I can do for you.'

He looked at me surprised, but sat down on the hill beside me and we stared at each other for a long time.

Then Harald told me the story of his rebirth.

'I awoke burning on a funeral pyre on a long boat sent out into the sea. It was a fitting death for a King.'

After I'd left the village with Maria, the Vikings had returned, taking the bodies of their dead. It was a mystery where their King's sword had gone and this caused much debate over whether he had died a warrior's death.

'I couldn't enter Valhalla if I didn't die with my sword in my hand. But then my brother noticed that my fingers were broken. And they assumed that the demon who attacked me had stolen my sword.'

I nodded.

'My brother was declared the new King and he did his duty in performing the right burial.'

'How do you know all this?'

'I was in a strange state. I couldn't move or open my eyes yet I was aware of everything, almost like I was in a dream. I heard their voices, saw their debates in my mind's eye. But I was helpless to tell them I was alive. I just couldn't wake up. It was almost as though, by listening to them say I died, that I believed it. Even when my brother insisted they take me home for my funeral.

'Back in Sweden they piled a boat with twigs and kindling, placed me on it, and set it alight, sending it out into the sea, never to be seen again. I would be pulled away by the current on the Skagerrak Strait and it would lead me to my heaven. Or so they thought.

'As the fire caught and began to eat into my flesh I awoke. I was in agony. I beat at the flames lapping up my chest. My beard and hair caught fire and suddenly my face was alight. My eyes felt like they were melting in their sockets. Sheer instinct made me throw myself into the water to douse the flames and as soon as the fire was out the pain stopped. A different kind of ache began in my skin. I didn't know then that it was my body repairing itself. But suddenly I was bobbing on top of the ocean and I could see again.'

I nodded as Harald glanced at me to see if I understood what he said.

'The boat had been captured in a strong current and I was halfway out to sea with a longboat that was rapidly burning to ashes. I stared around. I couldn't see any coastline and I was totally disorientated. But as the moments went by my body became stronger again. I raised one of my burnt and blackened hands up above the water only to see it turning pink once more, the flesh plumping out as the skin knitted together like magic before my eyes. I was shocked but elated. Odin had smiled on me. He was saving me. And so I began to swim. I'm a strong swimmer. All Vikings learn to swim when they are young,' he said proudly. 'It's paramount to our survival.

'I swam miles without stopping to rest. I didn't have a compass and I was confused and disorientated and so I swam in completely the wrong direction to home but I was trusting my survival now to Odin. And I knew he wouldn't let me go wrong.

'I never tired, even after hours of swimming.

'Morning was drawing in. It was still a long way, but strangely my eyes could make out details of a dry and welcoming beach. I kept going, my body felt strong but my mind was weary. There was an almost painful hunger gnawing at my insides.

'I reached land by the following evening and exhausted, I dragged myself onto the beach and slept.'

'I guess you learned the hard way that you were a blood sucker,' I said, feeling guilty and responsible for my carelessness.

'Yes. But the island I had found was uninhabited. It was animals I fed on at first. I thought maybe I had died and that this was my Valhalla. It was a strange time. My entire life ran before my eyes. I tried to reflect on my past wondering what I had done to deserve this hell. I had been a good Viking. I couldn't come up with the answer. I'd been a brave warrior, a worthy King and Viking. Part of me believed that it was the loss of my sword that was the problem. I was in some kind of limbo, never allowed to cross over to the true heaven. My whole life had been a failure.'

I cringed as he talked. How many bastard offspring had I produced over the years without understanding that there was a genetic link? I didn't think there were others, but then I had only just learned about Harald. It was a big world and there could be many more of us that I knew of.

'I stayed on the island for several weeks before the urge to leave became so intense that one day I just got back in the water and swam,' Harald continued. 'And I swam for so long, that I truly believed I was lost in some hell between heaven and earth.'

'I can see that,' I answered.

'Eventually I arrived in Scotland.'

'You swam the entire North Sea? That's some feat.'

'Yes. I don't know how long it took. I just kept on going and for strength I fed on the blood of larger fish. Sharks mostly. Then I found land and people. My true nature surfaced. I made my first kill and then I remembered you attacking me, your superior strength and speed. That was when I realised I was a demon. And a demon made me.'

'A vampire,' I corrected.

'I have never heard of that before ... witches, demons, banshees and sirens but never this ... vampire.'

'There must have been something like us in your folklore?'

Harald shook his head. I began to wonder when the history of the vampire even began. There were rumours of our kind all over Europe. It was well known – in my time anyway. But where did those rumours actually start? Perhaps I was responsible for more than I thought. I didn't really like the idea that I might have been the source of all vampire lore as well. I shook my head. No. Not possible. The myth must have been around much longer than that.

'Well that's what we are,' I continued. 'Vampires. And as you've already learned we live off blood. Just out of curiosity, did you wait around to see if any of your kills rose?'

'No. I wasn't curious, I was vengeful. I also didn't really know that this could happen.'

I smiled. 'Lust for revenge I understand.'

'And now here you are – my maker.'

'Yes. But like I said, there's no point in us fighting. You've already learned the hard way that we can't die.'

'And you have my sword,' he said again, holding out his hand for it.

'It's my sword now,' I said.

And Harald stared at me, both confusion and surprise colouring his cheeks.

I decided that the least I could, and should, do was teach Harald to be careful not to make more vampires, so I suggested he keep his fangs to himself and hunt using a knife in future. It was a self-fulfilling prophecy that he would therefore not bite Caesare and the future 'me' would. But all this had already happened in my timeline, and I believed it was impossible to change anything that had happened in my past.

'I guess it's time I taught you a few things,' I said. 'Rule number one. Don't touch my sword ...'

Fate Takes A Hand

There is a doorway open beside Caesare's body. I walk around it and glance through, but all I can see is a garden. It is like Adonai's garden but not entirely the same; it is not somewhere I have been before. I stare at the opening: I have no intention of crossing. Why would I want to plummet myself back into the past once more? That would be really stupid.

Caesare's body breathes. It lives but there is still emptiness.

'The lights are on but there definitely isn't anyone home ...' I try to smile at my own joke but my sense of humour won't return. The sadness in my heart is eating away at all of my memories and I don't believe there is any hope for the future.

'The future is bright ... The future is orange.' Even stupid advertising slogans are not funny anymore.

I leave the room, closing the door on Caesare and the gateway.

'It can sit there and rot! I won't go through and you can't make me this time.'

I go up to the surface. It's a beautiful day and despite the approaching winter the sun is shining. It reflects off the river and the castle is stunning against the brilliant blue backdrop of the sky. It is almost too perfect to be real. I imagine it as an oil painting. The river is swelling beyond its bank because up until today the rain has been incessant.

'Morning,' says a man as he walks across the bridge. 'Lovely castle isn't it?'

'Yes, she is ...' I answer.

I turn away as he tries to make more small talk. He's around forty and very attractive but I'm anti-social these days. I don't expend energy on humans unless it is to feed from them. There really is no point in becoming involved in their fragile lives. I walk down the hill towards the turret on the edge of the river.

'I've never done this before,' says the man. He is following me. 'You're a very beautiful girl and somehow I just have to tell you.'

I glance over my shoulder but keep walking. 'Please don't follow me, I'm not interested.'

'I just want to talk to you. I know it will sound crazy but ...'

I stop. Turn.

'I said I'm not interested. You don't know what you're getting into here. Now please leave me alone.'

The man blushes. I notice he has amber coloured eyes and auburn hair. 'I'm sorry. I wasn't trying to pick you up. I'm a medium and ...'

'What?' I almost laugh.

'I'm getting a message for you. I know it sounds insane. But I have to tell you; then I'll go away.'

I fold my arms across my chest. 'Okay. Knock yourself out.'

'It's from someone called, Chez ... No, that can't be right. It's a foreign name. Tell me again ...'

The man gazes off over the river, nodding his head as though responding to some whispered conversation.

'Not from, but about someone. Chay-zar-rey. Does that make any sense?'

I stare at him. 'Who are you?'

'My name is Simon Greer. I told you, I'm a medium.'

'You have a message then?' My arms tighten around my body.

'Chay-zar-rey needs your help. But you have to go through the door to find out how. I know it doesn't make any sense at all,' Simon continues, 'but these things rarely do.'

'Thanks.' I feel cold and I pull my coat closed and around myself.

'Does it mean something to you?' he asks. 'I like to try and make sense of these fragments for my own sanity.'

'Yes. But I think it's a trick and I'm damn well not going through the door!'

I turn to walk back up the hill leaving Simon staring up at me.

'A trick? But that doesn't make sense. The dead don't play tricks and they don't lie ... One more thing ... '

I stop. 'You are very naive Simon. Tell Adonai I won't be his pawn anymore.'

'Adonai?' Simon shakes his head. 'No, it was a female spirit ... her name was Maria ... She says to tell you she's your guardian ... She says, "Be brave".'

I reach the top of the hill and hurry back to my lair being careful to cover my tracks. My heart is beating hard in my chest as I close the door, once again underground. Then I climb the stairs and stand outside of Caesare's room. Already self-doubt is slipping in. Maybe I can learn something through that doorway. Maybe the answer to all of this insanity is there.

I back away and go to my bedroom. Throwing myself on the bed I lie silently listening to the beat of the castle's heart. I drift back into my depressive sleep feeling the vibration of the ley lines as they ripple over my aura. Only this time I don't let the power in to soothe me. I want my pain. I want my melancholy. I want my heartache. At least then I know I am still alive.

The Lair

I idled away some of the years with Harald. No more doors came to take me into the past or the future and this strange friendship between me and the Viking King began. I didn't let him into my heart or my bed. I'd learned my lesson and I wasn't going to love again. I couldn't stand to be ripped away from yet another world that I'd grown attached to.

Harald drifted in and out of my life.

'I'm going hunting,' he'd say, and that usually meant he'd heard of someone corrupt and important that he wanted to stalk. He was like the proverbial cat with a mouse.

I never asked him when or where but I knew what he was doing when he left for months on end.

My vampiric powers grew with every passing year. I learned to bewitch humans with some form of hypnosis that grew stronger than the original vampiric persuasion I'd once used, and King Edward's own soldiers built my lair underneath Rhuddlan castle. None of them ever remembered working like mindless zombies as they dug down into the earth. Here the ley was at its strongest and I used that power to make them forget or to heal the aches and pains they felt from the hard work. I was not a cruel puppeteer, but manipulating them was fun and it became something of a distraction throughout the years.

Also, it was a base. A home. A resting place where I felt safe and it was always the place that Harald returned to find me. I also knew that Rhuddlan would be there throughout the centuries waiting for me, even if I had to traverse yet another door and time.

I distanced myself from the world, choosing instead a hermetic lifestyle. I only emerged from my lair to feed, and occasionally, when I felt restless, I attended the banquets and balls that took place in the castle. I fell into a state of fugue. The years passed by and I barely even noticed when in the Sixteenth Century Harald took a ship to Rome, intent on looking for the son of a Pope who was known to be incredibly corrupt.

A small part of my heart reacted with anxiety when I made the connection, but I stayed in my lair and let the ley power take away the pain. It was like being perpetually on morphine. Rhuddlan Castle cosseted me. She got me through the lonely long years, helping me take a step back from the reality of living in a time I didn't belong. She cared for me like a mother nurturing her child, and in return I looked after her.

I didn't interfere with Harald, even though I knew he was brutal and cruel. It wasn't until much later that I shared my knowledge of witchcraft or the doorways. I never told him about my ley power because I believed giving him that knowledge wasn't necessary. He did mostly 'check' his food though and for years I managed to persuade him to stay away from Sweden as that would be the most likely source of vampire gene carriers.

'I don't understand why it matters so much to you that we don't make more of our kind,' Harald commented once.

'It's obvious really,' I said shrugging. 'More of us, means more likelihood of discovery.'

'But humans can't kill us.'

'No. But that doesn't mean they won't try. And a few centuries of being constantly hunted could become very tedious. Besides, who is to say they can't capture us?'

Harald laughed. 'I can break trees like twigs.'

I sighed. 'I know, Harry. But the thing is we don't know what the future holds. One day humans will invent weapons of mass destruction. They will build huge holding tanks and bunkers. I can't imagine that either of us will be able to smash our way through ten feet of concrete and steel.'

'You do say the strangest things, Lilly. Weapons of mass destruction? Holding tanks? Steel? I have never heard of these things.'

'Well, you will do eventually.'

And it wasn't my imagination, nor was it a lucky guess. I knew these things would exist in the future, and as a girl born in the late Twentieth Century I knew that there were secret agencies that may well be devoted to investigating the existence of the supernatural. Call it paranoia, but it was all so very possible, and Gabi and I had been so careful to avoid detection for those very reasons.

'It doesn't matter that you don't understand,' I continued. 'Just trust me when I say we really need to be careful. Don't do anything that might expose you to humans. We're monsters. We're the bogeyman. We're the thing that goes "bump in the night". And when people are scared they are unpredictable. It is best to appear benign to them. And if you do reveal yourself, then kill all witnesses.'

Harald smiled. 'That's just the way I like it anyhow.'

I let him go without further warning and watched his ship sail out into the ocean before returning to the castle where I fell into a coma-like sleep. I didn't give him any advice at all about how to deal with Caesare, and I never warned him that my past self would be there waiting for him.

Harry's Return

'Very funny!'

Harald shook me. I'd been dreaming of the corridor of reflections and the long hibernation left me feeling drowsy and drugged. I slowly opened my eyes and stared at Harald in confusion.

'How did you do it?'

'What ...?'

'You were there. In Rome.'

'What ... month is it?'

'October.'

Months had passed. I had slept the entire time that Harald had been missing and this was a new revelation. I could sleep some time away. Interesting. And very pleasing.

'How did you do it?'

'Do what?'

'How did you get to Rome before me?' Harald said.

'I didn't. I've been here the whole ... Oh!'

Harald stared at me.

'Lilly, I've always known you were holding something back. You appeared out of nowhere the night you changed me. You also materialised out of the blue here, in Rhuddlan, centuries ago now. Isn't it time you told me the truth?'

'Harry, I ...' I sat up on my fur covered bed. The lair had evolved from over the years into an underground mansion. I was in my room, on a large four-poster bed. It was the fashion of the time and a status symbol of the aristocracy. I loved my comforts and still deep down craved the technology of the future and so all the latest things were installed into the lair as they became fashionable.

'Well?'

'Harry, I just don't know where to begin. It's very complex. But tell me did you ... bite Caesare Borgia?'

'No. You know you did ... You saved him. Why did you do that Lilly?'

I shook my head. 'It was meant to happen. He had to live, Harry. Otherwise you and I wouldn't be here right now.'

And then I explained the paradox as simply as I could to him.

'I haven't seen a door since I arrived in Rhuddlan. And I don't think there will be one. Everything is done now. My meeting you was the final part I play in all of our futures.'

'How?'

'I taught you to be careful when you feed ...'

'But then, I disguised myself as Borgia and fucked and fed on his sister.'

'I know,' I nodded. 'I knew you wouldn't be able to always control yourself. And as I've said, I have no control at all on what happens. I walk through a doorway and I find myself in the middle of something. That's what happened when I bit you.'

Harald ran his hands through his hair. He was confused and couldn't believe that it was possible to travel through time. He found it even harder to understand that I was from a far distant future and had been trapped in the past for centuries.

'I know it's hard to take in. But you'll just have to trust me, Harry.'

'I want to know everything. I want to see these doors.'

'Like I said, I don't think there will be anymore. I now just have to be patient and hang around until my own time.'

But of course I was wrong. I hadn't counted on the next door. Or Harry's curiosity.

Chapter 46 - Present
Parallels

The door won't leave me alone and sleep is all I crave, but I hear the sounds of a river flowing through a green and vibrant world. The music of the breeze calls my name as it whistles gently through the trees. I'm hounded by the songs of birds, the slow hiccup of frogs and the pounding of horses' hooves on a prairie.

The door hums beside Caesare's body and I can't see one without the other being a constant reminder of my failings.

As I stare at his body, the medium's words ring in my ears and the temptation is almost painful. *I can save him.* Perhaps. But the tricks of fate have played their hand against me too many times.

Daily the doorway becomes clearer. I can see through it. There is a magical world that changes with a thought. Sometimes I see the river; at others I see a garden with unusual fruit. At times there is a large citadel on the horizon, the entrance guarded by a huge gate. Silent tiny people walk the streets or open the doors and windows in houses that are carved into the pure white rock.

'I've seen this place before,' I murmur to Caesare's still form. 'I can't remember how or where. Maybe it was a dream ...'

And there is the house. A huge mansion that seems out of place in the middle of the street. It looks a little like the house from which Norman Bates' desiccated mother stared out on the world. Or worse, some kind of freaky insane asylum. I imagine it full of dead lunatics walking with zombie slowness around the corridors. My mind's eye sees them rise from decrepit beds of rotting soil. Their hands – shedding decaying flesh – reach out to me as their empty eye sockets cry a silent, black, unholy plea.

But for what? I am not the saviour of the dead. And I fucking hate zombies.

I step back from the doorway, unsure of what I have really seen. I watch the unspeaking, small figures as they are swallowed up into the rock, screaming wordlessly. I blink. The garden is there again. It's beautiful and perfect. I can hear the river flowing.

I'm losing my mind. I place my hands over my ears and scream in frustration.

The ley circle around Caesare vibrates and I stare at him again. Is he failing? Will the body now die and begin to rot?

You've got to help him, the medium, Simon Greer, had said. *Only you can do it.*

I shake my head. The past is still punishing me and what did I ever do to deserve it anyway?

'Self-pity gets you nowhere,' I say shaking my head again but I can't clear the thoughts or the images from behind my eyes.

I glance at the door. The world beyond briefly looks like Adonai's Eden.

'I can't go back there. I can't start all over again.'

The image blinks and shudders and again the exotic garden returns. Plants and trees, grass and bushes, all so familiar and yet so unique.

There is definitely a parallel, but to what point I just don't know. It's almost as though the door is trying to tell me something, but how can I trust anything it shows me?

I step into the ley circle and take hold of Caesare's hand. *Can you feel me? Do you know I'm here?* I press his cold skin to my cheek. He's in stasis and the ley is holding without any trouble. My fears were unfounded. I rest my head on his chest and feel him breath, but there is still no heartbeat. How could there be? Lucrezia ripped it out …

Harry's Door

The impossible happened as we travelled to Scotland.

After a few centuries passed I'd finally agreed to visit Sweden with Harry and we planned to catch a cargo ship from Leith that would take us to Stockholm. We'd been travelling by coach to Edinburgh, but just as we reached the outskirts the coach driver pulled the horses into the courtyard of an inn to allow some passengers to depart and those of us who were staying on board were given time to stretch our legs or get refreshments.

It was a hot summer day, and as we climbed down from the carriage, Harry saw a young barmaid come out of the inn with jugs of ale to sell to the weary travellers. He was immediately interested.

'Behave yourself,' I warned. 'We haven't got time for any of your usual exploits.'

Harry laughed and went up to the girl but I suspect it was more about leering at her ample cleavage than sating any thirst for ale. He bought some anyway. Then went and sat down at one of the outdoor benches.

The laughter of children drew my attention and I stared across the courtyard at a group of boys and girls playing tag. The oldest was no more than nine. Two little boys were chasing three girls around one of the benches. Their clothing was basic but clean, but their playful screeches and screams soon irritated the barmaid.

'Clear off, yee mangy pests!' she yelled, and the five children stopped screaming and ran off out of the courtyard, presumably heading to the small village we'd passed on our way in.

A few of the other passengers joined Harry as he sat down in the sun swigging his ale.

It appeared idyllic, but there was a wrongness in the atmosphere. The hairs stood up on the back of my neck. I turned around, facing the entrance to the inn, and then glanced at the stables.

A stablehand was feeding water and hay to the horses. The animals were jittery, moving and shifting constantly within the confines of their harness, and following my time spent with Bellina I'd learnt that horses were extremely sensitive to atmospheric anomalies.

The heat made the courtyard appear hazy but I couldn't see anything out of place that would justify my sudden anxiety. I glanced at Harry. He was talking to the woman passenger who was carrying a hat box. He was bored. I wondered if I should rescue him or leave him to suffer the woman's waffling as she sipped on her glass of sherry, but as I turned my head towards the coach once more, something shimmered beyond the courtyard.

At first I could only see it out of the corner of my eye. Then the sun fell on the watery substance and reflected for an instant, sending kaleidoscopic rays of light all over the courtyard.

'Oh my God!' I said.

'What is it?' Harry was instantly by my side.

'A doorway ...'

Harry observed the blurred anomaly as it shimmered beside the courtyard entrance to the inn.

'Anyone could stumble through that,' I murmured.

Harry walked forward. I grabbed his arm and pulled him back, 'Be careful. I don't know what will happen if the wrong person crosses over it.'

'How long is it since one appeared to you?'

'Four hundred years or more ...' I shook my head. 'I never expected to see another.'

Harry walked around the spot, pressing and touching the air around it.

I glanced around at the passengers. They were blissfully unaware that anything was wrong.

'There has to be a reason it's here. But I'll be damned if I'm going to find out. Come on, let's get out of here. The coach driver is mounted and ready to leave.'

'A moment,' Harry said. 'I'm curious and I need to examine this in order to understand all you told me.'

'I know but – hurry.'

I had let him walk closer, ever aware that the coach was about to depart while I cast a worried glance at the passengers as they began to board. The old woman was still clutching the hat box that she'd insisted on carrying on her knee for the entire journey. An old man with a goatee beard, I'd assumed he was her husband, helped her up into the carriage. A well-dressed man of around thirty climbed up behind them. He carried a fancy cane and had a habit of polishing the silver handle with his leather gloves.

I glanced back at Harry. He was very close to the anomaly.

'Be careful!' I warned.

But Harry didn't look at me, instead he plunged his hands through the doorway.

'What are you doing?' I called, running towards him.

The watery gloop sucked at his arms pulling him forward and before I could reach him his entire body was pulled through the gateway.

'No!'

The door froze over, locking me out as though it was saying, 'only one customer per ride'.

Then the image blinked and shivered, disappearing completely from view. I turned around to see if any of this had been observed, but it was as if nothing had happened.

'Miss?' called the coach driver. 'We're ready to leave now. Where is your brother?'

I gazed back at the place where the gateway had been and I had no idea what to say to the driver, or what to do. Harry had disappeared into time, and the thought made me feel very scared indeed. I just didn't know why.

The Garden Welcomes

I feel like I have come full circle from the beginning of time to the present. Maybe this means it is finally the end of my journey. I'm not sure, and actually I don't give a shit, because if there is a chance that I can save Caesare then I know now I have to take it. I have been haunted for days by dreams of his tortured soul locked behind a doorway that only I have the key to. The doors will not be denied, I have always known that and so to try to refuse is futile.

In my dreams Caesare awakes, but he is a cold revenant, an empty shell, and he's crazed with bloodlust. Whether this is just some unreasonable fear I don't know. I can't help but make comparisons with my past. The past, present and future are all intertwined, or at least that is what Maria Serafina believed. I had always thought it was just because of my displacement from my own time.

The thick, gloopy membrane that covers the opening of the doorway, begins to thin out as I walk towards it. There is an excited whisper echoing through from the other side. This garden waits for me and the flowers chatter like children in a toy store.

Caesare lies inert beside it and I reach my hand through the ley and stroke his chest. I massage his face with my finger tips and then push back his hair from his brow. Loneliness is killing me as surely as any disease. If I save him I may save myself.

I back away from the body and turn to face the door once more, opening up still further as I step forward towards my destiny. I stretch out a hand to feel the water-skin substance and my hand passes completely through. I see my fingers waggle on the other side. Then I walk forward and through, forcing myself not to look back.

The garden welcomes me like an old friend. I feel the power on the air. It is a created world, not a natural one, and it is ley power that built it.

I suddenly know where I am. This is the Allucian city, under the Alps. Of course, it stands to reason. After all, this is where it started for me.

I walk the landscape unobserved. It feels like early morning. The fake sun is barely peeking out from behind the white and unnatural cloud. To the untrained eye this world would seem to be so real, but I can see the fake joins in the scenery. It looks like a badly constructed set for a low budget science fiction film.

I find myself before the gates to the city. Around me the streets are deserted. The world of the Allucians seems empty of its creators. Surely this is a time before the city disintegrated? Yet there is no one around.

So why am I here then?

The gates are locked and without a second thought I leap up and over them, landing smoothly on the other side.

I walk the main street. Nothing stirs. It really feels like I'm in the middle of a zombie film, after the apocalypse. Any minute I expect to see the dead rising and rushing towards me. I laugh at my own vivid imagination. As if that would actually make any difference to me anyway ...

It is strange though. All the worlds I've visited so far have been real, but this one is so obviously false.

I see the mansion ahead. It is completely alien to the rest of the environment. Close up it could be any haunted house, in any scary movie. That, of course, is what this whole city seems to be about. It is a disguise, a ruse, a painted prison, but to hold who, or what?

I climb the stairs leading up to the front door and at the top I stare at the long, pull bell.

'You've got to be kidding me,' I murmur.

It is delightfully corny. Should I ring and wait for 'Lurch' to come and open the door for me? I smile at the silliness of it all and push against the door. It opens at my touch. I half expect the predictable creak but the door makes no noise at all and that is when I notice it. There is no sound. That is the point.

Before I passed through the portal I had heard water, birds, wind. Now there was nothing.

'Another trick I suppose?'

I enter the mansion. It seems more solid than anything else here. It is in fact completely real and I consider how that could be here at all, but then I know that the corridor of doors is nearby, I can feel it. After all I've been here before when Lucrezia talked about it to Gabi and me, all those years ago in the café at Harvey Nicholls. Then she'd somehow summoned the house and the corridor and I had become lost. We had speculated then that the magic of the place meant that once you'd been here, you could call it back and be there again. But that was long before I knew anything really of the doors, or ley magic. Lucrezia had clearly known enough to cause the anomaly that led me to this strange and tiresome destiny.

'Not Lucrezia,' says a voice.

'You!'

Adonai stands in the hallway staring at me through his characteristically odd-coloured eyes.

'Everything that has happened, everything I've been through. You caused it!'

Adonai smiles and shakes his head sadly, 'No, Lillith. If only that were the case. I have tried to guide you, help you find the way forward, find your way home even.'

'Well, I'm not Dorothy and you're sure as hell not the fucking Wizard of Oz! Next you'll be telling me that all I have to do is tap my ruby heels together.'

Adonai shakes his head again. He doesn't get the joke. 'You've come so far, Lillith. The last hurdle is almost travelled.' He waves his hand towards the doors which lead to the corridors. 'Pick a door and the world will become right again.'

'Fuck you. I'm not playing your games anymore.'

Suddenly there is a burst of activity outside. I hear the movement of people. I walk to the main door and glance out over the street. A horse pulls an open carriage towards the gates. There is a cute little girl sitting in the back and the driver is barely three feet tall. The gates open noiselessly and the carriage clatters through. People slowly begin to come out onto the street and start their daily routine. A housewife with a basket walks off in the direction of the market. A little boy plays a form of hopscotch on the pavement. An old man hobbles along the street with a walking stick. Not one person is of average size; they are all perfectly formed but miniature.

I look back at Adonai as he waits patiently.

'I know what this is: Toy Town. You've created a world in which to play with people's minds. None of them are real.'

'They are real people, Lillith.'

'No. And it's Lilly. You've been playing at creation again, only I'm not sure if this is the first or the last attempt.'

I remember our first meeting, many years ago. Adonai had no form, and no name. I gave him both.

'Nothing exists without a name, Lillith. You of all people should know that.'

'Then try getting my name right for a change. It's Lilly.'

A shuffling, scraping noise vibrates around the entrance hall. I glance up to see the balcony lined with small babies. They peer down into the hallway, their golden pupils glinting in the light.

'Ah. The hell kids have arrived. Nice touch by the way, Adonai. I can see why Lucrezia found them so intimidating.'

Adonai laughs, 'Did she now?'

I try to work out what is going on in his mind. What is he hinting at? I shake my head. I mustn't forget I came here for something. I have my own agenda now and I'm not going to be distracted.

I walk past him and through one of the entrances to the corridor, examining the many doors which line it. There is a renaissance doorway with marble pillars for a frame; one is made of rotting wood and is covered with seaweed and moss; another is made of different strands of hair, all colours and all lengths; the next is metallic with no handle. A hundred thousand doors and everyone is different. Finally I reach the one that Lucrezia had pointed out the last time I was here. She had said that this door had a ward on it and I can feel the power oozing from it. The door has strange symbols carved around the frame and is made of solid oak. It is strangely familiar – and regal. I recall that the Allucians are holding a King prisoner. That King is presumably a vampire of great power. Lucrezia had believed that this King was the source of the Allucian power. That somehow the Allucians were draining him, as if they were the vampires.

I reach out and focus on the ley power directly under the mountain and I tap into it. The ward on the door flares up and I can see a pentagram as well as my own emblem, the triskele, marked on the door. Curious.

'This doesn't make sense. The doors only allow you a one-way trip. So why lock this one? If you sent someone through there, then they can't get back can they?'

Adonai shrugs. He begins to scrutinise his nails in a typically human manner. I know he is anything but human, although what he is I'm still not sure.

I reach towards the door with my power, searching for signs of threat. There are none. 'The Allucians lied,' I say softly. 'There is no King. The power source is the ley. How did they learn to tap into it though? Who showed them?'

I put my hands on the seal. It is icy cold.

'What's behind here?'

I glance back but Adonai doesn't answer.

The power is only weak. Nothing to a practiced ley witch like myself. It is some form of binding spell, but it could only hold those who did not have the skill to recognise its simplicity.

'Some so-called powerful vampire King couldn't be held in by that.'

'Not in,' says Adonai finally.

'What ...?' I frown at the door. It just doesn't make sense. 'Not in, then ... it must be keeping something out.'

'Bravo!' says Adonai.

I give him a look that I hope conveys my irritation. 'The Allucians are scared of something then? Mmmm? But what?'

Adonai doesn't reply. He is not really planning to help at all. The babies gather around his feet to watch my progress with their golden eyes. They appear so benign but really are creepy. The hair stands up on the back of my neck. I wish they'd go away.

'Koochi-koo,' I say. 'Tell the brats to clear off before I get hungry.'

I bare my fangs. The babies back away. I really don't like the thought of having them behind me, though I can't say why. After all, what could they do to me?

'What's behind here, Adonai?'

'Nothing,' he answers.

'Then why the ward?'

Adonai smiles.

'Oh my God. Of course. The doors aren't one-way at all! These points are closed deliberately. They are to stop someone or something using them to get in and out of here at will.'

'Very good.'

'And that's how you froze me out. That's how you've manipulated me like a puppet to do everything, and be anywhere that you wanted.'

Adonai merely stares at me, an expression of alarming innocence on his face.

'Who the fuck are you?'

Adonai says nothing. Behind him, another door opens and the old gypsy witch, Carmelita, enters the corridor.

'It's all been a ruse. But why? What did you hope to gain?'

Carmelita gives me a brown-toothed grin, 'Miranda has returned to the fold at last. Welcome home, my dear.'

Chapter 49 - Present

The Allucians' Destruction

I'm still tapped into the ley power when the fury hits me and I crack all of the seals on the doors. Carmelita steps back and Adonai's blank face briefly flushes with confusion. They obviously don't know how much my power has grown in the last four hundred years, and it is all because of Rhuddlan. The castle has taught me how to manipulate the ley, and so now I pump as much energy into the corridor as I can.

I glance again at Adonai, the babies and Carmelita. All of them have backed away. They stare at me with matching expressions, guarded but wide-eyed. I can sense their fear in the perspiration that suddenly beads Carmelita's brow.

The door beside me springs open, and Harry tumbles out and forward, pitching into my arms.

'What the fuck ...?'

'Lilly ...'

He's freezing cold.

'How long has he been trapped between this world and his own?' I demand.

'Not long,' Adonai replies.

Carmelita laughs with renewed confidence, she is getting younger and younger by the minute. Now she is a small and perfect Allucian. Her hair is a shiny black; her pupils a perfect pit of warm chocolate and the skin a dark olive colour. She reaches to Adonai and takes his hand.

'How long?' I demand again.

'A few weeks,' Carmelita answers. 'Not long enough to become insane.'

'My love,' Adonai says, raising her fingers to his lips.

'You're an *Allucian?*'

'The first of a new breed,' he answers, and his odd-coloured eyes change to a perfectly matching gold.

'L ... Lil ... y,' Harry stutters. 'S ... so ... cold.'

'How did he get here?' But of course I know. I had known all along that something must have happened to him when he stepped through the doorway back in the Sixteenth Century when the portal had been meant for me, but I hadn't expected this.

I have to get him out of here, back to the time he left. I glance at the gaping door and back down the corridor at all of the others. I help Harry stand and pull him along as we hurry down the endless corridor.

It isn't easy to know which one at first. I pull his freezing, exhausted body several feet before the answer comes to me. I open up the ley power and let it search for me. Energy pours down the corridor ahead of us as I half drag, half carry Harry forward. A white hot light explodes up ahead as we reach the door. The ley has found its target. There is a strange emblem that is burnt into the wood like a brand. It is three small crowns. I reach out a hand and touch the frame then pull back my fingers as if they have been burnt, but it isn't heat that I felt. For a moment I felt the strange coldness of icy waters, just as a rush of sound poured into my ears. It was the sound of the ocean, being slapped by huge oars. I've found the right door.

'You're going back,' I tell him. 'And you're not going to remember what happened at all.'

'How do you know?' he asks.

I see the spot, remembering it happening as clear as if it were yesterday.

'Because I'm waiting for you on the other side ... This has already happened for me in the past.'

'I don't understand ...'

'You shouldn't have crossed through. Those bastards trapped you for the hell of it. Time to go home,' I tell Harry.

With that, I open the door, pushing him through with one fluid movement. Then I close it quickly behind him, knowing that Harry will suddenly materialise at my feet in another century, bruised, chilled and disorientated. He will never remember the weeks he spent trapped in the cold film between doorways. Nor will he remember that it was I who freed him.

I walk back down the corridor towards Adonai. I'm determined to get to the bottom of it all. I'm totally sick of his stupid games.

'What's your real name?'

'I'm Adonai. You named me. As you did my brother and sister.'

Two of the babies begin to stretch and grow, warping into Eve and Adam.

'Nothing exists until it is named, Lilly.'

'What about Carmelita? I didn't name her and yet she exists doesn't she?'

'Ah but you did name me,' Carmelita replies. 'In your dream. You put the words in my lips when I introduced myself.'

'This is insane. I'm leaving now and there's nothing you can do to stop me.'

'I don't intend to stop you. But aren't you forgetting something, Lilly?' Adonai says.

'No ...'

'You came through the door to find something,' murmurs Eve, but it is as if she speaks with their collective voice.

Caesare! I almost forgot about him in the confusion, but then there is nothing here that can save him. He has his destiny yet to fulfil in this world.

Adonai smiles. Carmelita laughs and Eve mimics her cruel snigger perfectly.

'There's nothing you can do,' says Adam repeating my thoughts. 'How can you possibly save him?'

'I'll save him because you're going to help me,' I answer.

They laugh again as if I had said the funniest joke they had ever heard. Adonai shakes his head and smiles. 'Of course we won't help you.'

'No? Then this world, this fake and dangerous toy town, will crumble.' I feel down into the ley line beneath my feet, drawing a circle of protection around me.

'What is she doing?' cries Carmelita.

'Stop her!' Adam yells.

Adonai frowns. He too reaches for the ley power. I feel him pressing against my control, but fury strengthens my resolve and I push him off. Carmelita joins the fight, but I have had much more experience since we last met, and Rhuddlan has strengthened me.

'Go to hell!' I say coldly. 'I'm taking this place down. You're not screwing with my life again.'

I send the ley power out. It ripples over the underground cavern, pulling down all of the illusions that the Allucian children have created. Their whole city is a lie. I sense the rocks swallowing the houses and street as it vibrates back through the ley. In my mind's eye I can see the garden disintegrate, the fake blue sky falling in on the now rotting grass and then I see them. Lucrezia, Caesare and another Allucian woman, rushing through the destruction. I stop.

Adonai and the babies have scurried away in fright. I wonder briefly if they have travelled through the doors to some distant safety, but no. I still sense their presence in the house. And I can't destroy the house as I'd planned, taking them all with me, because Caesare and Lucrezia will be crushed too. Instead I send out the ley circle. It surrounds the house, keeping back the mountain rock as it tries to reclaim the stolen space, but the ley will hold indefinitely. I doubt that the Allucians will attempt to break my hold now.

I turn back to the door that once held the ward that kept Harry captive in an icy, interminable hell. I replace the magic, making it strong enough to discourage Lucrezia from trying to use it. I don't know exactly what else may lie in wait behind this doorway, but whatever it is, I need my children to stay clear.

Then I run down the corridor searching for my return door to the future. I'm getting the hell out of Dodge, before Caesare and Lucrezia see me here.

Stockholm

It was weird at the time how Harry just reappeared in Stockholm. He fell out of nowhere at my feet, frozen and shaking. I never even saw the door open, and it closed immediately after he tumbled through.

'What the hell ...?' I said, totally unaware that I was almost repeating the words and actions of my future self in the corridor of doors.

It was several weeks since I'd seen him and I had only just stepped from the ship that had brought me to Stockholm, and began my exploration of the city. Later he was to ask me why I'd completed the journey after he'd vanished, but I couldn't explain the strange compulsion I had to continue on. Even though I was worried what had happened to him it had been essential I came to Sweden.

'You have to understand,' I said. 'I can't let myself really love anyone or anything again. At any time it can be taken from me.'

'But we've been companions on and off for hundreds of years ...'

'I know. But one day you were there, the next minute gone. That is how my life has been. And now any security I had has gone once more. I'm not sure if a door will appear again to take me to some point in time where I need to fulfil my destiny. '

He couldn't remember what had happened to him of course. Only that he had been extraordinarily cold. He'd felt paralysed and trapped and it was as though he'd been there for both minutes and years.

'I've never felt anything like it.'

'You weren't meant to travel through the door. It had been sent for me for some reason. Perhaps that's why you didn't go anywhere in particular. You mustn't do that again Harry.'

We hunted. I checked several victims before we found one that was safe: a sailor from Germany. There was no trace of the gene in him and so I let Harry guzzle his blood down until he felt restored. He came back to full strength with what seemed to be no lasting physical ill-effects, but Harry was never really the same after that. He became much more pliant, and he stopped going on his long 'hunting trips', favouring the shores of his homeland to anywhere else in the world. It was hard to get him to leave Stockholm for any length of time. I was never sure, but I always felt he suffered from a strange agoraphobia. He liked to be in public places, he could leave the castle, but leaving Sweden caused him intense pain.

As for me, I worried about the implications of missing another journey through time when the moment eventually arrived, but began to consider if fate would solve the issues another way.

'I may have to go again,' I warned Harry. 'If another door appears, then I won't have any choice.'

'Why do you keep saying that?' he asked.

'I have to be prepared, and so do you. But if it does happen, it's likely we'll meet again.'

But the doorway didn't reappear and I went into the future the normal way, travelling through time with every passing day.

'I was a good King,' Harry told me as we explored Sweden.

He told me of how he had worked with his people to unite them all under one ruler. Until his reign there had been other Kings. Sweden was divided into three areas. Harry was the first to rule all. The way I saw it he had a very selective memory. I hadn't forgotten that he was a rapist, that I'd killed him, and then he'd become an immortal rapist and blood-drinker. Nice.

But he wasn't really upset that I'd bitten him. Harry loved the power he had as a vampire, but I still struggled with his abuse of women. Often his feeding still accompanied rape, and his victims rarely survived, but I tried not to interfere too much. After all, he did still have urges. I just wished he would try seduction a little more.

Once we were both in Stockholm, Harry found his world much changed. Gone were the marauding Vikings of his day. Stockholm was a busy trading centre and the people were far more civilised. Gone were beliefs of the Vikings too. Christianity had taken over, so Harry had to reconsider his nature.

'How can my people have lost their faith and their beliefs?'

'Christianity is a strong force, Harry. In my world about a third of the world's population are Christian.'

But Harry couldn't understand how the old faith could just be deemed blasphemy.

'Surely my Gods are the ones blasphemed here?'

'I don't know,' I answered. 'I've seen no evidence to prove or disprove any religion. And mostly over the years I've watched humans use it as a way to justify killing others.'

We entered Stockholm society and began an exploration of the new culture. There we had to be more careful than ever, because almost every potential victim I tested had a strain of the vampire gene somewhere in their ancestry.

'You sure did put it around,' I sighed.

'No matter,' said Harry. 'We will just kill when we feed.'

'Make sure your lips don't touch the raw wound then,' I warned. 'The infection could be in our saliva.'

We posed as brother and sister, just as we had before. Harry was then free to court and dance with the local aristocracy or the local whores as he deemed fit, but he always preferred to take by force, a habit I struggled to get him out of.

'I'd love to hear her scream as I break her in,' he said as he studied a shy Princess from a distance. 'I like it when they squirm, and the fear in their eyes is delicious.'

'You're such a complete bastard! Leave that poor girl alone, I won't allow it Harry!'

'You have double standards,' he replied. 'You kill, take blood. It's all the same: still rape.'

I shook my head in denial, 'I kill the deserving. You defile the innocent. How can that be the same? At least take someone who is a menace to society. You might find it far more exciting.'

But who was I kidding? Did some of the men I tortured to death really deserve it? All because they dared to desire me ...?

Even so, I showed him how the thrill of killing the strong and wicked was far more exhilarating than destroying the innocent.

'To see the fear in the eyes of a rapist, murderer or corrupt politician who has abused his power is very stimulating.'

Harry was surprised. 'You feed off fear as I do.'

I couldn't meet his eyes. It was true. Deep down I was no better and no worse than he was.

'Just leave the virgins alone,' I warned. 'Rape is sick. There are plenty of women who are willing. And you might actually enjoy having someone who wants you back.'

So Harry experimented on his home ground. He was in his element there, he felt safe and happy. He had come home, and somehow my words sank into his brain and slowly over the years he changed and evolved, just as the world around us did.

Occasionally I returned to Wales, or England, depending on my moods. But Harry preferred his homeland. Though often he visited other nearby countries to enjoy the freedom of the hunt more easily. It pleased me no end when he began to take lovers instead of victims.

'Taking by force has started to leave a sour taste in my mouth,' he said one day.

'Oh? Why's that?'

'I think you are actually beginning to rub off on me ... Besides, the blood tastes sweeter during passion.'

'Yes. It does,' I smiled.

For a moment I actually felt some parental pride. My child was learning. He was growing up.

The Corridors Of Illusions

I hear Caesare and Lucrezia enter the corridor behind me and I cloak myself, using my ley power rather than my vampiric skills because I can't decide on a door to take. Vampires cannot hide from each other, but a witch can hide from anyone if she's strong enough. I glance back down the corridor. I want to watch this story play out even though I already know the end result.

Caesare hurries to the door I warded. He pounds his fists on it, calling to see 'The King'. For a moment I wonder why he wants to see Elvis, and I don't understand why he's drawn to the door but then I remember and give myself a mental shake. Lucrezia told us that the Allucians said they held a King: the 'King of Vampires' in this hallway, behind a sealed door. Now I knew that wasn't true, except that they could have been referring to Harry, trapped as he had been behind that very door.

'Where is he, Lucrezia?'

'Not there, brother,' she answers moving to the door opposite. As she draws closer to the door I hear a woman screaming farther down the corridor beyond them.

'No. Not that one! Don't open it!' cries a beautiful Allucian woman as she runs towards Caesare.

Lucrezia back-hands the woman sending her tumbling across the marble floor. Her head cracks on the slabs and I smell blood seeping from her.

Caesare takes a step back from the door and stares at Lucrezia surprised.

'Illura ... ?'

He begins to move towards the girl's prone body.

'She's of no importance. Open the door, brother. Then you'll see ...'

'There is no King, Lucrezia. I told you. Our ultimate maker is a woman. But I am curious. What is this place?'

'These are the doors of time.'

'What diversion is this of yours? Ever since you came to me in Paris, telling me you'd found an amazing secret. It has been one game after another.'

Lucrezia shakes her head, her mouth dropping open. 'Caesare, you offend me. All I've done is try to help you. You said you'd changed and so I offer you this olive branch.'

'You promised me answers but all you give is riddles.'

Lucrezia strokes Caesare's arm provocatively but Caesare shakes her off.

'Where is this so-called King of yours?'

Lucrezia points to the door.

I'm confused. This is a far different scenario to the one described by Lucrezia. I'm at a loss as to what to do.

Caesare reaches the door. It is covered in cobwebs and mould: a doorway of decay and decadence. A black residue drips from the walls as though they are bleeding black blood. I take a step forward, but find my way barred. A blockade has been constructed from ley power and it feels impregnable. I was so busy hiding and protecting myself that I was unaware that someone else was using this to their advantage.

I glance down the corridor once more and see a dozen pairs of glittering gold pupils all focused on me.

'Little bastards!' I whisper under my breath. 'I'm not finished with you yet.'

'It won't open,' Caesare says, tugging at the handle. 'Help me.'

But Lucrezia backs away from the door and stands at the other side of the corridor.

I see Adonai; he raises his hand and the door illuminates. The handle begins to turn and Caesare pulls the huge and ugly portal open.

'Don't go in there!' I shout, but my cries remain unheard.

I pound on the barrier, but I can hear my calls and banging echoing back around me. Caesare can't hear me, no matter how much I shout and call.

I reach for the ley power, twisting and pulling it. I tear at minds with feral telepathic claws. The babies yelp and I feel their collective strength lessen. I push harder. Then I feel the barrier pop as they finally give up. They scurry away as I begin to run back down the corridor.

Caesare crosses the doorway.

'No!' I call, but already the door is closing behind him.

'Lucrezia!'

Lucrezia turns to me. I let her see Miranda's aspect as I approach. I want to identify myself and find out what the hell is going on, but as she sees me she backs away. Then she runs back down the corridor and opens a door herself. She jumps through before I have chance to get my hands on her.

'You bitch! You lying, fucking bitch! I knew it! I just knew you were no good! You tried to fool us all.'

I stop at the reeking mouldy door. Caesare has only just crossed. It may not be too late. I reach for the handle.

'There's only one outcome to this. I have to get you out of there before you're trapped and insanity sets in.'

'Lillith.'

I glare at Adonai.

Then tug the handle.

'Lillith. That door is barred to you.'

'None of them are barred to me. Everything you say is a lie!'

I pull harder, and then reach for the ley power to help me, but the power slips away refusing to assist in this fool's errand.

'I came here to help him. He has to heal. He has to live.'

'Why? Because you want it? Because you have to continue to fight against fate? Why not let him go? You could go back to Gabriele; no more doors will ever appear to affect your life again. I can promise you that.'

'Are you crazy? Are you trying to get me to make deals now?'

'Why not?' Adonai answers.

'Go to hell. I'm seeing this through and I'm getting the outcome that I want for a change.'

'You can't. It is done ... it is finished.'

'Don't you fucking quote the Bible at me! You're nothing, Adonai. You're just some weirdo Allucian who uses ley power. Why have you done this? All of this! What the hell was it all for?'

'Without you the vampire gene does not exist,' Adonai answers.

'Why do you even care?' I retort.

Then I see it. I realise that the ultimate paradox is one of my own making.

'You feed on us!' I say. 'My energy gave you life. Lucrezia and Caesare were feeding you, when all the time they imagined your powers were helping them. Or at least Lucrezia did. Because I know now that she lied about her brother bringing her to you. She brought him didn't she?'

'It's true we cannot exist without you,' Eve says, appearing abruptly beside Adonai, 'but we can offer you so much in return.'

'I won't play your games. You've been manipulating me for hundreds of years. You can all rot in hell for all I care.'

I think again about bringing the whole of the mountain down on top of them.

'You can't destroy us, Lillith. We still have to take your future-self back in time to create the vampire lineage,' Adonai says. 'Therein is the ultimate paradox.'

'But that is where you are wrong. That's already happened you see, because I'm living proof and so, Adonai, I can no longer be fooled. Now open this goddamn door or I'll bring this roof crashing down on your fucking heads.'

The door springs open.

The Final Adventure

I look through into an abyss of black ink. It is a world filled with blood. Somehow I know that the blood is from every victim ever taken by my children and me. The carnage of the vampire gene lies ahead and Caesare is lost within. His soul has fallen victim to guilt. He will stumble around for centuries, his mind becoming more lost. His insanity growing.

'It has already happened,' Adonai says. 'Time means nothing inside the mind. He's already insane. There's nothing you can do to save him.'

So time has passed in the minutes between him going through the door and this moment. I grind my teeth together and clench them tight. I glance at Adonai and then back into the charnel house.

'Caesare!' I call, and the wind within grabs my voice, whipping it in and around the gore covered walls.

It is like a padded cell, only the walls are cushioned with body parts. A torso protrudes half absorbed from a wall; a hand reaches out, the fingers still moving; blood pours in rivulets down bare brick; veins and arteries lattice the ceiling, bursting periodically to rain down on the room like a gruesome sprinkling system. The floor is covered with internal remains, some of them so mangled I can barely make out which body parts they once were. Blood. Gore. Sinew. Fluid. Cracked bones and broken dreams. It is a place out of the deepest, darkest nightmare.

I steady myself, placing a hand against the wall inside the door. Something moves under it and I pull away hurriedly, seeing a pair of female lips there, tongue licking out where my hand had been.

I hardly recognise Caesare. He's covered in black ichorous blood and it eats into his skin like virulent festering bedsores. He writhes in pain as though in ecstasy, but his mind is too far gone to even know the difference. I reach out my hand to him, but his animalistic brain sees me as more fodder for the horrific canvas. He crawls on his elbows, jaw snapping and snarling, fingers clutching at air like the legs of dying spiders.

I want to step back. Oh I so want to step back, but I hold my ground.

'Caesare ...'

My heart hurts so much that I can barely breathe. I watch my friend crawl to the door. What do I do? Do I close the door on him, abandoning him forever? Or do I let this monster out?

'Your choice,' says Adonai. 'You already know of the rampage he goes on.'

'It's not his fault. You did this.'

I glance back at the struggling figure. His progress is slow to the door, the gore, hands, legs, arms, lips, all grab at him, trying to hold him back.

But his eyes are on me, and he drags himself forward. I know I can't be the one to free him. It is too much of a responsibility to bear. What if he creates new monsters? His mind is too befuddled to remember to take care.

Hands emerge from the wash of blood on the floor and grasp him, but he pulls away, dragging himself ever forward. I begin to close the door. A terrible howl pours from his lips. It is a guttural sound of pain. He screams to me for help but can't find the words. Instead there is this animal cry that ends in a sad and lonely whine. The door is half closed and I stop.

'If only there was something there. Something left to give me hope.'

His eyes meet mine. His lips smack.

'I'm nothing more familiar than food ...'

'M ... M ... Mother!'

I throw back the door and almost step inside before I realise how very foolish that would be. I glance over my shoulder and see Adonai and the others. They seem poised to react to whatever I choose to do.

I step back from the door. The last thing I need is to become trapped in there as well.

I reach out for the ley power again, and this time it responds, licking up through my outstretched palms and surrounding my body. I have to be careful not to touch the contaminated blood. I force the ley outwards, firmly placing a cordon around the door.

I stare at Adonai. I'm furious. Adam and Eve hide behind him and the babies slink back in fear. I have no idea where Carmelita is.

'You evil fucking bastards. Just try anything and you all fry,' I say, then I charge the ley with an electric current.

I glance back at Caesare.

'You have to crawl to me, darling. I'll keep the door open, but I can't come in there.'

I think I see a spark of recognition in his eyes. I think he understands me, but I'm not sure. Maybe this is completely crazy, but I have to try. That is, after all, why I crossed the doorway back into this world. I have to claw him back from the abyss.

Body parts grip the remaining rags of his clothes, ripping them back and from him. They peel off like a bloody second skin being shed. He heaves himself forward, sliding in blood and gore, leaving a deep trail through the carnage. The walls weep mucus and bile. The ceiling cries bloody tears, but he's focused now, he has a goal.

'Yes! That's right. Come to me, darling. Remember me? I'm getting you out of here.'

His hand stretches towards the threshold but as he reaches out his skin begins to bubble and blister. He pulls back yelping like a scalded animal.

'Don't give up! You're almost there!'

'M … Mother.'

'Yes! Remember!'

He inches forward again, his hands extend over the threshold and grip the floor despite the agonising pain that distorts and burns his skin. He drags himself forward. As his head crosses, half of his face seems to melt and disintegrate. He cries, but pushes on.

'Keep going! It will all heal. You're immortal, nothing can kill you.'

I sense a movement along the corridor from me and turn to see the babies cowering farther back. Adonai gasps as he sees the destruction of Caesare's face.

'Don't move, any of you!' I warn. 'I swear to God if you try anything I'll fucking tear you all from limb to limb. Then I'll personally throw your remains in this hell you've created.'

Caesare is halfway into the corridor before I reach for him, helping him cross the final bit. Finally, he falls into my arms and I hold him as he sobs like a baby waking from a bad dream. Gore and slime cover him, but I don't care. He seems more lucid, as though the animal, instinctive side of him somehow was left behind in the room beyond the door.

Then Carmelita makes her move. Maybe she is the most powerful one among them, or maybe the most stupid, but I see the shock even on Adonai's face as she dives forward, using ley power to break my cordon. She hurls herself at me and I know what she's trying to do, long before she reaches me. She's trying to push us both back in. I let go of Caesare, dropping him to the floor as my arm swings back and I back-hand Carmelita as hard as I can.

A crack echoes through the corridor as my arm hits her and I feel her neck break. The force throws her body halfway down the corridor and her corpse skids along the polished floor until it comes to a halt almost at the feet of Adonai and the Allucian babies. There is a collective whimper as they stare at Carmelita, so easily slain by my vampiric strength.

'Lilly ...' Caesare gasps.

'I have you. And we're getting the fuck out of here.'

'But how ...?'

The Allucians stare back down the corridor, their expressions now emotionless. Adonai bends down over Carmelita's body, his fingers slowly stroking her face. Maybe now he understands the evil he has done me through the pain of his own loss. Then he slowly picks up her body and walks away, leaving the corridor and the babies behind in his grief.

I can't explain it yet. I don't even know myself, but when I look back into the bloody room I can see another figure working its way forward, but being pulled back time and again by the debris of his kills. I think Caesare's physical form still remains in the room, but it is gaining ground. Getting closer to the exit. I glance at the creature at my feet, and again gather him up into my arms. This is, I know, Caesare. His essence. His soul.

And that's what I came for.

I lift him up. He's weightless. I run down the corridor without looking back at the Allucians, but I hear them scream as Caesare's physical body leaves the room and stumbles towards them.

I use the ley power to search the gateways. This time I will control where I end up.

I run and run. It seems like forever. Behind me I hear the faint animal howl of the beast Caesare mingled with the screams of the babies. I don't give a fuck if he kills them all.

'Mother!' his body calls and I stop, glancing back briefly to see him stumbling blindly after me.

This is the insane creature that came into my world and which Lucrezia eventually destroyed. But now I know Caesare's essence was never in there and did not die.

I run forward once more. I have what I want, what happens to the ruined form behind me is irrelevant.

The ley ignites as I near a doorway. It is white and stark. It is a twenty-first century door, painted white and plain, with the minimalist cleanness I prefer. White hot light glows behind it. I hug Caesare to me and reach out with one hand.

'Mother!' the monster calls again far behind me, but I ignore him.

The door opens and I'm blinded by the light on the other side, but I can make out shapes. Yes! It's Rhuddlan. Holding Caesare close I throw myself forward and through the door. Like Dorothy in *The Wizard of Oz* I've learnt that I had the power within me all along. I'm going home. And I'm taking Caesare with me.

Home

I wake on the grass, lying out in the open beside the river. I feel disorientated and for a moment I don't remember where I am or how I got here. I glance up the hill. It is midday and the sun is high in the sky. I sit up.

'Fuck!'

Memories flood back.

I search around me. Caesare's body is nowhere to be seen. There is also no sign of a doorway – which I think is probably a very good thing anyway. I did not want the revenant to follow me through.

I leap to my feet looking around. Then close my eyes and search for his aura but come back blank. I run over the entire grounds, searching in every place but there is no sense of his aura anywhere. I become frantic.

Jumping unseen from the bridge I press myself against the wall until I find the hidden panel. My fingers shake as I key in the entry passcode. It takes three attempts before I get it right.

The door opens and I hurry inside passing rapidly through the several security doors until I am in the inner sanctum.

Rhuddlan vibrates and shudders above me. I pause and let her power wash over my skin, cleansing and calming my aura. Her presence can never be denied. Who am I to ignore the wisdom of this ancient deity?

'Okay. I hear you. I've got to keep calm.'

I walk, slowly now, up the stairs and stop on the landing outside Caesare's room. I search ahead. The ley circle is still in place. His body is there, but for a moment I'm afraid to enter. I pause outside, my heart beating hard in my chest. My breath begins to wheeze and I realise I'm having a panic attack. This is insane! I take a deep breath, force myself to calm down.

Opening the door I find that he is still in stasis. I close the door behind me and step closer to examine his body for the hundredth time. His skin has colour now, a slight blush that wasn't there before I left. I step into the circle and walk around his body as I have so many times in the past week. He floats in the air as though on an invisible bed. His face is serene and beautiful and for a moment I'm lost. His long lashes lie like tiny fans on his cheeks. Lots of women would kill for lashes like those.

'Sleeping beauty,' I whisper, but feel cynical.

Nothing stirs. Still I wait expecting re-animation at any moment.

Hours pass.

I stand transfixed and then suddenly crumble.

I kneel beside him. I have failed. Somehow his soul didn't cross through the doorway with me, but I could have sworn I felt him in my arms all the way through. Then there was nothing, just me waking as if it had all been a bad dream.

I laugh harshly. 'I'm a monster for fuck's sake. I am a nightmare.'

I stroke his cheek. Tears push against the back of my eyes but I swallow them down.

'I need to let you go, not torture myself like this by keeping your body here.'

I'm so sorry!

I stroke his face, his hands, his arms; all for the last time.

'I loved you, Caesare. More than anything. But it was all so brief. I wish I had never let them force me through their wretched doors. Why didn't I realise sooner that I could fight them?'

My hand massages his chest and rests on the barely healed wound on his breast. I massage where his heart should have been, pressing my hand against the cavity.

'I thought I could save you, but it was impossible.'

Where was his soul now, if it hadn't crossed with me? Was it still in the corridor waiting for me to return? The thought was unbearable.

'I can't do this. I can't go on forever wondering. It has to stop.'

I lay my head on his chest and let the tears come.

I sleep. I dream that his hand rests on my head, gently caressing my hair. I hear his whispered words.

'Lilly ... you didn't fail. I'm here.'

I wake from my fugue state and look into his face. His eyes are open and they smile back at me from a flawless face.

I can't believe it. I think maybe I have lost my mind after all.

Epilogue

Warning

'My journey has finally ended,' I tell Gabi on the mobile. 'I'm ready to meet.'

I give him the castle's address and wait patiently as he flies across the country to meet me again. It doesn't take long as he's only in Manchester and I am in North Wales. By car the trip would take an hour and a half. Gabi reaches me by air in fifteen minutes.

I have not seen him for hundreds of years by my timeline but Gabi has only missed me for ten short days. Even so, to him it must feel like a lifetime.

He lands silently in the castle courtyard. I watch him for a moment as I stand unseen inside one of the turrets. He stares around the castle, raises his arms as he feels the energy surrounding him. He turns a full circle. His face is shining with elation. A surge of love comes into my heart. He hasn't changed, he's just as I remember and his sensitiv soul can feel and love Rhuddlan just as I do. The castle clearly likes him. I feel her power massage his aura lovingly.

'She's beautiful isn't she?' I say, stepping out of the shadows.

'Lilly!' he gasps dropping his arms by his sides. 'You've changed!'

'I warned you I'd be different,' I say but my voice is warm and soft, none of the cold standoffishness remains.

My hair is long and wavy. It hangs over my shoulders and down to my waist like a golden cloak. I'm wearing a purple velvet dress, which fits and accentuates my curves, and although I haven't aged or changed physically other than my hair, I wonder if he can tell that now I have lived longer than he has.

I stare into his eyes. *God, he's so beautiful.*

'Gabi,' I say, and I hold out my arms to him, surprising even myself with how much I want to touch him.

He's in my embrace, his arms around my waist, showering kisses on my face, neck and hair. I hold him, revelling in the feel of his skin against mine after so long. It still feels so good. Perhaps it feels even better than it had.

'My darling!'

'Er-hem!'

I glance over Gabi's shoulder and see Caesare. He's standing with folded arms, appearing for all the world like a cuckolded husband. I laugh and push Gabi back and away, still holding onto his hands, so I can look in his eyes.

'This is going to be so weird and confusing for you. I have someone for you to meet.'

Gabi turns. Caesare and he stare at each other.

'Who ...?'

'This is Caesare.'

Then I explain in the simplest way possible. 'I have everything written down for you in my journal. The whole story. But what you need to know right now, what's most important is, that Lucrezia can't be trusted.'

'Everything she told us over the last few weeks was a lie?' Gabi asks.

'I don't know. Probably not everything. She told her story with some basis of truth except that: she was the one who found Caesare and took him to the Allucian city. He didn't kidnap her. That was a lie. She was definitely working with the Allucians. Although I'm not entirely sure what she had to gain from it.'

Caesare had told me that Lucrezia coerced him into coming to the Allucian city. He'd trusted her, but once there found he couldn't leave. This was a complete reversal of the elaborate story she had told us.

'How can you be sure?' asks Gabi glancing back at Caesare – and if looks could kill – '*He* could be lying to you.'

I sigh. I'm not ready for the macho stand-off shit just yet.

'I believe what I've seen with my own eyes. And what I heard in the corridor of doors. Lucrezia hasn't been truthful. I spent seven years with her as Miranda though and during that time she was, well, a nightmare to be frank. She was openly promiscuous, vicious and unfeeling in her choice of victim. And she certainly omitted her outlandish behaviour from her description of those days. Although that wasn't enough for me to feel too concerned. However, all along I had suspicions because there was this feeling of wrongness.' I shake my head. 'It's hard to explain. Maybe call it female intuition. But please, come downstairs to my rooms, I'll give you my laptop and all will become clear.'

Gabi stares back at me and his eyes are sad. 'She behaved strangely after you disappeared too. I suspected that somehow we were set up, but I didn't care to pursue it because you phoned me to say your were safe. What else am I going to learn from your journal?'

I nod, squeezing Gabi's hands in mine. 'Caesare and I had a relationship.'

'Have ...' corrects Caesare with a slight smile.

I smile back at him. 'Have.'

'And that's it,' says Gabi. 'I've just lost you, only to find you have him.'

I feel like my heart is going to break. There has to be a better solution. Why should any of us suffer now? I let go of Caesare's hand and walk away into the centre of the courtyard. I raise my arms upwards and soak in the power of Rhuddlan.

The men say nothing. They wait. It is almost as though they realise that this crucial communion with the castle will resolve all issues. And it does.

Rhuddlan's wisdom pours into me. There is no need for anyone to be alone anymore.

I drop my arms, open my eyes and walk back to Caesare and

Gabi. Standing between them I wait for a moment then I turn to Gabi, pulling him to me. I hold him. I kiss his lips with the passion for him that I've held in check for centuries. He's paralysed for a moment, but then returns my kiss pulling me tenderly into his arms. He never could resist me, or I him.

It only took seconds to realise that I still love him, will always love him. Besides we're vampires, if not adults. The human world's rules don't apply to us. I can love who I damn well please.

I release Gabi, and take Caesare in my arms. Hugging him to me I see that he understands the situation completely, and he's been through so much that petty jealousy would be a waste of energy. His lips meet mine and his love pours into my aura.

I smile at both my men, and the three of us embrace on the green grass of Rhuddlan, protected by her walls.

The castle shivers. Rhuddlan is happy to have us all here; as long as we don't break her rules. I share her feelings with Gabi and Caesare.

'Never shed blood on her grounds, and this ancient Lady will always keep us safe. It was a deal I made with her years ago.' I tell them.

Both men nod, and then they hug me again. I know the group hug thing is a cliché – but there's a lot to be said for it.

We hold hands as I lead them back to my lair. I feel so happy, so complete that I don't want anything to spoil it.

'What about Lucrezia?' asks Gabi much later as he puts aside the laptop. He is now up to speed on all that I've been through. 'We should find her and make her answer a few more questions.'

'Yes. I have a score to settle with her,' Caesare says.

'Shhh! No searches and no scores to settle. It's finished. Nothing is going to separate us.'

At least for now I want my happy ending.

Killing Kiss
by Sam Stone

He's looking for a girl; not just any girl, and dark-haired, brown-eyed Carolyn is the one.

But does Gabriele Caccini, a student at Manchester University, really know what he wants? When a beautiful curvaceous blonde comes into his life he starts to question his motives and emotions; even a seventeenth-century vampire can do that.

Alone in the modern world, limiting his feeds to one a year to avoid detection, Gabriele reflects on the origins of his immortality and questions why it is he who should have the vampire gene, when over four hundred women have not survived his killing kiss . . .

But at a house party, a fellow student spikes Gabriele's drink with drugs and his self-indulgent musings are suddenly turned upside down . . .

Futile Flame
by Sam Stone

Gabriele searches out Lucrezia, who reveals to him the horrors of her teenage years in the house of the Borgia's in the 16th century, and the possessive obsession of her brother Caesare who cannot accept that his love for her is unrequited. Her transformation as a vampire gives her freedom to escape for a short time, but leads to the terrifying world of the Allucian's; throwing her back into the arms of her now much stronger and powerful brother, two centuries later.

Gabriele discovers that Lucrezia is just as much a victim of her past as he is.

Hateful Heart
by Sam Stone

Lilly, Gabriele and Caesare's vampiric life at Rhuddlan Castle is disrupted by the arrival of Amalia: a new vampire created by Lilly's one-time companion, Harry. They learn that Harry is dead, killed by some powerful weapon wielded by a mysterious time-traveller known only as Carduth. Realising that their own lives are now in peril, the quartet begin an incredible adventure through time and space. They must track down Carduth, and somehow disable the weapon, before they too succumb to its fatal effect.

Also seeking Carduth are the remnants of the historic order of the Knights Templar who have been tracking a mysterious box for many centuries as they covet the power which rests within.

And all the time, the box is travelling, wending its way through time to seek a deadly revenge on the carriers of the vampire gene.